PENGUIN BOOKS
THE ELEPHANT AND THE MARUTI

Radhika Jha lives in Delhi and is a writer and a dancer. Her first Novel, *Smell*, published by Penguin Books India in 1999, was translated into several languages, and won the Prix Guerlain in France in 2002.

This is her second book.

The Elephant and the Maruti

Stories

RADHIKA JHA

PENGUIN BOOKS

Penguin Books India (P) Ltd., 11 Community Centre, Panchsheel Park,
New Delhi 110 017, India
Penguin Books Ltd., 80 Strand, London WC2R 0RL, UK
Penguin Group Inc., 375 Hudson Street, New York, NY 10014, USA
Penguin Books Australia Ltd., 250 Camberwell Road, Camberwell,
Victoria 3124, Australia
Penguin Books Canada Ltd., 10 Alcorn Avenue, Suite 300, Toronto,
Ontario M4V 3B2, Canada
Penguin Books (NZ) Ltd., Cnr Rosedale and Airborne Roads, Albany,
Auckland, New Zealand
Penguin Books (South Africa) (Pty) Ltd., 24 Sturdee Avenue, Rosebank
2196, South Africa

First published by Penguin Books India 2003

Typeset in Sabon by Mantra Virtual Services, New Delhi
Printed at Pauls Press, New Delhi

CONTENTS

acknowledgements

I would like to thank R.C.C. for explaining the finer points of roasting a leg of lamb; V.K. Karthika and Shantanu Ray Chaudhuri, my editors, for their suggestions; Laura Susijn for believing stories are worth writing; Charles Buchan and Katha Poggendorf-Kakar for their comments; Philippe Picquier and Simone Manceau for shedding light on what was missing in 'Beauty'; The Charles Wallace India Trust and the English Department at the University of Kent, Canterbury, for a much needed three months to finish the book; and finally, my father, Prem Shankar Jha, whose comments, editorial skills, and faith, I banked upon.

the wedding

Meenakshi, daughter of Bunny Kapil
weds
Sanjeev, son of Mr and Mrs P. K. Agarwal
Date: Saturday 21st April, 1995
Reception of Baaraat: 7:30 p.m.
Wedding: 8:00 p.m.
Venue: Lucky Farms, Chhatterpur

The wedding card was hand delivered by a courier service that specialized in weddings. Along with the invitation, the delivery boy handed me a little visiting card. 'Shaandaar Services,' it said. 'Biggest and beste mariage party dipand on good delivary. No one is forgot.' He looked smart, with his gelled hair, ponytail and fake Western boots.

A little awed, I opened the crushed raw-silk envelope. Inside was the most extravagant card I had ever seen. It had a real gold Ganesh on the front, which, once it was detached, became a pendant on a thin gold string. I stared at the names on the card. I knew two Sanjeevs, one was a nephew and the other was married, and I couldn't remember knowing a Meenakshi at all. I am sure I would have remembered the girl that went with such a pretty name.

It had been a season of weddings.

Starting in October, when the earth cooled just long enough for the women to bring out their silk saris, the wedding invitations began to arrive. At the beginning of the season only five of my fifteen female classmates were married. By April, only three remained unmarried. Apart from the weddings of my peers, I also attended a score of less important marriages—of the greater and lesser cousins, twice or three times removed. This would be my twenty-fourth wedding this year.

I weighed the Ganesh pendant that came off the invitation card in my palm. It was beautifully made, and heavy—a dancing Ganesh, one foot in the air, holding a flask of wine in one hand and Shiva's drum in the other. The elephant-headed God's sleepy, half-closed eyes and sensual mouth that turned down slightly at the edges gave him a somewhat dissolute air—and I felt almost certain I had seen it before. I tried to recall at which museum or exhibition I might have seen it. But the memory remained elusive. Finally I gave up—the card as much a mystery as the ones getting married. I slipped the pendant into my purse.

For the rest of the week I couldn't stop touching the little Ganesh, fingering its smooth flowing lines, the crooked mouth under the pointy tusks, the S-shaped curve of the trunk. On Friday I remembered. *It was Barra*. Barrabundla was getting married, and Meenakshi was Barrabundla's real name!

It all came back in a rush. The pendant was a copy of one Barrabundla had worn constantly in boarding school. It was a good-luck Ganesh made by her maternal grandfather, a goldsmith in Lahore. But that was before Partition.

We were poles apart. But in school Barrabundla and I were in the same class, and had beds right next to each other in the dormitory upstairs. Fate, it seemed, had decided we were to be friends. Barra was always in trouble with the teachers. Almost every Sunday, when the rest of us lolled around the city in 'civvies', poor Barra was stuck in detention.

I remember how the detentions began. It was math period.

We were studying quadratic equations. Barra was staring out of the window, singing softly to herself. The teacher, Mr Sandas, a burly, six-foot graduate from the National Sports College, Patiala, who doubled as cricket coach for the school, told her to stand in the corner facing the wall. Barra refused, saying she was claustrophobic. Mr Sandas looked confused. 'Class–what?' he shouted. Barra didn't reply. She was looking at the mist coming through the windows. He walked up to her desk and towered over her, his thick eyebrows in a straight black line. 'Get up. Tell it again—class phobic you said?'

The entire class laughed.

Finally he had her attention. 'I said claustrophobic,' she replied.

He still didn't understand what she meant. I don't think he had ever heard the word before. So he told her to get out of the class. She picked up her books and left, smiling hugely.

'Report to my class for detention,' he shouted after her retreating form.

Barra went to the classroom dutifully that Sunday, albeit one hour late. The teacher wasn't there. He had left a note scrawled in large uneven handwriting on the blackboard: Come to my house at the Commons.

The 'Commons', where the master lived, was strictly out of bounds for girls. Barra couldn't decide what to do. If she went there, the senior mistress (girls) would probably punish her. If she didn't go, Mr Sandas would probably report her to the headmaster for missing detention. Eventually, she made her way down the steep hillside to the cottage perched just above dhobighat—the abandoned stable which was now the school laundry.

When we all came into the dorm at teatime Barra wasn't there. She didn't show up for dinner either. At night, just before lights out, Barra came rushing into the dormitory. She looked tired. She changed and got into bed.

'So how was it?' I asked sympathetically.

She looked at me without seeing me. 'Great. Did you know that thirteen and seven are sacred numbers and with them you can build a building that will reach the sky?'

'Really? I didn't know Mr Sandas was into magic numbers.'

'Yes, and human beings have numbers too, something to do with their names adding up. That's why certain people are very powerfully attracted to each other. I'm a thirteen, he's a seven.'

'What? That's ridiculous. I bet he's just making it up.'

'No he's not. It comes from algebra.'

I was impressed. 'Is that what he taught you at detention? Why doesn't he teach us this stuff in class? It would make class so much more interesting.'

'He's a very interesting man.' Her voice went suddenly deep. Then she turned her back to me and went to sleep.

Next Sunday she was on detention again. Only this time Barra was on time. The Sunday after that was the same. It became normal for Barra to disappear at nine in the morning on Sunday and return after nightfall.

Eventually they began to suspect something was wrong. It was nosey Nanda, the senior mistress, who got suspicious because Barra's grades in math got worse, even though she was in detention doing extra math classes every Sunday. So they set a trap one Sunday. Nosey Nanda and her lover Fats Futtehalli sneaked up to the classroom on the second floor of Burns Hall where Barra was supposed to be in detention and peeked in through the closed windows. The room was dark and silent. Barra wasn't there. Eventually they found her, stretched out unconscious on the hard wooden floor of Mr Sandas's empty flat, stark naked except for the sports master's black-and-red silk cape, the one he wore to dinner each night, summer or winter. In one hand Barra held tightly onto Mr Sandas's photograph and in the other was an antique fly swat with a heavily carved silver handle, the kind used by tantrics in their rituals. As for Mr Sandas, the sports master, maybe the spirits he worshipped had warned him of what was to come, for he had already left in the middle of the night. Barra was quietly withdrawn from school.

She joined day school in Delhi and I never saw her again, till last year, when on the night of my twenty-fifth birthday, I bumped into her in the bathroom of the Mumtaz Hotel. Though I hadn't seen her for a long time, it was impossible not to recognize her. Because by then everyone knew Barra.

Her name, Barrabundla, came from her size. Her body was like a tub of ice cream, moist and sticky, melting into folds of breast, stomach, hip and thigh. All this abundance was encased in skin the colour of a mango kernel, cool, smooth, and slippery. Men liked her. They liked to hold her. Stomach, breasts and soft ample buttocks, she drove them mad with desire. Only, it was she who ate them in the end.

For ten years she had been the undisputed queen of the Delhi social scene. There was no party to which she wasn't invited, from the annual Polo club ball to the ruling political party's 'meet the citizens' mixers. Every Friday night she entered the ultra fashionable Blues Bar exactly when the place was teeming with bodies, and there were lines of hopefuls outside. The management kept a table at the head of the room for her that stayed conspicuously vacant till she got there, pushing her way through the bodies, a touch on a butt there, a little squeeze of a hip here. She held court till dawn, bestowing and receiving favours graciously. On Thursdays, she was to be seen at the Camel Court, the exclusive nightclub at the Sheraton. On Fridays, if there wasn't a party to be had, she would throw one, at one of her boyfriends' houses. And on Saturdays, she drank and danced at Darthvader, the country club-cum-nightclub just outside the city limits where they served her breakfast at seven.

But it wasn't the clubs that made her famous—Barra's name was always on everyone's lips, and in all the magazines. Sometimes she was rumoured to be writing a book about the men who had been her lovers, other times she was featured on the fashion pages, not modelling clothes, but talking clothes, like the 'outfit' Pooja Mehra, the latest little starlet, was wearing at the Camel Court last weekend—'She has terrible taste, poor little darling, and skinny shanks too'—or explaining what self-expression through make-up was really all about. Whether it was politics or philosophy or art, or her current boyfriend, or her opinion of Delhi's gays—'I have many gay men friends, some

I have even known intimately'—Barrabundla made news.

The bathroom was crowded with young things applying lipstick, brushing their long straight shining hair, pulling their short tight skirts slightly higher over their long, skinny legs. In that crowd, Barra and I stood out.

She glanced at me incuriously. Then her eyes widened.

'My god, it's you, isn't it, darling?'

'Hi, Barra.'

'It's been ages. Where have you been hiding yourself? Did you stay at that ghastly school till the end?'

I began to laugh, terribly pleased she had recognized me.

'So tell me, are you happily married?'

I shook my head.

'Any plans?' she giggled.

'Not really, I'm working in a newspaper now. And you?'

A shadow fell on her face. She looked at the skinny bodies in the mirror. 'I'll have to do it sometime. Maybe today, maybe tomorrow.' She giggled and winked at me in the mirror. 'Better tomorrow than today, you know what I mean?'

'Yes, I know.'

'All brides look the same. It's terrible!'

Lucky Farms was at the southern end of Chhatterpur village, amidst a wilderness of unmarked dirt roads flanked by high broken-glass-tipped walls. At first the road was fairly broad, polished granite and wrought iron gates on either side. The names on the gates ran: 'Mehra Farmhouse' (in gold etched on polished granite), 'Kul Dhan' (Sunny Sidhu, Bunny Sidhu, and Tiger Singh Sidhu), 'Anandparbat', 'Streedhan' (S.N. and Minni Verma). The road began to turn and twist upon itself, and the walls on either side grew higher. Eventually, the farmhouses dwindled into building sites surrounded by barbed wire fences and here and there the odd field could be glimpsed, still intact.

Just as I was about to give up, I saw the sulphurous glow of halogen lamps accompanied by dancing shadows. The car edged cautiously up the rutted road. To my surprise, it was remarkably free of the usual assortment of BMWs, Mercedes, Toyotas, and Maruti Esteems. In an empty construction site nearby, I noticed a decorated white horse and a bedraggled group standing around the gas lamps of a wedding band. They looked dwarfed by the huge walls around them. I felt a twinge of nervousness—perhaps I had come to the wrong place after all.

The road turned sharply to the right and I was suddenly confronted by huge black gates, eighteen feet of pure iron sheet, crowned by iron spikes. From the spikes dangled a few bedraggled garlands of marigolds. I parked beside the road and rang the bell. A little square of light appeared in the uniform darkness of the gate. A suspicious Gurkha face peered out.

'Lucky Farms?' I asked hesitantly. 'Is there a wedding going on?'

The guard slammed shut the window in response. A minute later, a crack appeared in the iron wall. Then it widened just enough to let a human being pass through.

Inside the gate, green, red and blue fairy lights garlanded the rose bushes on either side of the drive. An outdoor bar marked out one corner of the garden in empty crystal glasses. In another corner was the buffet with empty silver chafing dishes sitting on unlit fires. The immaculate lawns were empty of people. The mandap, where the wedding would actually take place, wasn't to be seen.

Instead, I found myself the sole occupant of a long sandy driveway decorated with marigold and rose petals. More yellow and pink petals littered the path that led to the sprawling white single-storeyed house set into the side of an artificial hill. A lackadaisical waiter told me to follow the path around the house to the back and step through the windows. I followed his directions and, within minutes, found myself in an enormous hall. The floor was black-and-white like a chessboard, made entirely of huge 3x3 feet slabs of Italian marble and polished black granite. To one side of the room was a marble fountain with a crystal swan at the centre. From the swan's mouth a slim stream of rose-coloured water trickled out. The room was bathed in the cold moon glow of tube lights hidden in curly baroque cornices on the walls. Heavy velvet curtains of brinjal-purple covered the windows that lined the opposite wall. The elaborately carved rosewood sofas were covered in the same material. The carpet had huge pink roses on a yellow background. It took me a few minutes to notice the people.

The average age in the room was around fifty-five, average weight 195 pounds, and most of it fat that sat stolidly on hips, thighs and butt, or hung pendulously as flaccid gut. The men wore corsets and droopy moustaches and stood against walls or behind their wives' chairs. The women, mostly wives, sat in a crisp Kanjeevaram row on velvet sofas and talked in whispers, barely audible above the buzz of the central air conditioning. There were no smiles, and no laughter. Only soft drinks and small eats circulated.

In the midst of all this colour, Barra's mother looked like a widow rather than the bride's mother, dressed as she was in a simple white Bengal cotton sari, no make-up, no false eyelashes, no beehive hairdo on her head like she used to have when she came to visit her daughter in school. All that had been shed three years ago when Barra's mother learnt that her husband, Barra's father, had a mistress in a little flat in Kidwai Nagar, right down the street from Barra's grandmother's house. So Barra's mother took sanyas and went to Rishikesh where she lived for a year with a sadhu and retrieved her peace of mind.

Barra's dashing, young-looking father wore all black. The only white in his outfit was his hair, tied back in a ponytail. His mistress wore peacock blue sequins, her knee-length hair braided with diamonds. She laughed louder than all the rest, and kept asking where 'darling Barrabundla' was. Barra's mother maintained a detached calm, ignoring the other woman's loud remarks—nothing betrayed her irritation except the slight twitching of her left eye.

The air was hot and heavy despite the presence of the split air conditioners. The open bay windows sucked the cool air out into the sultry spring night. The women fanned themselves with paper napkins. Then a high-pitched female voice disturbed the lethargic silence. 'Where's the lovely bride?'

'She must be in the pink room,' another voice replied.

'Are they going to stay the night here then?'

'Yes. It belongs to the groom's uncle, he makes BIC ballpoint-pen refills.'

'Really? The girl's family couldn't find a place of their own to hold the wedding in?'

'Sshh ... I know, I know. But the father is an alcoholic, a womanizer, and a gambler. They say he even gave all his wife's jewels to his mistress. You see the sapphire set she is wearing now.'

'Who? Where?'

'The woman in the blue sari—that's her.' (Pointing at Barra's father's mistress.)

'And the groom? What does he do?'

'Oh, he does watch straps, but I hear he wants to branch out into costume jewellery.'

A young fashionable entered, her face a mask of perfection. A thick line of black eyeliner made her eyes mysterious, dull gold eye shadow accentuated the curve of her eyelids, and her lips were painted a bold red and outlined in black. On her skinny body she had put a jumpsuit in dull metallic copper. Around her neck she wore a typically tribal silver choker. She stopped for a second at the entrance, her face registering dismay at having come too early. Then she tossed back the long black hair that fell artlessly across one side of her face, and tripped through the room, heading for the back of the house where I guessed all the young people were hiding. I followed her.

A maze of marble corridors led from the salon with its velvet sofas to the bridal chamber. A brass plate implanted in the door proclaimed its name: the Rose Room. I peeped in, thinking maybe Barra was in there getting dressed. The floor was carpeted with more roses and marigolds. The satin curtains were rose coloured too, with silver fleur-de-lis embroidered on them. Plump rose-coloured sofas with heart-shaped, pouty red cushions lined the walls. In the vases on the low mahogany tables, bunches of flame-coloured gladioli and white tuberoses added to the confusion. In the four corners of the room, miniature fountains sprayed rose-coloured water from the miniature penises of laughing cupids. Attar of roses hung in the air, clung to the curtains and the heavy furniture. The centre of the room was dominated by an imposing rosewood-canopied bed. A gold counterpane was draped over it—also littered with rose petals. Prominently displayed on the vast bed was a set of shocking pink lingerie and a tiny nightdress, all sheer and lace. Everything was ready and waiting, so far nothing had been touched. The cushions on the sofas sat primly upright. The rose petals on the floor and on the counterpane had not been touched. In a corner, a small brown-and-white bundle caught my eye. Barra's spaniel, Dotty, raised her head, a question in her mournful eyes: where was Barrabundla?

At that very moment, Barra was speeding through the streets of Delhi at ninety kilometres an hour with Shiv and his new wife Parvati in their new Maruti Esteem.

In a whirl and flutter of peach-coloured silk, she arrived.

'Oh, I'm so sorry I'm late. I sort of lost track of the time,' she apologized lightly.

'On your own wedding,' her mother said dryly.

'So what, why should you care? It's not your wedding, is it?'

'Thank god it's not my wedding. I would have died of shame.'

'Thank you. Now will you get out of my wedding chamber, mother?'

Actually, Barrabundla was nervous. At six that evening when she should have been getting ready, she had locked herself into the bathroom, and lying naked on the black-and-white tiles, she had consumed tons of ice cream. When her friends arrived to escort her to the farm at seven, Barra was still in the bathroom. At eight, when the banging on the bathroom door became like ceaseless gunfire, Barra opened the door.

'I'm ready,' she announced, rivulets of sweat running down her body through dried ice-cream fields. Then she puked.

The group of friends who had come to escort her to the farmhouse weren't too surprised. They had been expecting something like this. Barrabundla was known for her surprises—that's why they all crowded to her parties. One time, rumour had it, she let five guys do it to her at the same time. Fact or fiction? The women swore it was true, the men, they weren't so sure. But what they were sure of was Barra's unfailing kindness and her good humour, and her booze. And so she had many friends among members of the opposite sex. The women? One didn't count the women—they simply went where the men went.

Shiv and Parvati dumped her in the shower. They slapped her a couple of times, and Shiv pinched her sunflower nipples one last time. The women dried her and crammed her body into the lush silk lehnga weighed down with rhinestones and sequins. They slipped the short kurta over her head and crammed in her breasts into the right pockets. There was no time for the dupatta, so they left it for later, once they reached the farmhouse which was still a good hour away.

'So Barra, how do you feel, now that you're going to be married?'

'Am I? Of course I am,' she giggled. 'Who am I getting married to?'

'Silly, to Sanjeev, yaar.'

'Gosh, I'd almost forgotten about him. Where is he?'

Sanjeev was standing in the muddy parking lot outside the farmhouse gates along with the rest of the baaraat. He was doing what he always did when it involved a date with Barra—waiting. But waiting suited him. He liked sitting around, his huge gymnasium muscles at rest, thoughts flying randomly through his head, and nothing more expected of him than to wait till Barra appeared and took charge.

It was the same with her ritual of getting ready. Barra would never let him watch her. It spoiled the surprise, she said. So he was forced to wait in her bedroom, an overweight fly caught in a tumbled nest of clothes, dirty lingerie and sheets, while the spider prepared herself in the bathroom. From behind the bathroom door sounds would emerge: water running, Barra peeing, Barra gargling, flush pulling, paper tearing, shower curtains rustling, a scream of pain, Barra hurting herself, panting Barra, chuckling Barra, Barra talking to herself. From under the door little whiffs of Barra smell would reach his nostrils, filling him with longing. To Sanju the bathroom was Barra's temple—a place of magic and mystery, honesty and deceit that were applied in layers to befuddle the mind. In a trance he would lie before the locked bathroom door. Slowly, his body would melt and seep through the crack between floor and door—become water and fall in curtains over her naked back, arms, breasts, stomach, hips and thighs, or become steam and settle like diamonds on her pubic hair, one with her body.

But waiting was purgatory for the rest of the baaraat party. The heat was thick as chocolate, clogging the pores and choking the lungs. A roll of thunder broke the waiting air but was smothered almost immediately.

At last a light rain began to fall. Out of the darkness a million mosquitoes appeared and began to attack the waiting people. The halos of light around the band-walas' kerosene chandeliers began to dance, thick with tiny fighting bodies. The rain soon soaked the women's fine saris, and the men's silk kurtas, freeing the odours of dried sweat, old cigarettes and mothballs, feeding their misery. For Sanju though, the rain also fed his longing—the scent of dry earth and sweat potent reminders of Barra.

As soon as she emerged, Sanju would rush into the bathroom, shut the door, and breathe deeply—pulling her essence into his lungs. Then he would unzip his pants and stare at himself in the mirror, his member swelling between the pots and jars and womanly disorder around the sink.

'Fuck man, your horse just farted,' Gothru announced through pinched nostrils.

'No shit.'

'Yes shit, he just done it.'

'Shit. Where is she?'

Sanju was nervous. The horse they had provided him, a huge white carthorse, scared him. When he had tried to mount, the horse almost fell onto his forepaws like a camel. He had grabbed the creature's hair to steady himself, and the damned beast began to reverse. He had fallen down and his gold coat got muddied. Everyone, even his best friends, Bappi, Gothru, and Sunny, roared with laughter.

'If that's the way you're going to mount your wife, Sanju,' someone shouted from amongst the baaraat, 'you're not going to get very far, you know.'

'Shuddup!' Sanju yelled angrily.

Someone brought a brush and tried to scrape the mud off his coat. That only made things worse because the mud was wet and spread like peanut butter across his coat.

He tried again. This time four men held the horse, one holding on to each leg. He stood beside the horse and tried to think of mounting Barra. He grabbed the horse's mane firmly with his left hand, put his right foot into the stirrup and, holding the saddle with his other hand, heaved himself onto the horse. The poor animal almost jumped sideways in shock and Sanju fell forward, reaching blindly for something to hold on to. He grabbed a handful of hair and tried to place his other foot more firmly in the stirrup. The horse yowled. Sanju let go and grabbed the saddle. 'Hold the horse, will you,' he snapped at the men beside him. They were staring at him strangely. He looked up and realized with awful suddenness that somehow he had got onto the horse backwards. 'Oh God,' he groaned. This time there were only a few laughs as he slid off the horse.

Then, just as he was about to hoist himself up a third time, Gothru had a brainwave. 'Hey man, hold it. I've got it,' he shouted. He grabbed a chair and placed it next to the horse.

Sanjeev stood on the chair and then hoisted himself onto the horse. It was easy.

'Gimme a cigarette, yaar.'

'Sorry yaar, this is my last one.'

'Go ask the band-walas.'

'Actually, what I need is a drink.'

'You'll have to wait till Barrabundla arrives, for that.'

His sister waddled up to him, dark and threatening in her gaudy red salwar-kameez. 'Where the hell is she?' She saw Sanju's mud-streaked coat and squeaked, 'What have you done to yourself? Do you know that the achkan you're wearing cost twelve thousand rupees? Now we won't even be able to give it to the sweeper.'

'Oh stop it, sis. You'll get married soon,' Sanju said wearily. But that only made her angrier.

She sneered, 'Better not get married than marry the kind of girl you are marrying. What a shame for our family. She's even late to her own wedding!' A sudden thought made her face clear a little. 'Is she going to come? You're sure she hasn't changed her mind?'

'Shuddup. She promised.' Sanju wished she would go away.

Bappi came back with the cigarette. Sanju's sister left in a hurry. She hated Bappi as much as she hated Sanju, but unlike Sanju, she feared Bappi too. Once, when they were all in school, Bappi had stuck bubble gum all over her head for stealing their porno magazines and showing them to her mother. She'd had to have all her hair shaved off and it had never grown back to the same length.

'The band-wala wanted ten rupees,' Bappi said, grinning.

'What? That's robbery,' Sanju screamed.

'Yeah, I know. But he said, "It is a wedding after all, sahib,"' Bappi replied.

'Okay, okay, did you get the matches?'

'Oh shit. I forgot.'

'Go get them, you fool. For ten rupees a cigarette, at least they can give us a free light.' Sanju was yelling in irritation. It felt good to let it out. Sanju's uncle heard him. He walked up to the horse and held up a light. Sanju bent down and inhaled deeply. The cigarette glowed red.

'So what is it you see in her, beta?' his uncle asked, walking up to the horse and standing on tiptoes. This uncle was his mother's brother, the BIC ballpoint-refills magnate and a bachelor. Sanju was his heir. He was already quite drunk, having helped himself liberally to the booze lying in the dicky of the Maruti Esteem that had been following Sanju's carthorse at a discreet distance. 'Why did you choose this woman when your mother would have found you a princess? What is her magic?'

Sanju was tongue-tied. He knew that his uncle, the only one that mattered, emperor of the BIC ballpoint-pen refill trade with a market share of seventy-eight per cent, was trying to help him, trying to tell him that he was on Sanju's side.

The uncle continued to tease Sanju good-humouredly. 'Come on. Explain to me, yaar. I am just a poor bachelor, unversed in the ways of women.' He laughed at his own joke and winked conspiratorially at his nephew. The entire family knew that he frequented a brothel in Churiyanwaligali, and was the long-time lover of a Muslim dancer called Shabnam.

Cornered atop his four-legged friend, Sanju took a long drag on his cigarette and began, 'It's ... she gets under your skin, mamaji.'

His uncle looked at him, uncomprehending.

'N-n-no, no, no,' Sanju tried again, 'it's just that ... well, you can feel her on your skin even when she's not there, like perf ... her smell ... ' He tailed off, miserably aware of how stupid he sounded.

He stared down into his uncle's virile moustached face. It was shining wet, little rivulets of sweat pouring down each side of his nose and into his moustache. He thought, how could he explain to his uncle, in his cheap white suit of some shiny unknown fabric, who had introduced him to the whores of old Delhi, that Barra's essence, the core of her seductiveness, lay in the complex cocktail of odours that enveloped her, flowed around her when she moved, and clung to a man when she left him, driving him crazy with longing.

'Her smell?' His uncle laughed. 'Is it her perfume then? What a simple trick to fall for. And to think I could have bought you an entire perfume factory with a harem in the middle—if that

...ntrapped you with. Really, beta, I'm disappointed.'
...his head. Little drops of sweat flew in all directions,
...g the light.
'No mamaji, it's not a perfume specifically, it's ... it's her
smell,' Sanju tried to explain.

He had long tried to decode the various ingredients of the
Barra magic, and failed. In the places they went to, her smell was
diluted with alcohol and cigarette smoke, so Sanju was left chasing
after her in the girly, roses-and-cream smell of her soap. Or in
the deodorant she used; or in the acrid medicinal smell of her
pimple cream and the smell of her face powder, dry and slightly
bitter; or in the sluggish petroleum smell of her lipstick, and in
her vaseline and her nail polish and her Oil of Olay moisturizer.

Apart from these mundane smells that were nonetheless the
foundations of her charm, there were the more personal smells
of her hair, her sweat, her skin, her pee—mushroomy odours
that rose smoky, like burnt milk and baby puke. Sometimes he
caught the dry, powdery smell of her upper arms in the odour of
ashes, her sweat in the gently overflowing gutters of the monsoon,
and her inner thighs in the smell of incense and overripe fruit
and vanilla ice cream. In the smell of a wet campfire he smelt her
hair, and sitting in a car, filling petrol at the garage next to the
biggest fruit and vegetable mart in Delhi he smelt her mouth.

'Mouth,' he said aloud, the word bursting out of his lungs
like a sigh.

'Her *what*? You sound like a man bewitched. Has she really
bewitched you as your mother keeps telling me?' His uncle's eyes
began to bulge.

'Of course not, mamaji. Mother is just jealous that I didn't
marry someone of her choosing. She's a lovely woman, gori,
beautiful hips and skin. And her grandfather was ICS.'

'And poor. What do we want with such people? What do
they know about business? And they will expect us to feed them.
As it is, you youngsters ... dowry is not fashionable, is it? What
was good enough for your elders isn't good enough for you. Is
it?'

'No mamaji, it's …'

'So how did you meet her? How long did you see her before telling your bechari mother? And where did she get her name? It is not even a Hindu name.'

'I met her at a party,' Sanju snapped. The heat was getting to him and Barra's lateness was beginning to worry him too. A muffled groan from Gothru made him look down. He bit his tongue in horror as he realized who he was talking to.

'A party was it? Nowadays one gets married at parties.' His uncle's voice was deceptively soft. 'Whose party?' he barked. 'Was it Sunny and Gothru's party? Or Minnu's?'

'No, mamaji, it was someone else's. Someone you don't know.'

'I know all about your famous parties, and the disco dancing and drinking.' His uncle was shouting now, in an uneasy blend of English and Punjabi.

Sanju tried miserably to shush his uncle, whose drunken voice kept getting louder. Cars drove by the sandpit, the passengers staring curiously at them.

Suddenly, Barra's brother appeared. 'She's come. We'll be ready to receive you in five minutes.'

Everyone was abuzz. The band-walas lit their gaslights and tuned their instruments, the horses neighed and stamped their feet, the camels rose, the members of the baaraat put on their rose-coloured turbans. Someone handed Sanju his, which was bedecked with real gold, the veil made of thousands of little American diamonds. The women, led by Sanju's mother and sister, began to sing.

The band began to play *Amma dekh*. The little nieces and nephews in their lace-and-sequin dresses and gold miniature achkans began to dance. Gothru got his mother shaking her enormous but muscular ass next to his skinny, shaggy one. Bappi twirled his sister around. Barra's brother, an avid polo player like his grandfather, came to Sanju and fearlessly grabbed the reins of the horse. He was to lead them in. The party heaved and shuffled into a disorderly line, and slowly proceeded down the dirt road to the big black gates. Someone had put flowers on them and so they looked less forbidding. Guests were entering in droves. Sanju watched them through his veil; there was no one he knew.

A posse of beautiful girls lined the driveway, holding diyas in their hands. Clumsily, he dismounted. Someone giggled. Girls, he thought, they were all so damned superior, wiggling their asses in your face at the Camel Court, smiling, asking for a 300-rupee bottle of beer, and telling you to go to hell the next minute.

Cameras flashed, the crowd (now around 500 people) clapped and cheered. From under the combined onslaught of the military band's enthusiastic rendition of Mendelssohn's wedding march, and the baaraat band's equally spirited version of *Choli ke piche kya hai*, Barrabundla appeared. She wore the traditional ghaghra of all Punjabi brides. But it was silver-grey and black instead of red or pink or any of the other colours brides normally wear. Huge silver roses climbed up her stomach, encircled her breasts, and erupted in pearly splendour over her nipples. The tight silk top stacked her flesh into neat upright compartments of waist, hip and breast.

She waded sedately through the crowd, stopping here and there to say hello to a particular friend—a politician with a purple birthmark like an ink stain on the right side of his face, an Austrian count, her eunuch hairdresser Isaac, Ayesha and her designer boyfriend. Then there was Randy, the Australian DJ at the Encounter, the latest and trendiest nightclub in town. Sanju recognized the woman he was with, randy Ritu. Shiv, whose father made the Maruti headlamps, was there too with his bored-looking wife, the daughter of General Rawat. They swarmed around her, hundreds of faces and heads Sanju had only seen in magazines. He searched the crowd for his friends. He couldn't find them. They're probably at the bar, he thought bitterly.

Alone on the dais, lost in the dense shadows created by Barra's brilliant entry, Sanju felt suddenly small. She's taking ages to get here, what's wrong with her? When she finally stepped on the dais he said bitterly, 'What took you so long?'

'What do you mean?' she said, her big smile freezing.

'Beti, you look wonderful, just like a bride,' one of Sanju's many widowed and indigent aunts gushed.

'I mean I've been waiting here for almost three hours, that's what. I almost went back home,' Sanju said belligerently.

Barra's face slowly turned purple. 'You can still go,' she said. 'I'll find someone to marry me right here from among the guests.'

She stepped forward before he could say anything. 'Does anyone here want to marry me? This is your chance, because Sanju here is having second thoughts. So I'm going to count to three. I'll marry the first one who steps onto the dais. This is your lucky night, guys, 'cause Sanju here doesn't quite know what he's giving up. Some of you out there aren't so stupid, I know. One ...'

The band stopped playing. Silence. Then a few hesitant, hurriedly choked laughs. Barra continued, 'Come on, Shiv. I know you want to. All you have to do is change your religion and then you can have two wives, or divorce that cow you have with you.' The laughter grew bolder.

'Two.'

Sanju's uncle stepped up, waving his hands, smiling, sweating. 'Come on, beti. Sanju was only joking. You also only joking, no? It's a good joke. Very funny. Now you two must marry quickly or the auspicious hour will pass, and it will be unlucky. Must not joke with fate.' Sweat was pouring down his face.

Barra's father stepped up and quietly handed her a garland of marigolds. On the other side, Sanju's mother handed him his garland. She wouldn't look him in the face. He felt her shame and anger. 'Sorry, ma,' he mumbled. The baaraat band began to play furiously—to make up for its earlier lapse. The other band joined in. Now a shehnai could be heard too.

Sanju turned humbly towards Barra; but she was smiling at him now. 'I'm sorry darling, it's you I want to marry,' she whispered. She picked up the garland of marigolds. Her body swayed towards him, enveloping him in her warm milk-and-honey smell. She kissed him, running her teeth along his lower lip, just as he liked, as she had taught him to like.

two

hope

It is forty-three degrees outside and the sun has turned the tarmac into a glutinous swamp. The furnace breath of the 'loo' makes the dagger-shaped leaves of the eucalyptus trees dance. They are the only things that move with any grace or energy.

'Eight minutes for us to get through,' Sheila remarks, eyeing the mosaic of cars and buses ahead of us.

'Yup,' I smile. Waiting is a pleasure with her beside me.

'I'm glad I don't drive. There are just too many cars in Delhi now. Too many cars and too many people in this city.'

My hands let go of the steering wheel. Does her remark include me?

On either side of us cars squeeze into every inch of free space till none remains. I turn the vent of the air conditioning more fully towards myself, and retreat into the music coming out of the car stereo system. My mind fuses with the voice of the singer and I am as close to bliss as one can be on a hot summer's morning in Delhi.

A year after I moved from Bihar's crumbling capital city, Patna, to Delhi, to take up my job as special correspondent with the *Business and Political Monitor*, Sheila and I bumped into each other at the Kalkaji market one Sunday morning. She had just finished buying milk while I was still in line, waiting to do so. Using her prerogative as a woman, she had skipped the queue. When she saw me she said, 'If I'd seen you earlier I'd have got you your milk as well.'

Sheila is the most beautiful woman in the office. And a great writer. Her English is flawless. She never has to search for words. And she is independent and single. Which is why she scared me so much that I never spoke to her until the day we met at the Mother Dairy booth. The next day she walked right up to me in front of the others and asked if I could give her a lift home. I had just bought my car—on a lease finance scheme sponsored by the company that owned the newspaper—and was very proud of it. I had spared no expense on accessories—special paint, air conditioning, and even a stereo with four speakers. In spite of this, when Sheila eased her long jean-clad legs into the car, I felt more like a badly dressed country boy than a warrior who conquered the metropolis each day in his brand-new chariot. When she asked if she could ride with me the next day and the next, the feeling grew within me that a true warrior had to have a beautiful queen to protect. And Sheila was that jewel, given to me by Delhi, my new home.

An insistent knocking cuts through the web of rhythm and melody in which we are cocooned. Greasy pictures of women made to look sexy are plastered onto the windscreen and the boy who has put them there suddenly appears on the other side, his eyes pleading.

Sheila purses her lips primly. 'I wonder what that young boy thinks about having to parade around with half-naked women clutched to his chest. They shouldn't allow them to sell such things on the road, it's obscene.'

The boy's eyes draw me in. He would make a good cover for a hard-hitting issue on Delhi's urban disaster: with his glamorous cover girls and anxious eyes, and Humayun's tomb in the distance. I turn to tell Sheila but she is staring disgustedly at a man outside who presses his broken veined nose to her window, waving orange rags. Sheila and I shake our heads furiously at him. But he doesn't leave immediately, he first stares at her, drinking his fill of her beauty. No sooner has he gone than another man takes his place and tries to sell us small plastic statues of Hanuman, Ganesh and Lakshmi. His voice is a thin, tired drone, and his words run seamlessly into each other. Sheila and I exchange glances.

'It only gets worse. There's no place to breathe any more,' Sheila says. 'It's become a veritable invasion.' I hear the ragged edge of panic in her voice.

'They're hardly an army,' I feel forced to say.

'Yes, but that makes it worse. You can't reason with poor people. They won't listen to anyone. They just have to be sent back.'

'Sent back? Where?' I squirm uncomfortably.

'I know you think I'm being inhuman,' she says, 'but I'm just being practical. Look at them, would they be selling junk on the streets if they could find something better to do here?' Suddenly, she becomes animated. 'Did you see last Sunday's papers? There was a story about how a thirteenth-century tomb just disappeared because Bangladeshi squatters had built jhuggis, using the stones. And it wasn't even front-page news! How is that different from the Afghans destroying Bamiyan, you tell me?'

'They were Taliban, not Afghans, for a start,' I correct her. Something must be bothering her today, I tell myself.

'Taliban are Afghans,' she insists. 'They're Muslims, no? And they're doing the same thing here.'

She must have received bad news last night. Maybe a close relative was dying. We come to another crossing and I look around nervously for beggars and salesmen. Miraculously, the crossing is clear. Sheila rants on, 'Do you know, in my flat I only get two hours of water a day. The jhuggi colony below gets water all day long. I can't wait for the bulldozers to come and clear the place.'

Appalled, I say, 'But ... those are their homes.'

'Since when have parasites had the right to a home?' she counters coolly.

I turn to face her. 'What's bothering you today, Sheila? Is something wrong?' She looks away, and is silent. Then she says, 'You may be used to beggars where you come from, but I'm not. There were hardly any in Delhi when I was growing up. Now look at it. I just can't take it any more, the way their eyes fix upon you, demanding more, no matter what you give them. And when you give to one, ten more arrive.'

I look away, at a loss for words. To call a human being a parasite sounds like blasphemy, a challenge to the gods. My eyes fall on a man waiting at the kerb beside me. He is standing comfortably on his crutches. His clothes are clean. Only the empty leg of his trouser neatly pinned back and the way his eyes knowledgeably scan the passing cars betray his profession. Our eyes meet and instead of twisting his face into a grimace of despair, he smiles. I stare at him in surprise. *Beggars aren't supposed to smile.* Beggars are the city's wishing wells, our guards against misfortune. Beggars have to look miserable.

But the missing leg decides me. Hurriedly, I fish in my pocket for a coin. But Sheila seems to have jinxed me. The coin escapes my fingers and remains hidden somewhere in the folds of my trouser pocket. The beggar watches me sympathetically. I roll down the window. 'I'm sorry, I can't find any change right now,' I tell him. 'I'll give you something next time.'

'Doesn't matter,' he says calmly in Hindi, 'I'll be here.'

I laugh, amazed at his attitude. 'All right, next time then, I promise.'

Beside me, Sheila sniffs but says nothing.

That evening Sheila is going to a party in central Delhi after work, so she doesn't drive back with me. One traffic jam follows another and I let people edge their cars ahead of me. I am in no hurry to get back. The evening stretches before me with nothing but the television for company. At the Moolchand Crossing, I see the man still standing on his crutches beside the road. How tired he must feel standing all day on two bits of wood just to make a few rupees, I think.

'You're back quickly,' the beggar jokes, recognizing me.

'I said I'd be back, didn't I?' I have a five-rupee coin ready and hand it to him.

He smiles. 'Thanks. But you needn't have. I made more than enough money today.'

I stare hard at him. Is he trying to get something more out of me? My eyes settle on the crutches and the empty leg. Pity washes away my doubts and I slip the money into his shirt pocket.

'What happened to your leg?' I ask.

He laughs. 'I had it amputated because it kept getting injured and since I couldn't feel it, the flesh would fester. It looks better like this, don't you think?'

Cut off! My blood freezes. 'You're a *leper*,' I blurt out.

He looks surprised. 'Of course.'

'God, I'm so sorry. I didn't realize.' My hand itches suddenly.

'No, no ... don't worry,' he says quickly, seeing my involuntary action. 'I'm cured now.'

I hide my hand. 'Yes, but ... I mean ... it must have been terrible for you.'

He laughs strangely. 'It wasn't so bad, it brought me to Delhi.' Then he adds, 'You'd better go, your light's changing.'

The next day I tell Sheila about the beggar as we drive to work. 'What do you make of that?' I finish excitedly.

'So you met a beggar who likes the city. Why shouldn't he? He gets everything he needs, and he doesn't have to work for it.'

'But he likes life, in spite of being a leper and having to cut off his own leg. There's something very noble in that. Don't you think?'

'I don't know what you mean. Sorry,' she says coldly.

I don't know what exactly I am trying to say, either. Something about the leper touched me, filled me with awe, and frightened me. I had hoped she would understand—the way women seem to understand these things. I had hoped she would be as impressed as I was.

At the crossing we see the leper again. He is wearing a bright purple shirt today, clean and neatly ironed. I take out some change.

'How are you today?' I ask, handing him the money. Sheila watches us.

'Fine,' he says. His smile warms me.

'What's your name?' I ask impulsively.

'Shibu, Shibu Mondal,' he replies.

Gradually, Shibu Mondal becomes part of the morning routine of fighting traffic while Sheila complains about the invasion of her city. I look forward to his smile, his air of being content with not moving too much. Even Sheila has begun to smile when we approach the crossing. Sometimes she teases me, 'Got your change ready? Or shall I give you some?'

Then one day he isn't there. There is a hole in the road where he normally stands, and thin Bihari labourers are picking desultorily at it. I stare at the spot, feeling bereft. When the lights change, I crawl away, still scanning the sides of the road for him.

'Don't worry. He'll be back. He's probably on holiday,' Sheila says.

A week later, the road has been mended, the hole filled. But Shibu Mondal hasn't returned. I worry about him, wondering whether the leprosy had come back.

'Leprosy doesn't come back, silly,' Sheila laughs.

'But … what if it did? He would hate to go back into a lepers' home, I know it. Those places are worse than prisons.'

'As if this city is any better,' she says sourly.

'Well, he doesn't think so,' I reply hotly, tired of her constant carping. In a sudden flash of empathy, I understand what has attracted me to him. 'He loves this city. He sees the good in it.'

'What good?' Sheila sneers as we drive past the vegetable market at Garhi. 'If you weren't a Bihari, I'd think you were joking.'

I brake sharply as a herd of cows noses its way through a litter of discarded fruit, newspaper wrappings and vegetables, delicately choosing what to eat. There are at least twenty-five of them on the road. We wait for them to cross. To me they look quite beautiful, islands of tranquillity in the manic swirl of Delhi traffic.

They have a completely different effect on Sheila. She turns to me, a haunted look in her eyes. 'Look around you with the eyes of an educated man for once, instead of constantly comparing this city to that backward-looking shit-hole you came from.'

I stiffen. Am I never to be allowed to forget that I don't belong here?

'This city is being strangled by overpopulation,' she continues, oblivious. 'Look at them, see how many calves there are! These are not strays. Their owners have deliberately left them to forage on the roads and in the waste bins, so that they do not have to spend anything on feeding them.'

'But look what efficient garbage managers they are,' I joke.

Sheila's face takes on the expression of disdainful wonder that I most hate. 'Garbage! With buildings sticking out like mushrooms, that's all that's left here. In less than twenty years this city has become nothing more than a giant breeding ground for bacteria.' Her face fills with despair. 'How I long to get away from it; but there is nowhere to go.'

'What do you mean, nowhere to go?' I make it clear I think she exaggerates.

'This is the only place where I can live safely as a divorcee.'

'How ... have you thought about moving to Bombay, or Bangalore?' I ask, concern for her overwhelming my wounded pride.

She laughs wildly. 'You don't get it, do you? Bombay was taken over by the hordes a long time ago. To get away, the rich built upwards and suffocated the city, cutting out the sky. Bangalore is a fake, a parvenu. It's a village with an army cantonment in its midst. This city was different. It was full of space, of sky, of gardens and flowers. But they'll do a Bombay on this city too. Because that's how the *bloody politicians* make their money. They'll let the hordes in, push down the standards, and bury the individual in a crowd of hungry stomachs.'

We finish the drive in silence.

Sheila has infected me with her despair. Even in the air-conditioned calm of the office I fail to shake off a sense of impending doom. Delhi seems a charmed city to me, a city full of possibilities, a city that is alive and constantly growing. But for Sheila, growth was the root of the problem. Could there really be too much growth? Was Delhi growing into a hell? What kind of a hell would it become: a lawless ghost town like Patna, or something different? Somehow it didn't seem possible. Someone like Sheila could not exist in hell. Sheila doesn't know what hell is. She flirts with despair because she has never really seen it. By afternoon, I feel as though my body is on fire. At five I realize I am running a fever, so I finish my story and go straight home.

The fever keeps me in bed for two days. The air conditioner had broken down the day before and the room is suffocatingly hot. In my fever I feel the walls pressing in on me. Is this what Delhi is doing to Sheila, I wonder. On the third day, the fever subsides. I get out of bed shakily, walk to the living room, and pick up the newspapers that have piled up by the door. I sit down at the dining table and begin reading. But I can't concentrate. Where is Sheila? How had she got to work? Did someone else give her a lift or did she take the bus? I hope she took the bus. I tell myself I am glad to have been spared her gloom and doom scenarios. Let someone else have the pleasure for a change.

I get up. Normally, I like being on my own in the flat. But today I feel lonely. I go out onto the tiny balcony. The sunlight bounces off the concrete walls of the other apartments and blinds me. I see not a soul. There is no sound to be heard; even the dogs have disappeared. Everything is so hard here. Hard as concrete. Our words bounce off each other's surfaces. Where do they go? I think of Shibu. Where could he be? On some other busy crossroad, full of people to talk to, or tied to a bed in some nameless leprosarium. Somehow, I cannot shake off the feeling that he is in trouble. He had seemed so happy at his crossroad, there was no reason for him to change.

The doorbell rings. I go to open it, my heart beating like a sledgehammer. A stranger stands there, holding a battered leather medical bag from the fifties, just like the one my father had carried.

'I've come for the air conditioner,' the man says laconically.

I stare at him. From his very first words, I know he is from Bihar and a wave of nostalgia engulfs me. I am taken back to the huge house by the Ganga where I grew up along with twenty other cousins, never knowing what it was to be alone. My nostalgia colours the man's features and he even begins to look like one of my cousins.

'This is number 317, isn't it?' the electrician asks impatiently.

I do something I have never done in my year-long stay in Delhi. 'Where in Bihar are you from?' I ask.

He looks stunned and then wary. 'From Gaya,' he says. 'But now I live here,' he adds quickly.

I know that defensive reflex only too well. How often had I used those same words, the last time with Sheila.

'You were expected three days ago,' I say to the electrician, speaking the way one would to a younger brother.

He shrugs and looks sulky. 'I was told only today,' he lies.

Suddenly, he ceases to be a fellow Bihari and becomes an unreliable Delhi electrician.

'Come along then.' I show him to the bedroom. He begins his work. I decide to make some tea. As I pour the tea into a cup, he reappears.

'I've finished,' he says.

I look up, surprised. 'That was quick.'

'The job was easy, and I don't believe in wasting time,' he replies. His accent is like the soft breeze of the east, easing the loneliness in my heart.

'Have some tea,' I say.

'No. Thanks. I should go,' he replies. But his face softens.

'I'm from Bihar too,' I say, handing him a glass of tea. 'I moved here thirteen months ago.'

'Yes, I know you are from Bihar,' he replies. 'I can hear it in your voice too.'

We look at each other for a moment and begin to laugh.

'How did you get here?' I ask after the laughter ends.

'How did I get here?' He shakes his head and grins. 'I didn't want to come to the city. But we were four brothers, you see. And my father only had six acres of land.'

I nod and wait.

'It's a long story,' he demurs, looking at his watch.

'Come on, sit down and tell me,' I insist.

He looks surprised but accepts my invitation. Putting down his bag of tools, he takes the tea I hold out to him. But he remains standing respectfully.

'When my father told me I had to leave,' he begins, giving an odd laugh, 'I went around the village asking people about Delhi. They told me all kinds of stories. Delhi was full of gold, it was full of criminals. People were rich but they weren't human. But everyone seemed to know someone who had gone to Delhi and become rich. So I decided to come and try my luck too.'

'And did you succeed?' I look at his polyester trousers and none too clean shirt, his worn-out bag and scuffed leather chappals, and prepare myself for a hard-luck story. But what Kishan Singh tells me goes far beyond my wildest imagination.

*

When Kishan Singh left the village, his father gave him a hundred and fifty rupees. He tried to give the money back. It seemed a fortune. But his father insisted. 'You'll need it,' he told his son. 'It's bad luck to approach Goddess Lakshmi empty-handed, and Delhi is the Goddess Lakshmi. If she smiles on you, you'll be rich. If not … ' He looked away. Kishan Singh decided then and there that he was going to be rich.

'I'll bring you double, or I won't come back,' he promised.

The train journey from Aurangabad, Bihar, was long and slow. People tried to talk to him, for he was a good-looking young man. But he didn't respond. As the train neared Delhi, he noticed a change come over his fellow passengers. They lost interest in each other and stared out of the windows or at the walls, clutching their belongings to them. They wouldn't meet each other's eyes. When the train arrived, they all leapt up at the same time, and pushed their way out as quickly as possible. Kishan Singh remained in the compartment till he was alone. He remembered that he hadn't asked his fellow travellers if they knew Khakroli, the place where his cousin lived. He looked out of the silent compartment and was stupefied by the noise and by the speed at which everything moved.

Kishan Singh's cousin lived in a patch of wasteland on the

Sultanpur-Badarpur border, nearly fifty kilometres from the city centre. It took Kishan two days and almost all the money he had to get to the place. When he arrived, Nandan Singh, his cousin, wasn't there. He looked around him bitterly. Nothing moved. Everything was brown and dead. The ground, cracked and alkaline, was rimmed with white. In the middle, beside a dead tree, stood a tube well, and beside it a corrugated iron shack. A huge lock on the flimsy door indicated that someone actually lived there. Kishan Singh sat down in the shade of the shack and waited.

When evening came and his cousin still hadn't returned, Kishan Singh walked to the nearest village. He asked the owner of a ration shop if he knew his cousin and the man laughed bitterly. 'Know him? Which shopkeeper doesn't know him here?' The shopkeeper stared at him suspiciously. 'Are you his brother? He owes me money.' Kishan Singh shook his head and ran back to the room to await his cousin's return. By now he was angry and very hungry. So he broke the lock on the door and entered the room.

It was a pitiful place. Bare, except for a charpoy, two broken chairs and a battered steel trunk which doubled as a kitchen table. There was no food on it. The kerosene stove looked as if it hadn't been used for several days. Hungry and tired, Kishan Singh lay down.

He must have fallen asleep because when he woke up a man was stumbling around in the dark, singing tunelessly. The man lit a lantern and Kishan Singh recognized his cousin, Nandan, his face swollen with alcohol.

'So you've come,' Nandan said, his face showing neither surprise nor shame, and extinguished the light. He lay down to sleep beside Kishan Singh and was soon snoring. Kishan remained wide awake. Tomorrow I'll go into the city and find a job, he vowed. I will never come back here.

A little later they were both awakened by a knock on the door. 'Who is it?' Nandan called out.

'I'm a truck driver. My truck's broken down on the main

road. Can I have a place to sleep?' a voice replied.

His cousin opened the door and a huge bearded man stepped inside, carrying a cloth bundle.

'Hey, can we have a light in here so I can see your faces? How will I know you aren't ghosts?' he joked.

A shiver ran down Kishan's back. Why was his cousin inviting death into the house?

When his cousin finally managed to light the lantern, his doubts were confirmed. The man's face was dominated by two hard black eyes and big white teeth which he flashed all the time.

'That's better,' the truck driver said, sitting down. 'Tell me, where can I get some food? Is there a town nearby where a hungry, thirsty man can get some satisfaction?'

'The village is a kilometre away,' Nandan replied foolishly.

'My god! I've been walking for two hours on the highway. My truck broke down. I can't walk any further.' The man looked around. 'Can you give me some food? I haven't eaten all day.'

'There's no food. It's finished,' Kishan said quickly, wanting the man to leave.

The truck driver noticed Kishan and his eyes narrowed. 'Well, I have something that will kill the appetite,' he said with a flash of his teeth. He reached into his bundle and pulled out a pouch of country liquor. 'Here,' he thrust it at Kishan.

'I don't drink,' Kishan told him, pushing it away.

But Nandan's eyes brightened. He reached for the bag eagerly. Soon, he and the truck driver were happily drinking and playing cards.

Hunger kept Kishan awake but he pretended to sleep. When his cousin went outside to take a pee, the man suddenly loomed over him, a broad knife to his throat.

'Give me your money or I'll kill you,' he whispered.

Fear made Kishan's tongue move like water. He gave the man the thirty rupees he had left and begged him not to kill him. 'I just arrived from the village and have an old father to support and three sisters to marry.'

The last bit made the man put his knife away. 'All right, I'll spare you,' he said gruffly, 'but don't say a word to your cousin or I'll kill you both.'

Just then, Nandan Singh returned, singing. The truck driver hid the knife in his belt and turned towards him. 'Let's have another game, you're a lucky fellow.'

His legs shaking, Kishan got up and went outside. He needed to urinate badly. As he left, he heard the truck driver tell his cousin, 'Look, he's not even drinking and he needs to pee. What a woman!'

Nandan Singh's laughter rang in Kishan's ears as he peed. All of a sudden it was cut off and Kishan knew he was dead. He began to run.

The road met the highway on the crest of a hill. To the north he saw a great orange glow. He began to walk towards it. He walked all night towards the lights. In the morning he got a lift on a truck carrying cement into Delhi.

Kishan Singh pauses, takes a sip of the now cold tea.

'What did you do when you arrived?' I ask breathlessly.

'I worked as a construction worker on the Nizamuddin Bridge. It was worse than working in the fields because you couldn't stop until someone blew a whistle. And the contractor insisted on taking "rent" for allowing us to sleep on the site. There wasn't even a bush behind which one could defecate privately.'

When the whistle blew to signal the end of the day, Kishan's arms felt like lead. Now he understood how Bholu the bull, back in the village, must have felt. He sat down on the ground and watched as the wives started the campfires and cooked. The other construction workers were Nepalis and tribals. They had seen his sacred thread and kept their distance. One by one the men trickled back after washing in the river. They sat down beside their wives and began to play with their children. Slowly, the air filled with the smell of cooking and the sound of children laughing.

As he watched, a band of steel tightened around his chest. Kishan had never felt so alone. He wondered if he would ever see his father again. Night came and his stomach burned. He looked up at the stars, far away and pitiless. At last a man came up to him and offered him a beedi. Kishan refused, telling him he didn't smoke.

'Where are you from?' the man asked.

When Kishan told him, the man looked disappointed. 'I thought you were from Bangladesh, like me.' He got up and walked back to his family. Kishan's spirits dipped even lower. He looked up at the stars and contemplated death. Later, someone brought him food, and a smelly blanket. He was already three-fourths asleep by then.

'But how did you become an electrician?' I ask impatiently.

'On the site I got to know one of the electrical workers, a Rajput like me, but from UP. He gave me a piece of advice that set me on my path. "If you want to succeed in Delhi," he said, "you have to stop working with your hands and attach yourself to a machine. Let the machine teach you to be its master. Then this city will be at your feet."'

When the monsoons came, the work on the bridge stopped. Kishan decided he'd had enough of the city. The wad of money in his shirt bulged, and he decided to go home. But the night before work ended, all his money was stolen as he slept.

'I blame myself. I shouldn't have gone out in a city I didn't know with people I didn't know,' Kishan says to me. 'It was the last time I touched alcohol.'

Kishan Singh was staring at the water of the Yamuna, wondering whether he had the courage to commit suicide, when the electrician found him. An electrical appliance shop in Connaught Place was taking in apprentices, he explained. 'I know the boss, I used to work for him. It's all fixed.'

So Kishan Singh became an apprentice electrician for 150 rupees a month. He worked fifteen hours a day, ate one meal and at night was locked into the shop to sleep. At last he had a roof over his head, and it was free. In the morning he woke up to the rattling of keys in the lock.

Six months later he was a certified electrician signed up with a huge Delhi-based contractor.

'But the money I saved during that time went for buying my tools and my degree. A year had passed since I arrived in Delhi and I still couldn't send my father his three hundred rupees,' Kishan Singh tells me.

Kishan's first job as an electrician was at Bharat Heavy Electrical's (BHEL) Haridwar plant. BHEL, a huge government-owned enterprise, had plants all over the country. Kishan Singh spent two years in that holy city on the banks of the Ganga. At the end of the two years the company offered him a permanent job in the maintenance department. But Kishan had begun to miss Delhi. Somehow the city had managed to get under his skin.

His contractor welcomed him back and got him a good job with another contractor who was installing central air conditioning in a new, Connaught Place office building for the air-conditioning company, Blue Star.

A reflective smile lights his face.

'On the recommendation of my contractor, the other contractor put me in charge of all the workmen on the second floor. That was where my luck turned.'

One morning, when the work was almost finished and it was time to test the system, Kishan came in to find the contractor who had hired him, the manager from Blue Star, and the building contractor, all waiting there. He realized immediately that something was wrong.

'Who paid you to do it?' his boss barked accusingly.

'What are you talking about?' he asked, stunned.

'I want to know who paid you to sabotage my work,' his contractor shouted, 'and if you don't confess, I will not pay you.'

Suddenly, Kishan understood his game. The contractor was trying to get out of paying them. He stepped up to the man and looked him in the eye. 'I'm sorry. Someone must have made a mistake yesterday after I left. Just give me one day and I'll fix it.'

The contractor looked startled. His mouth opened and then closed. He looked at the building contractor who was looking equally stunned, and quickly looked away. But not fast enough. Kishan caught the look that passed between the two men. He fixed his eyes on the Blue Star manager who looked relieved and immediately agreed to let him try and fix the problem.

Kishan's boss was forced to agree. But as they left he said to Kishan in an undertone, 'Come outside with me, I want to talk to you.' The contractor then turned to the other workers and announced, 'I will give a reward for information on the person who did this.' Then he turned and walked towards the lift. As he got into the lift he told Kishan, 'You better listen and do what I say and I'll look after you. Just shut your mouth and don't let anyone do anything. The system must not work, okay?'

After the lift doors shut, Kishan faced his co-workers. Some were openly rebellious. 'He's not going to pay us, let's just destroy this place,' one said. Some of the others nodded in agreement. An older man grabbed Kishan's arm. 'Do something. How will I feed my family? My son is ill and my wife is going to have another baby.'

Kishan bent over the wires and examined them closely. He realized immediately what had been done. The connections to the different meters had been tampered with and odd wires that didn't match had been deliberately joined together. It must have taken a group of four men working all night to do it. But it wasn't impossible to fix. They would have to test all the wiring and replace the burnt-out bits. It could take them all night, possibly two days, but it could be done.

'We can fix this quite easily,' he told the others, jubilantly.

'So what? That's not going to get us our money. Our families will starve anyway,' one man answered.

'They won't starve if we fix it. They'll have to pay us then,' Kishan argued.

'But it will take hours. We need to find other work, or else our families will go hungry today. Besides, it's deliberate. I've seen it done. The contractor has done it to get out of paying us.'

Eventually, Kishan managed to persuade them all. They worked all day and through the night to rip out and replace the wires. They had barely finished when the electrical contractor came back with the manager of Blue Star.

'We've fixed it,' he told them proudly.

The electrical contractor couldn't contain his rage. He started to abuse them all, but especially Kishan Singh whom he obviously regarded as the ringleader. 'How dare you?' he spluttered. 'You think you know more than I do? You have probably made things worse, you uneducated fool.'

Kishan Singh had never had such foul language heaped upon him. He felt as if his head would burst. But somehow he controlled himself for the sake of the others.

'I am not working for you any more. I don't want your money,' he told the contractor, taking off his badge. 'But you'd better pay these workers or I'll find you and kill you.' He walked out.

The next day Kishan Singh went to his first boss, the contractor who had introduced him to the other man and told him what had happened.

The electrician pauses and takes another sip of his tea. Then he looks directly into my eyes and continues, 'The man was honest but he could not move against one of his own kind. He advised me to go and meet the general manager at Blue Star instead.'

When he arrived at the Blue Star office, the general manager shook Kishan's hand as if he had been expecting him. He asked Kishan to sit down on the chair in front of him. 'You realize, don't you, that you've saved us a lot of money,' he said. 'Your contractor was in league with the builder who had commissioned us to do the air conditioning. The builder was trying to use this supposed mess to get out of paying us and was in league with the wiring contractor who would have used the excuse not to pay you. We've sacked your boss and paid the workers directly and are taking the builders to court. I gather that it was you who persuaded the workers to set the wiring right.' He paused, a smile tugging at the corners of his mouth. 'Will you manage our next project for us?'

The electrician finishes his tea. 'That's how I got my first break. Since then, I've worked on many projects and between projects I do little jobs like this one.'

'So you must be a rich man,' I say, feeling a little envious.

'No, I am not rich,' he protests, laughing, 'but I have a house in Delhi and my freedom. My brothers are all well settled. One is an electrician like me, the other is a house painter, and the last one looks after the dairy farm I started on our land in the village. And all my sisters are married—the last one got married eight months ago. Now I am free.'

He takes the glass to the kitchen and asks my permission to leave as if he were still the peasant and I the landlord.

I walk him to the door. His story has me both chilled and elated.

'You must be proud. Not many people have been as successful as you. This is a cruel city,' I say, patting his shoulder.

He looks surprised. 'Of course not! There are lots of people like me in the basti.'

'Lots? You are being modest,' I say.

'No. I am telling the truth,' he insists. 'The paanwala in the house opposite me has two cars, a Maruti Esteem and a Zen. He started with nothing, like me. Today he is rich.'

'How did he do it?'

'You ask him.' He laughs, then becomes serious. 'This city is made of gold for those who want to work hard. Come to my home and I'll introduce you to any number of such people.'

I do not argue with him. After he leaves, I head for my bed. I can't wait to see Sheila and tell her about this. Then maybe she will be freed of her despair. The fever takes hold of me once more. But some of the inner restlessness has left me. I dream of a million Kishan Singhs floating into the city, fighting bloody battles and then growing roots here.

*

Two days later, Sheila and I are driving to work again. This time she insists on driving me. I feel nervous about letting her, but she is impossible to refuse.

'Sorry I didn't visit you,' she says as soon as we change seats. 'But I was afraid you had the viral. This city is so full of diseases,

I can't run the risk of infection. My immune system won't take it any more.'

'That's all right,' I reassure her, thrilled that she had thought of coming to visit me.

'So, how were your days at home? Enjoyed them?'

'Yes, it was quite exciting actually,' I reply, trying to sound like her.

'Exciting? Was there a James Bond festival on TV in the afternoons?'

'No. I met an electrician.'

She rolls her eyes. 'No! I don't think I can handle another poor beggar story right now. There's too much sadness in this city anyway.'

'I'm not going to tell you a "poor anyone" story,' I snap, stung. 'This is a success story of the most unusual kind.'

As we approach a crossing, the light turns red in front of us. She brakes sharply.

I grab the dashboard.

'Sorry. Eight minutes to wait now. You may as well tell me about your fantastic electrician.'

So I tell her about Kishan Singh. When I finish, she says nothing.

'So what do you think?' I prompt.

'What's the point of your story?'

I can't believe my ears.

'The point of the story? Don't you see, there are literally thousands of Kishan Singhs in this city.'

'And ... so what?'

I stare at her pretty face. 'It means this is not a dying place. This is a city of hope. People come here and become rich, like Kishan Singh. They struggle and fight to make a place for themselves, they risk death, but they succeed. Don't you find that amazing? This city is a growing thing, Sheila. Can you not feel it?'

'And for every man that makes it, there are ten others too dumb or too weak to make it. What do those people do? They swarm the roads selling their rubbish, they build shanties and filthy the streets, they create garbage that suffocates the rest of us, and when all else fails, they cut off their limbs and beg. Of course, some things grow on dung heaps. But does that make it a growing healthy place?' She laughs, pleased at her use of metaphor.

I am silent. I want to say that the city isn't such a horrible place. I want to tell her that it isn't so horrible, could never be, because it holds her. But I can say nothing. I try to push away the image that delights and haunts me each night, of a radiant Sheila driving me to work with no clothes on.

We drive in silence for a while, occupied with our own thoughts. Suddenly she says, 'I'm sorry. Sometimes, it's hard for me to see the bright side of things. This city used to be so beautiful. If only you could have seen it twenty years ago.' Then she adds, her eyes glowing, 'Your story was beautiful, you're obviously a total romantic. I like that. But, of course, you've got it all wrong. That's not what this city is about.'

'What's it about then? You complain about the people but you don't really see them. All you see is politicians, old buildings, corruption, cars—'

'Gosh, you're quite sexy when you get emotional,' she interrupts, smiling tenderly.

'It's the Bihari in me,' I reply, not willing to be mollified.

She bursts into laughter. 'I didn't know Biharis had a sense of humour.'

'When you come from the poorest state in the country, you have to have a sense of humour,' I say. 'You Delhiwalis have no sense of humour, you're too rich.'

'Touché.'

She leans across and squeezes my hand lightly.

I go still in shock. Then my body fills with helium and I start to rise. I feel I can climb Mount Everest with a bag of cement on my back.

The feeling remains with me till lunchtime when I remember that I have to interview the president of the Indian Cement

Manufacturers Association, Mr S.C. Gupta. Mr Gupta, who I suspect never finished school, is known only to meet journalists in order to humiliate them. First, he makes them wait for at least half an hour and then gives them a lecture on the uselessness of education. But I can squeeze a quote out of a stone—that is my talent. For, when someone tells me a story, I disappear inside the story and live it like a film. So people like to confide in me, to tell me things.

The cement king's office is at Nehru Place where there is never any parking, so I leave my car and take a three-wheeler instead. It is badly sprung and the hot air wages war on my skin, pricking it with a thousand needles. Deprived of my chariot of steel and speed, I feel small and utterly at the mercy of the traffic. I wonder if a lifetime of travelling in three-wheelers is the reason for Sheila's bitterness. The pollution and dust stream into my eyes and nose. I can hardly breathe. Five minutes into the journey, I am longing for the comfort of my car.

After Mr Gupta has had his fun and I have got what I wanted, I get back into the three-wheeler and try to sort out the truth from the lies in the cement king's crude meanness and hyperbolic boasting. At the Savitri Cinema traffic light I see a beggar on crutches. The cement king's words are forgotten as I wait impatiently for him to notice me.

To my disappointment, it isn't Shibu. This man's face is twisted into the usual mask of misery, his eyes trying desperately to convince you that he is a worthy object of your largesse. I shake my head and look away. But the beggar doesn't budge.

The driver reaches into his pocket and gives the beggar a rupee.

'What else can a man do if he doesn't have a leg,' he remarks. 'At least this way he can still be a man.'

'What do you mean?' I look at him, seeing him for the first time. He looks sixty. But his clothes are clean and his gaze, in the rear-view mirror, is direct.

'In a village a man without a leg is an object of shame, a burden to his family. Here he can make money and send it home to his family.'

'But what has begging got to do with being a man?' I still feel irritated that the beggar isn't Shibu. But my irritation is quickly giving way to shame.

He laughs. 'Perhaps you are right, sahib. I am not an educated man. But if you cannot bring money to your wife, what kind of man are you? That is what they would say in Bulandshahr.'

The lights change and the auto-rickshaw engine jerks, coughs, splutters and then stops. Horns blare and people curse us. Unperturbed, the driver spits, gets out and begins to push the machine across the road. Too uncomfortable to move, I shut my eyes as we cut right in front of furious cars to get to the side.

'What's the matter?' I ask the man as he looks into the oily black engine under his seat. Now that we are no longer moving, the heat closes in on us. Mirages dance above the tarmac.

'Don't worry, sahib, I can fix it. There is nothing I don't know about this machine.' He begins to tinker with the engine and, miraculously, within ten minutes we are back on the road.

'Machines love me,' he says, when we are rolling once more. 'I used to work on great big printing presses once. Enormous hulks of metal.'

'Printing presses! You worked in a newspaper?'

'Yes, sahib, I used to work at the *Statesman*.'

'Then what happened? Why did you leave?' I ask curiously.

'The machines changed, sahib.'

I remember vaguely the days when the giant rotary printers had still not been replaced by offset presses, and each page was first composed in metal. But this is the first time I have come face to face with one of the thousands who lost their jobs because of computers. 'I'm sorry,' I say, glancing at the man's face in the rear-view mirror. But he is concentrating on squeezing us between a bus and a Tata Safari. The traffic has come to a total standstill. I groan inwardly and wonder what has blocked us and how long it will take to clear. My blue suit and tie feel like a penance. I curse the city silently. Then I curse myself as well, as I loosen my tie.

'Great cities aren't made by people, but by people and

machines working together,' the auto-rickshaw driver suddenly says. 'Without one there cannot be the other. That's what makes us city people different from village people.'

'What do you mean?' His words have touched an answering chord deep inside me. I think of my beloved Maruti and how we conquer the city together each day, and curse myself for having abandoned it. I must have made a sound which the driver interpreted as disbelief.

'You don't believe me, sahib?' the driver's voice rises. 'I may not be as educated as you are, but,' he lowers his voice, 'my knowledge is based on experience, not books. When you see the real nature of something, it gives you something back in return, that is my experience. How else do you think Savitri could save her husband Satyavan? She saw the real nature of Death, and so Yama gave her back her husband.'

'The real nature of things? What do you mean?'

The deep emotion in the man's voice makes me think of Sheila and in spite of the heat my body comes briefly alive. I look at him in the rear-view mirror. In some ways he reminds me of Sheila, strong, unbroken, different. But unlike Sheila, his face is marked by suffering. He catches my eye and seems to have read some of my thoughts, for he says, 'Though I was born a Brahmin, I have long since stopped believing I am one. Poor men don't belong to any caste and hence they have no gods watching over them. But there are new gods being born all the time. This city is my god. She looks after me. Her railway stations are her temples. When I understood that, she gave me the love of my life.'

'The love of your life?' I sit up.

'Yes. I found her on the railway station. She was being chased by a group of young hooligans. I didn't stop to think. I just grabbed her and slapped her. "How dare you run away from me," I shouted. "I've been mad with worry." She looked up at me, shocked, terrified. I could feel her trembling. The other boys surrounded us.

'"Let go of her. She's ours," one of them said.

'I held on to the girl's hand even more tightly. "What do you mean she's yours, she's my sister," I said.

'"Really? Maybe she doesn't want to be with you. We own this station and we found her. She belongs to us now. Tax." One of them tried to grab the girl but she moved behind me.

'"You don't need a sister in this city. She'll only get in your way. Leave her and get out, before I break your bones," said the leader of the group, a short ugly man with sores on his arms. His voice was so calm, so sure of itself, that it made my blood go cold. For a second I thought of giving her up. Just then I saw a railway policeman coming down the platform behind the boys. "If you touch us I'll scream so loudly that the policeman behind you will be forced to come here," I told them.

'They looked around and began to get nervous. "You'd better go. I am going to count to three," I said. "Then I'll scream." All eyes were on the policeman now. Finally, the leader looked back at us and made a face. "Coward," he said. "And your sister's not that pretty anyway. There are fresher ones available." He turned and sauntered away. The others followed him. I watched them go, my heart pounding.

'Suddenly, I received a ringing slap on my cheek. "You dared to slap me," the girl said furiously, and began to cry. That's when I noticed how beautiful she was. So I took her home, back to my father's house. She was the city's gift to me and I wasn't going to let her go, or my luck, I knew, would go with her.'

Ahead of us, the traffic jam finally begins to clear. As he is about to start the engine, the auto-rickshaw driver turns around and looks at me.

'While I was still at the *Statesman*, my love left me, taking my luck with her.'

He shrugged his shoulders.

'Yes, sahib, she just walked out one day, and never came back. Some women are like that. You can love them but you cannot keep them. They are the gifts of God, given for a short while, then taken away.'

He starts the auto-rickshaw and continues, 'But I married

again, and my new wife gave me three boys—the younger two are twins. After I lost my job at the *Statesman*, I became a casual labourer again. Often, I'd wait half the night in front of textile mills, only to be passed over when the factory gates opened. Someone told me that the factories in Delhi were closing down because the owners were making factories in the countryside and that there were jobs to be had in Haryana and UP. So I walked a hundred miles into Haryana. For two years I worked as a boiler maintenance man in a factory in Hissar. Then the factory closed down and once again I was without a job. Other factories were also closing and there were many people more desperate than I was. I began to walk back to Delhi. On the way, my things were stolen. Even the clothes on my body were taken. The police picked me up and gave me a spare uniform. So I came back to Delhi in a police uniform. When I got to Delhi, the police here picked me up and put me in jail because they thought I had stolen the uniform. I stayed in jail for a month. When I got out, my hair had gone completely white, and no factory wanted to hire an old man. So I became a cycle-rickshaw driver.

'I would hire the rickshaw for five rupees, and make around twenty-five rupees each day. I didn't dare tell my wife. She would not have been able to face the neighbours. Then my son got sick. The doctor called it tubercular epilepsy and prescribed expensive medicine and good food. That's when I became a grave digger as well. All day I plied my rickshaw and all night I buried the dead. In the morning, I would beg a few roses of the flower sellers outside and give them to my wife, letting her think I had a flower stall.'

'This city has treated you terribly,' I say, even as we come to a halt at another traffic light. Sheila's strange bursts of rage, her despair, all seem to make sense, all of a sudden. She knows the city far better than I do.

'Terribly? What do you mean, sahib! This city is a devi.' The auto-rickshaw driver stares accusingly at me in the rear-view mirror. 'She gave me my auto-rickshaw. She … '

The light turns green and in a sudden eruption of diesel

exhaust, the cars and buses begin to move. I cover my face with a handkerchief to filter the fumes but in spite of it my eyes and throat burn. The driver coughs as he drives.

'She will kill you,' I cannot stop myself from saying, as the air clears. 'How long do you think you will be able to take in this smoke before it chokes your lungs? That is going to be your goddess's final gift to you, my friend.'

He looks troubled. Then he says, 'It's true this city may one day kill me. But none of my children have had to wait at a mill gate from five in the morning and do hard manual labour from morning to night as I did. And it was a city hospital that saved my son's life. None of our Hindu gods helped me. All my children know the taste of rice and wheat, and they can speak English. The eldest one even knows computers. With the help of this city, I have given my children a future, sahib.'

There is nothing I can say, for he is right. Success comes in different shapes and sizes.

'You still haven't told me how you got your auto-rickshaw,' I say as I pay him.

'Sorry, I forgot.' He laughs. 'The bulldozers came, you see. The hospital next door was going to expand so they tore down our basti. But they gave us land near Nand Nagri through the government. I sold that land and bought this. My wife works in the new wing of the hospital and they give us a room in exchange.'

We shake hands and part. 'Next time, sahib, I will take you for free,' he says as he drives off.

I spend the rest of my afternoon staring at the computer. The cement king's words are long forgotten. The story that itches to write itself is the auto-rickshaw driver's. Sheila drifts into the office. I try to catch her eye. She doesn't look at me, but goes straight to her telephone. I make up my mind, get up and knock on the editor's door.

'Come in,' he says and smiles when he sees it's me.

'Sir, I had an idea,' I begin.

'That's good, at least someone's still thinking here,' he says.

I wonder if I am supposed to laugh. 'Sir, I was wondering if I could do a story on Delhi.'

'What kind of a story?' he asks warily.

I lick my lips nervously. 'About small businessmen, electricians, auto-rickshaw drivers, people who've pitted themselves against tremendous odds in order to succeed. They represent the true spirit of this city, sir.' *They are the ones we should be writing about.* The unspoken criticism hangs in the air. I wonder if the editor is aware of it.

I shift from one foot to the other as I wait. He takes his time, taking off his glasses and cleaning them first, a sign that he's thinking carefully of what to say. 'Well, that's certainly an original idea. Twenty years ago, when I started as a journalist, one may have been able to sneak it in. But today we have to think of our readership, you see. The people who read don't want to know about those people and those people don't read.'

Those people.

I thank him and back out of the room. He looks relieved. At the door he stops me.

'How did your interview today go, Shailendra? Got anything interesting?'

For a few seconds I am at sea. Then I remember the cement king. 'Very well, sir … he gave me a good story, actually … and he didn't make me wait.'

We both pretend to laugh.

'I knew you'd be the one to do it. Can you hand it to me by this evening?' the editor asks.

I am being gently reprimanded. Not for the first time, I admire his tact.

That evening as we drive home, Sheila says to me, 'I saw you with the boss. What was that all about?'

'Nothing. I had an idea for a feature. He shot it down.'

'Really? What about?'

I look at her for a second, surprised by her curiosity. 'It was just a half-baked thing. There was no meat in it.'

'Come on. Don't downplay yourself all the time. Tell me what it was.'

'I wanted to do something on small-scale businesses and the men behind them.'

She laughs. 'You want to write about your electrician.'

'There are others like him ... why, just today I met—'

'—You met another one,' she finishes for me.

'Yes,' I say lamely, embarrassed.

She looks at me for a long moment. I feel the sweat break out on my back. 'All right, tell me about him.' So I tell her about the auto-rickshaw driver. When I finish, she simply says, 'Wow!'

I feel thrilled but say nothing.

When we reach her place she asks, 'Will you come up for a drink?'

'I ... I don't drink,' I tell her. The truth is that I have never drunk alcohol in front of a woman. The idea terrifies me.

Her face is turned away from me as she struggles with the seat belt. All of a sudden it comes off and she unfolds her long legs. 'Tomorrow then,' she says.

The next day she is unusually silent. Her perfume fills the space between us and I turn on the music to distract me. Still, I can feel her all around me. Only as we reach Moolchand is the silence broken.

'I wonder if ... '

' ... Shibu Mondal will be there?' she finishes in chorus. We both begin to laugh, self-consciously at the beginning.

The light is green and we have barely enough time to look for him.

'He wasn't there,' she says flatly as we pull away.

'I hope he is all right.' I meet her glance briefly, pulling away before I betray myself.

One afternoon, a few days later, I find a note on my desk. Even before I open it I smell her perfume. It is brief. *I have found Shibu Mondal*, it says. I look up over the partition. Her chair is empty. In the evening I look for Sheila again but she has still not returned. The office empties till I am the only one left. I wait. Perhaps she's in a meeting and has got delayed. At last, only the sweeper and I remain.

'Why are you still here, sahib?' he asks.

'I am waiting for someone,' I tell him coldly.

'Sheila madam left already. She left around four o'clock,' he says stonily, his eyes on the floor.

'What?' I feel naked. Does the entire office know we go home together? 'You're sure she went home, not to a meeting?'

'Yes, sir, I got her the scooter,' he says, briefly looking me in the eyes.

I stare at him in dislike. He has eyes that see too much.

'Well, in case she returns, tell her I have gone,' I tell him.

His expression is carefully blank. 'Of course, sahib.'

There is little traffic on the road now that rush hour is over. But soon the same gnawing loneliness that follows me around at home makes its presence felt in the car. I wish Sheila was beside me and wonder whether she went home early because she was going to find Shibu Mondal. I wonder if I dare go to her house. I come to the Moolchand Crossing and suddenly see Shibu Mondal standing at his usual spot in the middle of the road. I almost don't recognize him. His face has aged, and his hair has turned snowy white. I feel shaken by the change in him but try not to show it.

'It's been a while,' I say, handing him ten rupees. 'Where did you go?'

He doesn't answer. 'Where is your woman?' he asks instead.

'She's not my woman,' I say sharply.

He laughs. Clearly he doesn't believe me.

'You know nothing about her, or us,' I say defensively.

He says nothing at first. Then casually, almost as if he were talking about the weather, he says, 'She came and saved me. I was taken by the police and put into a leper hospital along with many others. They refused to listen when I told them I was cured. "We don't want lepers in Delhi," I was told. I had given up hope and stopped eating when today your woman suddenly appeared along with the director and they set me free. I don't know how she did it, but she is a brave woman. The hospital was awful, far worse than the other one.' He adds after a pause, 'She put me in a scooter, told me to come here and left. I would have left the city already, but I wanted to thank her first. You're a lucky man. Why haven't you married her yet?' His face becomes terribly sad. I am sure he is thinking about his wife and that he hasn't seen her since he got the disease.

'Where is your wife?' I ask.

'I don't know. Maybe she is still fighting in the jungle. Maybe she surrendered and now has a business. I heard the government gives surrendered militants money now to start a business.'

My heart leaps. 'You were a Naxalite?'

'That's what we were told we were.'

The irony doesn't escape me. Yet, I stare at him and feel a huge relief. He isn't just a leper—he is a hero.

'When, where?'

'It's a long story.'

'No, please tell me.' I turn off the engine to demonstrate my seriousness. Behind me horns blare.

His face breaks into a smile, the same warm smile I have been searching for all these days.

'Oh, all right, but you must promise to marry her.'

'If you come to the wedding,' I reply gaily.

He laughs and points to a parking area on the opposite side of the road. 'I'll wait for you,' he says.

'Are you hungry, sahib?' he asks when I arrive.

'No, thanks.' I get out and we move to an empty bit of kerb between two cars. He puts one crutch aside and rests on the other. A portrait of courage, I think sentimentally. Perhaps, I go still at the audacity of the idea, I could write about him for a daily newspaper under a pseudonym. No one would know except me. And Sheila. I can't wait to tell her Shibu's story. I look at him expectantly, impatient for him to begin.

'Freedom is a funny thing,' he says. 'I wanted to be "free" ever since I can remember. But what freedom was I never understood till this.' He looks down at his missing leg.

'I was fifteen when I ran away from my village and went to Barddhaman, the district capital. I had failed my tenth-class exam. I couldn't understand why. So I lied. When my family asked me whether I'd passed, I told them, "Of course I passed." They were overjoyed. The first person in the family to matriculate, and the eldest son too, was an event to be celebrated. They called the priest, asked him how much a small puja would cost. And soon the whole village knew about the puja and all of them invited themselves to it. After all, a matriculate could become anything, even a government officer. I wasn't too concerned. I had almost come to believe I'd passed the exam. I had studied for it anyway.

'Three days before the puja was to take place, a boy in my class from a neighbouring village came to visit a relative. He heard of the puja and laughed. "But he didn't pass. He failed. He never got a certificate. I was there, I remember." And he proudly showed everyone his certificate. Slowly, people began to ask about my certificate. At last the whispers came to my mother's ears. "Son," she asked, "can I see your certificate?"

'And so I had to run away.' Shibu smiles as he tells me this, but his eyes are shadowed with pain. 'Barddhaman wasn't as big as Delhi, but it had buses and cars and paved roads and three cinema halls. It all seemed wonderfully exciting to me at first. As I walked around, I felt happy I had escaped the village. A village was no place for a tenth-class pass. Of course, I conveniently forgot that I hadn't quite passed. In that new place, it didn't seem to matter.

'For the first week I wandered through the streets doing nothing except staring, much like I do here. The city seemed so exciting. I needed a job so I went into a smart office and told the receptionist I wanted a job.' Again Shibu laughs dryly.

'"I am a tenth-class pass and know how to read," I remember telling her proudly.

'"But there are no jobs for readers here," she told me. "Can you do shorthand and typing?"

'I turned and ran.'

The Elephant and the Maruti

Shibu stops and looks at me. 'Three times in my life I have run away. This was the second.'

'And the third?'

'Wait.' He settles himself more comfortably on his crutches and continues.

'Eventually I got a job selling newspapers at a stall in the railway station. It was a temporary job, I told myself, but at least I would be able to practise my reading. And I would meet important people with proper jobs to give. But I never did. People just streamed past me endlessly.

'One night, just as I was closing, I saw a man putting up posters on the outside of a train. *Grab your future*, the poster announced, showing a closed fist against a red background.

'"How do you grab your future?" I called out to the man putting up the posters.

'The man turned and glared into the shadows. "Who are you?" he asked.

'"I want to be like you," I said, stepping out of the shadows.

'Seeing I was just a boy, the man relaxed. He told me to come for some night classes his organization held each Friday.'

'You joined a Naxalite Working Group?' I break in eagerly.

'Yes,' he replies and continues, 'I joined the night study group, hoping to learn shorthand and typing. Instead, it was all talk. An old man who talked like a politician would give speeches about revolution and the evils of society. After two sessions I was ready to leave. At break time I went up to the teacher and told him I was leaving.

'"Why?" the teacher asked.

'"Because what you are teaching won't get me a proper job."

'The teacher didn't answer straightaway. He made me promise to stay till the end of the class. After the class, the teacher took me to a small hotel by the railway station for dinner. Over dinner he made me tell him about myself. After I finished, the teacher said very seriously, "If you want a job you have to fight for it. You have to make your own job. A man's job is not to work for someone else, a man must be free."

'"Yes, I want to be free," I agreed. "That's why I came. I thought you would teach us something useful like typing, English, so one could be free."

'The teacher stared at me as if I was mad. "A job doesn't make you free," he told me.

'"But a good job does. I am a tenth-class pass. I deserve a good job," I said.

'"Yes, you deserve a good job. If I could, I would give you one. But I am not rich."

'"Can you tell me how to get one?"

'Now it was the teacher's turn to be silent. At last he banged on the table. "If you want jobs you must be prepared to fight for them. The capitalists will not give them to you without a fight," he said, clicking his fingers under my nose.

'For another hour he kept me there, telling me how rich people exploited the labour of poor people and with the money they stole from us they hired more people for even less money, giving them barely enough wages to stay alive. At the end my teacher said, "Don't worry, I'll take care of you." They sent me for "training" to the tea estates.'

'So you became a real Naxalite,' I break in again, unable to contain myself. 'What did you do?'

'To begin with, all I did was pass messages, collect "taxes" from the workers in the tea estates and learn to shoot a gun. Then I was forced to guard a kidnapped tea estate official. I liked the man. He promised to give me a job when he got free. One day when I came to give him food he was gone. I learned later that he had tried to escape and they had killed him. Suddenly, I was being called a murderer and was being hunted by the army.'

My horror makes him laugh.

'There is nothing free about being in the jungle. You are a prisoner of your body. All you think of is hunger and cold and heat. Then you get diarrhoea and all you can think of is a toilet. After a while, even the fear of being caught doesn't touch you.'

I shudder, and he laughs again.

'I went south,' Shibu continues, 'travelling always by the light of the moon and the stars. I crossed into Bihar, into dacoit-infested jungles. One day I met a man who made guns. From him I stole a gun. Eventually, without knowing it, I crossed the border into Orissa.'

Shibu looks straight at me. 'You probably have never been to southern Orissa. No one ever goes there. There are no pukka roads and the jungle is thick, so thick you cannot see ahead more than a few feet. The people are very poor and there are no schools. No government officers go there, only forest officers and contractors.

'I had almost become an animal. An unfamiliar sound scared me more than killing a deer or even a human being. Then I got malaria. I began to see my family hanging from the trees. Somehow those apparitions guided me into a village in the forest. A farmer rescued me. He had a beautiful daughter. She was as beautiful,' he points at me, 'as your woman. But she looked more beautiful because she had no nice clothes or jewellery. She had only a cotton sari and flowers in her hair. Sometimes your woman wears flowers in her hair too, doesn't she?'

I nod, though I hadn't really noticed Sheila wearing flowers.

'When I became better, I told the family my story and they put me in touch with the Naxalites in that area. They were a stupid and uneducated bunch. For, in the forests of Orissa, there was no one to fight and nothing to fight for. Everybody was poor and had nothing—there were no wealthy landlords to target. But I wanted to be a leader, so I decided I would find an enemy. I forced the villagers to give us "donations" in order to buy guns. Then, with my private army I began to target timber traders and force them to pay tax to me. I even taxed those who came to buy honey and ayurvedic plants. I settled land disputes and took half of the land as payment. For three years I was the king of those forests. But it was when I killed a forest officer that I became famous. Once more the police knew my name. But this time I wasn't afraid of them. I knew the jungle better than they did ...' He pauses, remembering. 'Then I got this,' he says, pointing with his crutch at his missing leg.

'My woman noticed it first. She was the first to leave. After that the others began to leave one by one. But I had my gun and could still get what I wanted from the villagers. Then, the villagers informed the police and my remaining men and I were ambushed. Two of my men were killed. I escaped. Eventually, I got to Cuttack, about hundred and fifty miles away. The disease was clearly visible now, and my toes were infected, though I couldn't feel any pain.

'In Cuttack I tried begging but it was not like Delhi, people didn't give much. I went to the temple for food but there too they shooed me away. There is a hierarchy among beggars. Lepers are at the bottom.' Shibu touches his leg with a crutch. 'This disease is the best disguise. I wish I'd known it earlier. I wouldn't have had to run so much.'

I feel my heart clench. I let out a gasp of protest. Shibu pretends not to notice.

'In the end I decided to go back to Bengal,' he says, 'to my family. I managed to crawl onto a goods train bound for Puri and from there to Bengal. When I reached my village, no one recognized me. The children threw stones at me. I left. I didn't want my family to suffer again because of me. What had I done for them when I was healthy to expect them to take care of me now? I went back to Orissa. In Bhubaneshwar, the railway police caught me and transferred me to a government leprosy hospital near Puri.' His eyes become bleak. 'The hospital was worse than a prison.'

'My God,' I find myself saying. But I don't know if I am saying it out of sympathy or disappointment. Maybe I don't want my hero to become an object of pity.

Shibu senses it, because suddenly he is staring fiercely into my eyes. 'Leprosy is a terrible disease,' he says. 'It takes away more than just your freedom, it takes away your humanity. We were kept locked up like animals in a slaughterhouse with nothing to do except play cards and fight. The food was terrible and the patients would fight over food because there was so little of it. But soon I realized that I was wrong. The fights were not about food, but about feeling alive. For, only when they were fighting did they feel human.

'Unlike most of the others, I knew how to read. I asked the doctors to give me newspapers so I could keep in touch with the world. The doctors were delighted and encouraged me to read to the others. One even offered to teach me English, but what would I have done with it, sahib, except read more newspapers?' Shibu laughs. 'I even tried to teach some patients to read, but they didn't want to learn. "What for?" they said. "The world doesn't want us. Why should we care what happens to the world?" I couldn't explain why, but I knew that I wanted to go back into the world, and that I loved it. I wanted to see the beauty of the world again—especially now that I could not be a part of that beauty. When I was cured, I made them take off my leg.'

Shibu stops, his eyes suddenly filling with tears.

'For four years I stayed in that prison. After a while I forgot what it was like to live on the outside. But I never forgot what a beautiful woman looked like. When the day came and the doctor said I was cured, he offered me a job as an assistant in the hospital. He knew how difficult life was for lepers on the outside. Cured patients begged for that job. But I refused. I couldn't wait to see whole people again.

'After I was released I decided I'd see as much of India as I could. Two years ago I arrived in Delhi. But it still feels like yesterday. People here are quite beautiful compared with other cities.' Suddenly, his eyes bore into me. 'You don't know what it means to be free,' he says. 'I know. Freedom is being able to look at a beautiful woman, to examine each feature separately and then together and know they will be whole. That is what I do as I stand here. That is what freedom is.'

How I got home that night remains a mystery to me. My mind had become a stage on which scenes from the auto-rickshaw driver's life and Shibu Mondal's enacted themselves—with me as the lead actor. Sheila was there too, first as the auto-rickshaw driver's absent love and then as the Naxalite queen of the jungle.

In the morning I wake up feeling light-headed, nervous energy coursing through my veins. The heat presses into me, pushing me back into that region of not sleeping and not being awake where I had been all night. I think about how lucky I am to have Sheila's company to look forward to each day. How lonely the car feels without her. Suddenly, I know that I cannot wait any longer. I know it with a clarity and a conviction that I have not felt in a long time. Maybe the auto-rickshaw driver is right after all—this city *is* a devi, and that devi has given me its daughter, Sheila. With Sheila I can stop running away from marriage. For Sheila is freedom, she is the spirit of the city made flesh. Only she doesn't know it, it is up to me to make her realize that.

I bathe and shave hurriedly and get into the car, smelling of Old Spice aftershave. I stop the car in front of her house and honk. I am a little early, so I turn on the cassette player and settle down to wait. Ten minutes become fifteen and then twenty. No Sheila comes rushing out, papers on the verge of falling out of her leather bag. Finally, I decide to go up to her flat. She is never this late. I ring the bell. Nothing happens. I knock loudly on her door, imagining her lying in pain, or in a faint. As I get ready to break down the door, it opens. A sleep-softened Sheila stands before me.

'Shailendra!' She seems as surprised as I am.

'A-aren't you coming to work today?' I stammer.

A momentary annoyance drives the softness from her face. 'Didn't Shalini give you my message? I am on leave for two weeks.'

'Oh ... leave ...' I feel immensely relieved.

'But I'm leaving for good. I had meant to call you in a day or two to tell you about it ... to share my happiness with you. For you have been my closest, my most loyal friend.' A shadow of regret flits across her face and suddenly she will not meet my eyes. 'I'm getting married next month. He lives in Toronto.'

beauty

I did not notice that the singing had faltered, for I was busy watching a muddy monsoon pool from which a giant column of tiny flying insects was rising up to the sky. There were thousands of them, each no larger than an oversized mote of dust, a blur of rainbow-coloured movement that thickened the air. At first I thought they were just hanging in the air like an army waiting to go into battle. Then I realized that they were flying upward, not straight up as you would expect, but in spirals, thousands and thousands of them, so that together they made an enormous shimmering column.

There was a pattern to the movement. Each insect would fly upward in a half circle to a spot diagonally opposite its original station. After a brief pause, it would complete the circle and take a position a little higher but exactly above its initial position. Simultaneously, another would take its exact place just below while yet another took the place vacated by the latter. Every couple of circles, two insects would fly straight across the middle of the column and rejoin the original semi-circular path on the other side. In this way the column maintained both an inner structure and an outer form.

That's when the air left my lungs. Because the insects, I realized, were dancing. Only dance could explain the perfect symmetry of their motion. My eyes moved up the soaring, achingly beautiful column until they collided with the blue sky. Then I breathed again. I looked around to see if any of the others had noticed the dancing insects. Six hundred faces encircled by blue collars and red ties mouthed the words of 'All things bright and beautiful'. Most looked vacant, a few looked bored, a very few sang with gusto. No one was looking towards the dancing column. Disappointed, I turned back to the insects. In seconds, the rainbow-hued column obliterated the everyday horrors of boarding-school life.

So I was the last person to see what had made the choir catch its breath and turn ragged. Only when the restless shuffling of feet in the boys' line had disrupted the column of insects did I look towards the stage and see the teachers and prefects turned to stone. I followed their gazes to the right side of the field and saw what had caused the disturbance. Standing beneath the champak tree, dressed very simply in jeans and a white t-shirt, was the most beautiful girl I had ever seen.

I am especially sensitive to beauty because it has the capacity to hurt me. It's a secret I hide deep inside me. I am afraid to look at a beautiful thing because it has the power to pull my heart into my eyes from where anyone can pluck it out, play with it, and throw it away. Photographs are especially dangerous. One shouldn't look at photographs too often because they can tear a hole in time. People in photographs don't age or die the way real people do, the way my mother did. When the other girls sit around on each other's beds and flick through the latest *Elle* and *Cosmopolitan,* I stay away. Later in the night, or in the early hours of the morning, I steal the fashion magazines from the other girls' lockers, hide myself in the airing closet next to the bathrooms, and feast my eyes on those beautiful faces. After I look at a photograph of a beautiful girl I close my eyes. Behind my lids she comes alive, more real and more beautiful than on the page. Then the seconds pile up and entomb her, till she dwindles into a coloured dot. Only when the dot loses colour and turns black do I open my eyes. I don't open the magazine again.

So when I say that this was the most beautiful girl I had ever seen, I know what I am talking about. But it wasn't just me who felt that way. I turned around to look at the faces of the others.

The Elephant and the Maruti

Some wore little smiles, their eyes liquid with pleasure. Others looked angry, some fierce. Some were awestruck and even a little afraid. And the rest looked satisfied, as if they had just consumed a banana split or chocolate fudge sundae. One way or the other, the whole school was staring at her, mouths open.

At last I myself looked properly at the new girl, and was engulfed by the same emotions that were visible on everyone else's faces. Then I made my first mistake. I should have shut my eyes or at least looked away. I should have let the seconds mount till they had swallowed her, turned her into a dot and made her fade away. But I didn't.

The singing resumed, and suddenly I knew the girl's incredible beauty was nothing to be afraid of. I opened my eyes and felt the wet cool monsoon wind caress my face just as lovingly as it caressed the trees in their full monsoon skirts. And in the cobalt sky, the column of mosquitoes resumed their crazy dance. I began to sing with the others.

I am sensitive to beauty because I have so little of it. And because I am never allowed to forget it. All my life I have been surrounded by beautiful things and beautiful people. All my father's girlfriends were beautiful. I could have coped with that, for all of them were human and all of them were mortal. To me most seemed old and a few were overweight. But there was one person I could not compete with, one who never aged or grew fat, and whom I was not allowed to forget. My mother. None of my father's friends came close to her. My father told me so again and again. And I didn't need his words to know that he was speaking the truth. I had the photograph.

All my life it had stared down at me from the wall above the double bed. She was twenty-two when it was taken. Her face was slightly tilted, her thick curly hair pulled to one side and curled around her neck like a black silk scarf, showing off her high cheekbones and finely cut jaw. Her long straight nose, with its delicate, flared nostrils, set off the beauty of her full lips. A vase with a lily drooping artistically over her in an arc completed the picture. But these were details I only noticed later. The eyes dominated the photograph.

'No one could ever forget your mother's eyes,' my grandmother would say with a sigh, her eyes becoming unfocussed. Then they would get focussed again as she stared at me dispassionately. 'It's a pity you got your father's eyes,' she would say. 'But that is God's will. Such perfect beauty could not exist twice on this imperfect earth. She was too good for this world. And I, her mother, must have done something horrible in my last life to have to suffer the loss of such a perfect child.' She would shake her head, sigh again and stare into the television as if it could give her an answer.

'But aren't my eyes even a tiny bit like hers?' I would plead, opening them to their fullest. Her face would go blank the way adult faces do when their owners are about to lie. But in my grandmother's case it meant that her mind had returned to the past and she wasn't there any more. So I would turn away, knowing that when she returned to the present, she would choose a different topic of conversation.

But one day she surprised me. 'She had the eyes of a doe, your mother. When you open yours wide like that, you look like a frog. But yes, you too may grow up to be beautiful. If a frog can become a princess like Mandodari, why not you?'

A hush fell over our class when she walked in the next day. Behind her was our headmaster, wearing a dazed look on his face. 'This is Mandakini,' he announced to the class. 'She has come from Dubai.' A wave of shuffling and rustling swept the class. It began in the benches at the back, where the school bullies, the sports jocks and their hangers-on sat, and blew forward, filling the room with restless energy. The teacher made her sit at the front desk, the one touching his desk so that no one ever sat there. She sat down obediently, her back to the class. From where I sat in the second row, I could see her shoulder and her profile. I stared hungrily. I felt I was being carried away on a rip tide, I knew not where. She was like a breath of pure new air in the dull, stale atmosphere of the school. We were all greedy for her, desperate to grab a little of her freshness for ourselves before she mingled with the rest of us and became old and stale too. And so we all kept taking little looks, our glances like spoons dipping into her beauty and carrying away a little of it at a time. The geography teacher droned on. The classroom grew quiet and dreamy.

But the new girl's special quality didn't wear off. Not even after she was clothed in the same hideous grey uniform that we all wore. If anything, it made her even more special, because now her beauty surged straight out of her face, the rest of her body made mysterious by the shapeless, hand-me-down uniform that we all wore.

'What kind of a name is Mandakini?' Maya, the boss of our class, asked scornfully.

'It's a pretentious name, an attention-seeking name,' Anjali, her second-in-command replied.

The others nodded. 'We'll call her Skinny,' Maya announced. The others cheered and laughed and nudged each other in delight. Maya looked at Anjali and nodded. Obviously, it had all been rehearsed beforehand.

In the days and the weeks that followed, I noticed something strange about Mandakini. Whenever she entered an area, no matter how crowded, a hush fell over the room for a second and then a surge of electricity shot through the crowd. Movements became more expansive, laughter grew more frequent and voices became shriller—especially the girls' voices. People touched each other more and stood closer together. But around Mandakini, a small clear space developed, a thin cushion of air, sometimes hardly more than a few inches deep. But it was space nonetheless, a circle of emptiness and silence that was even more marked because it was surrounded by so much activity.

At the centre of that circle stood Mandakini, seemingly unruffled by the currents she generated. She didn't seem to care that no one spoke to her. She just stared challengingly into the space around her. As for me, I enjoyed her presence thoroughly. Whenever she was nearby, the world suddenly became more beautiful. I found myself noticing the colour of the sky and the new spring leaves, my friend Anjali's thick blue-black hair, and the strange yellow-green of the moss on the dormitory walls.

One day I walked into the common room to find Mandakini staring into the mirror, pinching the skin on her forehead to loosen the blackheads. Her face—all scrunched up, tongue sticking out—looked almost plain.

'You mustn't do that, you'll spoil your face,' I shouted before I could stop myself.

In the mirror, our eyes met. 'How does my face matter to you?' she asked insolently, not turning around.

'B-because you'll spoil your beauty,' I stammered, blushing.

Contempt took hold of her features. 'This school is obviously filled with lunatics,' she remarked to her reflection and resumed her hunt for the blackheads.

Anger made me forget myself. 'Your face doesn't belong to you, so you shouldn't spoil it,' I said.

'Really? Who does it belong to, then?' she asked sarcastically.

'To God.'

She looked suddenly nervous, her eyes darting to the side to see if there was anyone else there.

'I-I'm not crazy,' I stammered, my cheeks on fire. 'Your beauty is just another little bit of the world. But it has a purpose. It's been put into the world to remind us that He does exist. Your beauty is God's veil, you can't spoil it.'

She turned around and began to walk towards me. 'Is that why you aren't scared to talk to me?'

The question came as a surprise, but more than the question itself, it was the expression on her face that intrigued me. For on her face was a hunger not so different from what I felt every time I looked at her.

'The girls are jealous, and the boys afraid,' I said at last. 'You force them to think about what they have lost.'

'What's that?'

'The other world, the invisible one.'

'And why are you different?'

'I told you. I understand what your beauty means.'

'So tell me, for I certainly don't know what it means, though I've lived with it all my life.'

That was my second mistake. I should have left then, told her I was joking. Instead, I shared with her my greatest secret.

'At first I hated beauty,' I said slowly. 'Its sole purpose seemed to be to torment people like me who aren't beautiful. It was my father who one day told me that perhaps beauty had another purpose and he described to me what he had felt when, as a student, he saw a squirrel in a park in England. It was the first squirrel he had seen in months. All winter it had sat in its hole in the trunk of a tree and grown fat, eating the nuts it had stored there. In the pale sunshine of that morning it had descended from the tree for the first time, to forage and to explore and to greet the new year. With the three white stripes on its back, it was not very different from our gilhari, he explained. But the resemblance ended there. This squirrel was three times as large. Its body was the richest auburn he had ever seen, the white on its back purer than the purest white one could imagine. The sunlight reflected off its back and chest contained every shade of red, from an auburn so deep it was almost black, to the gentlest shades of orange and beige.

'It was then, he told me, that he felt sure that God must be some kind of a carpenter. All day he kept busy repairing, rebuilding, managing, and protecting this unruly world of ours. But then every once in a while, he took a little time off and did something that gave him pleasure, creating something that had no reason. At least no reason that linked it to this world of ours. Something designed to give *him* joy. Like the squirrel. It needed to be different from the female. It needed to be striking, so that it could catch the female's attention. But it did not have to be so incredibly, so breathtakingly, *beautiful*. That extra something was God at play; God reminding us that he exists, and that we have a duty to preserve and protect what he has built around us, including ourselves.'

I shut my eyes, feeling once more the sense of wonder and freedom that his words had given me. Then I looked at Mandakini.

'That's when I realized that beauty has a purpose, perhaps the most wonderful purpose of all. For it reminds us that God exists. Because he has no face or form of his own, or maybe because if we were to see his real face we would die of fright or be blinded by it, beauty is what he uses to hide his face. It is his veil, which he created because he knows it fills us with delight and pulls us to him.'

Mandakini didn't comment. I watched her nervously out of the corners of my eyes, willing her to break the silence. Her face was still, like a mask. At last she spoke. 'You're a funny girl, worrying about what God looks like,' she said in a queer tight voice. 'I never thought I'd meet someone like you in this dump.'

I felt overwhelmed by the compliment. We stared at each other uncertainly. Then I couldn't bear her beauty any longer and ran out of the room. I didn't stop till I reached the library, at the other end of the school.

That evening, while we waited for the dinner gong to ring, Mandakini crossed the invisible barrier surrounding her and came and stood beside me. A ripple went through the chattering throng, followed by a sudden diminishing of sound as everyone within eyeshot craned their heads to watch. 'I'm glad there's one interesting person in this school. I was getting tired of standing alone,' she said loudly so they could all hear. Another ripple went through the crowd, a scuffle of feet and angry whispers. The circle of space re-formed around us. I looked out at the crowd and then somewhat timidly, at her. She smiled at me and I forgot the crowd of hostile girls, forgot the school and its many miseries. I felt as I had when she had arrived, the day I discovered the column of insects dancing up to the sky. Before either of us could say anything, the gong for supper rang and we were forced to separate.

The next day, when I entered class, Mandakini beckoned and pointed to the empty place beside her in the front of the class.

'You may as well come and sit beside me, the boy who sits here is always trying to stare down my shirt.'

'But what if he wants to sit there?'

The boy in question was Nikhil, the class bully. He had been the bully since we were in class six when he had his growth spurt and whatever brains he had got transformed into muscle. He made up for his lack of brains with violence and had once hospitalized a fellow football player. So while we all laughed at him, pretending to wonder in which part of his body his brains were hiding, we were all scared of him too.

'I can't just take his place,' I said timidly.

'All right, if you're scared, I'll take his seat and you can have mine,' she replied, moving over.

A few minutes later, Nikhil came in. 'That's my place,' he said, glaring at me.

'No, it's not your place. I am sitting in your place. Would you like me to get up?' Mandakini asked sweetly.

He hesitated, then still glaring at me, went and sat down right behind us, banging his books on the table. He leaned forward and pulled my plait. 'I won't forget this, rat-tail,' he warned. But I knew it was a bluff. He was too much in awe of Mandakini.

The rest of the class straggled in. They all stared at me sitting beside Mandakini. I ignored them, my heart swollen with pride. The bell rang and Mr Trivedi, the political science teacher, walked in.

Beside me, I felt Mandakini go rigid.

Mr Trivedi was an odd man. While all the other teachers wore pants and navy or tweed blazers, Mr Trivedi only wore kurtas and chappals. While the other teachers smoked pipes, he preferred beedis. We laughed at his heavy Indian accent and the Hindi words that littered his speech. We laughed at the way he combed his five thin strands of hair carefully across the top of his bald head and tamed the luxuriant growth on the sides with sickly sweet scented hair oil. But most of all, we liked getting him angry so he would shout at us, his eyes full of unshed tears and his voice tight, cursing us for having the opportunity to study in one of the country's best schools and not taking it seriously.

But for all his oddness, Mr Trivedi was an exciting teacher, discussing the daily news with us like adults and encouraging us to argue with him. And we as a class responded because we sensed that, unlike the other teachers, Mr Trivedi actually cared about us, he cared about what we thought. For some reason that had to do with our being Indians like him. When one of us did a good essay he would read it out in class and unshed tears of pride would make his eyes shine as he read. Which is what made his cruelty to Mandakini inexplicable.

The very first day she appeared in his class, he singled her out.

'You, stand up,' he ordered. 'What is your name?'

'Mandakini Kaushal, sir.'

'So you are from UP then,' he said, looking pleased.

'No. I'm from Dubai actually,' Mandakini replied.

His face froze and his eyes bulged. When at last he spoke it was in a completely different voice, one we had never heard before. 'You're not Indian, you're from Dubai.' He turned to the rest of the class. 'Whoever heard of an Indian from Dubai?'

We all laughed and the boys at the back of the class stamped their feet and banged on their desks in approval. Mr Trivedi beamed, quite forgetting to correct them.

Mandakini didn't like being laughed at. It hurt her more than anything else. 'Well, I'm not from UP and I won't lie,' she said, shouting over the noise. 'My home is in Dubai, I've lived there ever since I can remember.'

The class went absolutely still. Everyone stared nervously at Mr Trivedi.

'Then why are you here?' he asked quietly. 'Why didn't you stay in Dubai? There are plenty of good schools there.'

Mandakini's face went bright red. 'My parents sent me here. How should I know why? If you have any more personal questions, you'll have to ask them. They'll be visiting soon,' she said, subtly reminding him that he was just a teacher, and it was her parents who paid the school's exorbitant fees.

Now it was Mr Trivedi's turn to look furious. 'This is my classroom, and while you are here not even your parents can save you.'

A tremor went through the rest of us. But Mandakini seemed unperturbed. She examined her nails as if she were bored. We waited for Mr Trivedi to do something worse to her. But he didn't. He just glared at her, then opened the textbook and began reading in a colourless voice. Though he ignored her and the class continued quite normally after that, the tension hung in the air for the rest of the hour.

After that Mr Trivedi changed. Every class began with, 'What does Mandakini think of today's events?' No matter what news item she chose to discuss, he made her sound stupid. His classes changed, they became a contest of wills between the two of them, with the rest of us the spectators. The girls loved it. Even the boys enjoyed it to an extent. They had all succumbed to Mandakini's power the first day and felt secretly uncomfortable when she was made to look ridiculous. At the same time, they felt united with Mr Trivedi, happy that he was putting a girl like Mandakini in her place. I felt a little on his side too. But for different reasons—Mr Trivedi was also ugly, like me.

So we all laughed with him and were secretly impressed by the way he managed to dim Mandakini's beauty. Mr Trivedi would look like a chicken that had just laid an egg. He would strut back and forth in front of the class, his chest all puffed, until he turned back to Mandakini and saw her expression. For Mandakini just stared at him mysteriously, and every once in a while, gave him a knowing little smile. Then his face would go as red as a tomato and he would find a way to punish her.

If she came late to class, he declared an on-the-spot quiz based on the previous day's lesson, and gave her a zero for it. In the weekly oral test, he regularly reserved the impossible questions for her. When she couldn't answer, he gave her a black mark. When she asked if she could go to the toilet, he always said no. At least twice a week he accused her of not paying attention, and forced her to stand facing the class with her fingers on her lips, or stand with her face to the wall.

Mandakini tried to argue with him. But that only gave him an excuse to increase her punishment. So after the first few times, she kept silent, not uttering a word of protest no matter how hard the question or how humiliating the punishment.

'So Mandakini devi, what taaza khabar do you have for us today?' Mr Trivedi asked one day, coming and standing right in front of us, so close he almost touched the edge of the desk.

'I'm sorry, I don't know what you mean,' she purred, giving him a bewitching smile.

He looked bemused. 'Are you trying to be cheeky with me?' he asked.

'Of course not, sir, I wouldn't dare,' Mandakini replied, looking even more enchanting in her faked innocence.

'Then what is it you don't understand, beti?' he asked more gently than he had ever done before.

'Your English word, sir, taaza. What does it mean? I have never heard it before,' she replied demurely.

My blood went cold.

Mr Trivedi's face darkened. 'You don't know what taaza means?' he said in a high silly voice, pretending to imitate Mandakini's faintly British accent.

'No, sir,' she said primly, 'I have never heard the word before. You see, I thought this was an English-medium school.'

You could have heard a pin drop. Then from the back of the class, someone laughed. The laugh was quickly smothered but it was too late. Mr Trivedi looked as if he was about to commit murder. 'If you weren't a girl … ' he began, his hands clenching into fists. With great difficulty he controlled himself, his eyes becoming bloodshot with the effort. 'Taaza means fresh,' he said finally. 'So tell us what news item you want to bring to our attention today.'

Beside me, I felt Mandakini's body slump against mine. Then I felt her straighten herself, as if drawing energy from me. 'My news for today is that Miss India Lara Bhatt was voted the most beautiful woman in the world yesterday.'

The whole class burst into relieved laughter.

Only Mr Trivedi didn't. 'So you think this is important news?'

'It was on the front page, sir, of the *Times of India*.'

'Really? Is that why you thought it was important?' His eyes flashed, and his voice roughened. 'Or is it that you like to imagine yourself parading half naked in front of men like she does?'

Staring up into Mr Trivedi's face I suddenly understood why he acted so strange with Mandakini. He couldn't help it. Her beauty was doing it to him. He was even more under its power than we were and being a strong man he was trying to break free of it. He didn't like being captured by her beauty. I felt a sudden empathy with him. Then I looked at Mandakini. She was biting her lower lip and trying hard not to cry. Behind us I could feel Nikhil boring holes into her back. And the boys at the back of the class were sniggering the way they did when they looked at the girlie magazines they kept hidden in their books.

'Come on. Answer me. Tell me what is so important about this event,' Mr Trivedi repeated, carefully neutral except for his eyes, which burned.

Mandakini was silent for a long time. At last she said in a small voice, 'It is important for India, sir. At least the world knows we're best at something.'

He gave a harsh bark of laughter, emotion flooding his face again. 'So you think that producing the most beautiful woman is like producing the supercomputer, do you, or the nuclear bomb?'

Under the table I reached for Mandakini's hand—it was ice cold—and squeezed it. She barely noticed. She and Mr Trivedi were locked in a struggle so deep that the rest of us had ceased to matter. 'Sir, a computer or a bomb is a work of the imagination, isn't it?' she asked.

Mr Trivedi nodded.

She continued softly, 'Our scientists are creators, they are therefore in a way, artists. But so is a beautiful woman a work of the imagination. Behind her is a team of talented artists—fashion designers, make-up artists, hairdressers, voice trainers. It isn't easy to create anything, even a dead thing like a computer. But a human being is a thousand times more complicated.' Suddenly, the docility evaporated. 'But nothing these artists do can work if the basic raw material isn't there. True beauty is impossible for a human to create. It comes from God. Lara Bhatt is important because she is proof that God loves our country, sir,' she shouted triumphantly.

I heard a few quickly smothered giggles. Now the class was silently laughing, not at Mandakini but with her. Mr Trivedi must have felt it too. But he pretended not to notice. His entire being was focussed upon Mandakini. Suddenly his lips began to move. 'It's a waste of time trying to teach you anything,' he said, in a voice blanched of feeling. 'You are spoiled, dirty. You don't deserve to be in a school like this. I don't know why your parents bothered to send you to school at all. They should have sent you straight to beauty school so you could learn to be the whore you really are.'

You could have heard a mouse squeak, we were so stunned. Mandakini's face was frozen, drained of life. Then, still sitting, she drew herself up to her full height and stared defiantly at Mr Trivedi.

'So then why do you make us read newspapers, if that is what you think of the beauty industry? The newspapers thought it was important enough to put on the front page. Are their minds as small as mine? Should they be demoted too?'

Mr Trivedi took a step towards her, looking as though he would strangle her there and then. Mandakini shrank back. The entire class gasped. Mr Trivedi suddenly remembered where he was. He took a step back, shock filling his face.

'You get out of my class,' he growled at her. 'Get out.'

Mandakini got up, looked once around the class with contempt, and walked out. My heart filled with love for her. She was so brave even at her most vulnerable. And she looked more beautiful than ever.

For the rest of the class we all pretended to be model students. We debated the women's reservation bill, and the right to information bill. We all tried to give good answers and make Mr

Trivedi smile. But all the while I could feel Mandakini's ghost gobbling our words. Then spitting them out, light and dry as husks.

Eventually, the class ended. We trooped out gratefully. Mandakini was waiting outside, chewing on an apple core. At last Mr Trivedi was alone inside and the two of us were the only ones in the corridor.

'Go and say you're sorry,' I whispered anxiously.

She grunted. 'It won't do any good.'

'Of course it will. He can't punish you when he almost hit you himself.'

The face she turned to me was old and somehow defeated. 'You want to bet on that?'

She turned and walked gracefully into the classroom. Mr Trivedi looked up at her as she neared the desk. I hurried out of the building and around to a window. His face didn't look angry, I thought, relieved. He made her sit down. The two of them talked for a long time. I began to get anxious. The next class had started ages ago. At last they both stood up. Mr Trivedi had his hand on her shoulder and was smiling at her. His hand came off her shoulder and he handed her the newspaper. I ducked under the window and waited till he walked out. Then I clambered inside.

'What happened?' I asked her as I came in.

'He wants me to copy this newspaper from cover to cover, word for word, five times.'

'You're joking! That'll take forever. He can't punish you like that!'

'It's not a punishment,' she said. 'It's for my own good. To educate me.'

'You can't be serious.'

'That's what he said.'

'I think you should report him to the headmaster. He called you a whore and almost hit you.'

She shook her head. 'I can't do that.'

'Why not?' I couldn't understand how one minute she could be so brave and another so defeated.

'You wouldn't understand.'

'Why? Why won't I understand?' She began walking down the corridor. 'I've wasted half of the next class waiting for you, so I think you should at least try to explain,' I panted, struggling to keep up with her.

Suddenly her mood changed. She laughed and hugged me. 'All right, let's bunk the rest of the class and go to the canteen and have a coffee. Then I'll tell you my story.'

It had begun two years ago in her school in Dubai. A teacher began to send her messages hidden inside the homework assignments. He was a married man, and when she threatened to show the letters to the headmaster of the school and to his wife, he began to cry. He said it wasn't his fault, her beauty had driven him mad. He swore he would never bother her again. So she returned his letters, all except one which she kept as insurance, and forgot about. Then the harassment began. Little snide remarks made in class that were aimed at her, then the humiliation of being punished, and finally the extra harsh grading. She complained to her mother. But her mother didn't believe her. Her mother even accused her of flirting with the teacher to better her marks and then making the story up because she couldn't handle the consequences. So she complained to the headmaster. She showed him the letter and asked that he fire the teacher.

'He looked at me and he stroked his beard with long, beautiful fingers. He gave me tea and talked to me for a long, long time. When I left his office I felt on top of the world and more than half in love with the man. Then he called up my parents and asked them to come and see him. I'd already told them what I'd done and so they were prepared. I took the day off from school. I painted my toenails and put henna in my hair. I felt happy. The henna was almost dry and like a helmet on my head when they returned. One look at their faces and I knew something was badly wrong. My parents told me that the headmaster had asked them to take me out of the school. He had told them that I was prone to strange fantasies and lied, and needed special care and treatment, which the school could not provide. He told them that I had made unfounded accusations against a very happily married senior teacher and therefore couldn't continue at the school.'

'But what about the letter?'

'I don't know. Maybe he destroyed it.'

'But why?'

Her voice became bitter. 'Probably because good Hindi and physics teachers are hard to find. Like good political science teachers.'

'But the whole class saw how he behaved. I'll come with you to the headmaster.'

Her face clouded, hope alternating with fear. 'No,' she said at last, 'I can't take a risk like that. If I have to leave this school too, they will send me to live with my grandparents in some village in UP.' She shuddered. 'I'll die if that happens.'

I grasped her hand and held it tightly. For a while we said nothing. Then it came to me. 'I'll help you with the punishment. I can imitate handwriting quite easily.'

She looked at me in amazement. 'You'd do that for me?'

'Of course,' I replied.

It took us a week to finish it. We would have finished it faster, if Mandakini hadn't chosen as public a spot as the Gandhi statue in front of the library to do it. The entire school saw us sitting there, hour after hour, copying that newspaper.

At first they just glanced at us. Then a few of them came by to see what we were doing. Not the boys of our class, but the seniors, tall, muscular men in trousers instead of silly shorts. They would walk by like gods, pretending not to notice us. Then, at the last instant, they would stop. They would ask us casually what we were writing so furiously, but their eyes would be on Mandakini.

'We're copying the wisdom of this newspaper so that we can become wise citizens of our great country,' she would say.

They laughed at that. We would all laugh. But their eyes, as they looked at Mandakini, didn't laugh. Then she would tell them she had been punished. 'Who punished you?' they would ask, looking surprised, their eyes suggesting amazement that anyone would dare punish such a beautiful girl. 'Because I said that producing beauty queens was an important national achievement,' Mandakini would answer. They would shake their heads, light filling their eyes, and beg her to tell the story. Mandakini would then tell the story of how Mr Trivedi lost his temper. But she made it sound so funny that the seniors would laugh even more. Mandakini would laugh with them. Then their eyes would drink in the sight of Mandakini laughing, and their laughter would roughen at the edges.

'And she?' one curious senior asked 'What did she get punished for?'

'Nothing,' I replied, blanketed in shyness, 'I'm just good at copying.'

'That's useful,' they would say, looking at me in disbelief. Then they would turn their attention back to the real object of the visit.

'She's helping me. She's my friend,' Mandakini was saying as I came out of my reverie, draping her body over me in a most intimate hug, a kind she had never given me before. I could feel every line of her body, and it was as if I was the senior and it was him she was draping herself over. I looked at the guy. He was watching us with moist longing in his eyes.

'Lucky friend,' he croaked, looking at Mandakini. 'Can't I be your friend too?'

They laughed together as if it was a huge joke. Mandakini glowed.

By the end of the term, the school had lost its shyness of Mandakini. The circle of space that used to surround her wherever she went had vanished and was replaced by a group of the school's most beautiful girls packed so tight they seemed like petals around the heart of a flower. After the circle of chattering girls came the boys, hanging darkly around her. Everywhere I went in school, the air hummed with 'Mandakini says, Mandakini wouldn't like … ' Top models were now regularly compared to Mandakini. But I was her special friend. She made that clear. I was the only one she could trust, she told me. The others were just there to steal some of the light.

'What light?'

'You know. The boys' light, the way they look at girls.'

'Oh.' I wasn't sure I agreed. The light came from Him, and shone through Mandakini. It had nothing to do with boys.

When final exams arrived, I could hardly believe how the term had flown. For the first time in my life, I was sorry it was over. How different it had been from last term when all I had wanted to do was escape. Now I didn't want to re-enter the silence of the flat in Bangalore—a silence that was broken only by the sound of my grandmother's knitting needles and the bhajans she played on her portable cassette player.

Mandakini and I finished the last exam, English Literature, together. As we stepped into the sunshine, I felt so light I could almost fly. It was a perfect summer day in the hills. The sky was a cloudless blue. The crisp, dry air was perfumed with the resinous scent of pine needles, cut grass and dry wood. It caressed the skin of my forearms like silk. I turned to Mandakini to share the perfection of the moment, but her face was troubled.

'What's the matter?' I asked.

She smiled absently. 'Oh, nothing.'

'Was it the exam?'

'Huh, no, no, the exam was fine. I'm sure I passed.'

'Then what's bothering you?'

She said nothing. So I told her how I felt about the holidays and how I would miss her. She didn't answer. Then she said suddenly, 'I won't be far. I'm staying right here for the holidays. But I'll miss you too.'

I couldn't believe it. 'Whatever for?'

'My parents are going to be in Europe. Dad's got work there and my mother likes the shopping. So I can't go home.'

'But … but.' I felt angry with her parents, which confused me for it made me feel somehow disloyal to Mandakini. 'Anyway, it's only two weeks of holiday,' I mumbled.

'Two weeks alone,' she said.

I couldn't help shivering. A place of ghosts is what the campus would be. Even most of the teachers would be gone. Mandakini would be lost.

'At least you'll be able to sleep as long as you want,' I said awkwardly, trying to make a joke of it. 'My grandmother wakes me up at seven. She just doesn't take no for an answer.' But Mandakini wasn't listening any more.

Gabriel Fernandez was waving to her. He was the most beautiful man in school, beautiful enough to be a model, the whole school said. He and Mandakini made a wonderful couple. Slowly he walked over to us, a lazy smile on his lips. I looked at Mandakini. She had her 'queen' look back on her face.

'I'm going to America, wanna come?' Gabriel said, waving an envelope in her face. 'I've got admission to Leo and Sayer College, Ohio.'

'No, thanks, I was there last year.' Mandakini was very cool. But even as she said it, her eyes laughed at him.

'Really?' His smile slipped slightly, and then righted itself. 'Come into a nice private spot and tell me all about it.' Without waiting for her reply, he grabbed her hand and pulled her away.

I watched them talk, Mandakini laughing up at him, he leaning hungrily over her, desperately trying to please her. They seemed to belong together, like two young trees. A familiar feeling swamped me, a feeling of beauty so tangible that it was as if I had eaten it and its taste was penetrating every last taste bud and nerve cell inside me. I looked away, feeling embarrassed. Suddenly, it came to me that every beautiful view needed a window to frame it. Without the window there would be no view. In Mandakini's case, I was that window. So I watched the two of them talk. But, all the while, another image kept superimposing itself on the first one, that of Mandakini, alone, walking the halls and stairways where she and I had sat surrounded by admirers all term long. I imagined her walking past the dark mango tree beneath which Gabriel had kissed her for the first time, the lily pond beside which they would sit and hold hands for hours. How could her parents be so selfish? Did they have no idea of what it felt like to be imprisoned in a boarding school? Could they not guess how desperately we longed for home? Had Mandakini's parents already forgotten that their daughter's beauty was also a cross, sometimes too heavy to bear? How could her mother be so selfish as to choose yet another trip to Europe over her daughter?

At that instant I made my decision: I would ask Mandakini to come home with me for the holidays. I could easily forge a letter from my father to the headmaster inviting her home, and Mandakini could forge another one from her parents allowing her to go with me. My father would be surprised to see her and so would my grandmother and the aunts, but they would soon fall under her spell like everyone else and forget to ask how she had got there. That was my third and final mistake.

It went so smoothly that at the time I felt convinced that what I had done was right. If God had given Mandakini her beauty, he must have intended me to be its foil. I had to be with her always, to watch out for her, to protect her.

The day school ended, our driver, Babu, came to get me as usual. But by the time Mandakini and I got into the car it was early evening. I could feel Babu's anger. He knew he would get an earful from 'sahib', and worse from his own wife. My grandmother too would be imagining the worst by now. But I didn't care. Mandakini was with me. It had taken her a long time to say goodbye to all her admirers and an even longer time to pack. But at last we were in the car and speeding down the hairpin bends towards the distant city.

It was a perfect evening. As I watched, the sky slowly darkened and a golden full moon rose enormous over the forest. Beside me, Mandakini was silent. But I was as intensely aware of her beside me as I was of the huge moon above the trees. Because of her presence, the moon felt closer.

Night came. But night was different in the forest. The darkness was more intense, somehow more fierce. It fought off the light from the headlamps, forcing it to remain confined to the narrow strip of road, turning the forest into a tunnel through which we sped. Every once in a while we saw a fox or a jackal, and once a deer leapt gracefully across the road. The forest was noisy. Even above the hum of the car I could hear the chirruping of cicadas, punctuated by the whoops, roars and whistles of bullfrogs, the occasional hoot of an owl or a nightjar, and the coughs, barks, and grunts of larger animals.

'So what are we going to do when we get to Bangalore?' Mandakini asked. 'This drive is giving me the creeps.'

'Uh, I don't know,' I said, wondering how she managed to remain indifferent to the overpowering presence of the jungle. 'I don't even know if anyone will be awake when we get home.'

'All the better. Then we can go straightaway and eat. I heard Bangalore has great pubs.'

'But the driver has to go home,' I protested, knowing Babu was listening in the front.

'Oh.' She sounded disappointed.

We completed the journey in silence. Babu also maintained his grumpy silence. Normally, I would sit beside him in the passenger's seat and he would tell me all about events at home while I told him what I had been doing at school. It was a seven-year ritual, and I tried to get him started by asking him all the usual questions. But he replied in monosyllables. Eventually, I gave up and stared miserably at the impenetrable darkness of the forest.

When we arrived at the apartment in Golden Enclave, my father opened the door, his face like thunder. As soon as he saw me he grabbed my arm.

'Where were you? We've called the school, the state police. I even cancelled an important business dinner,' he shouted.

'I'm s-sorry, we … we got late,' I stammered. In my father's vocabulary, 'business dinner' was a euphemism for an important date.

But he wasn't listening. He had just glimpsed Mandakini standing behind me. He let go of my arm abruptly.

'Papa, this is my friend Mandakini. I brought her home for the holidays. We're in the same class,' I said nervously, watching his face. But I needn't have worried. Before my eyes, the anger drained out of his face and was replaced by something I had never seen before, an expression at once servile and desperate to please.

It was this expression and the dark emotion that fired it which got us, barely an hour after we arrived, inside a real Bangalore pub. My father was like a man bewitched. He had forgotten about his party, he had forgotten to be even mildly angry with me. 'Young people, especially young women, have no idea of time. My wife was just like that,' he said to Mandakini, when she took the blame for our being late upon herself. Later, when Mandakini said that she would love to see a real Bangalore pub, because she had never been to one and had heard so much about them and this was such a night of first-times for her that she felt she just had to ask, my father brushed aside my grandmother's protests about the huge dinner she had cooked and hustled us into the car.

My father was a great one for Bangalore's pubs. He went to them at least three times a week. But every time I asked him what was so special about them, he laughed and told me to wait till I was eighteen and then I would see for myself. So over the years, I had developed a good understanding of what a pub really was. I had glimpsed the long lines outside. I had heard the older girls whisper feverishly about their evenings in the coffee shops on Saturdays. And I had seen *Saturday Night Fever*. A pub was a temple to beauty. I could picture the way the music and the darkness transformed ordinary people, cloaking them in beauty so that they were freed of fear and so could ask for and receive love freely. I dreamed of the night I too would enter those black-and-gold doors, how the darkness would be filled with a sea of writhing bodies. They would swallow me and I would give myself to them completely, for the dancers, the lights and the music were a single living thing, with the power to transform even me into something beautiful.

So, to say that I was disappointed would be an understatement. Instead of the intimacy of darkness and bodies, the inside of the pub was like an airport lounge, lots of empty dead space, harsh white light and over-loud music. The furniture stood out more than the people: brightly coloured amoeba-patterned sofas alternated with shiny black leather chairs, all built for giants rather than small Indians. Too-large black granite tables turned the people into isolated little islands. In between, bored-looking waiters in white jackets, black trousers, bow ties and black-and-white shoes took orders and served drinks. They looked exactly like penguins, I thought scornfully. Even the music was the same tired stuff that I heard in school, in the shops, and on Channel V. It wasn't surprising then that no one was dancing.

We sat down at a table in the centre of the room. My father immediately put his hand on Mandakini's arm and began to laugh and flirt, enjoying himself. I felt the ground shake beneath me. And yet some part of me wasn't at all surprised. They were only doing what adults were supposed to do in pubs. I watched them, feeling like a child staring at something I wasn't meant to see.

So I looked around at the other people. Most of them looked old and successful. Hairy forearms peeked out of starched white shirts, gold glinted around thick necks. Fleshy lips smiled and leered. The women had complicated hairdos, heavy hips, and powder that didn't quite match the colour of their skin. They sprawled silently in their leather chairs and velour sofas, blinking ever so often like lizards in harsh sunlight. They were all as ordinary as I was. Only Mandakini shone like a light, and of course my father, energized and transformed.

I was staring longingly at the black-and-gold doors of the pub, wishing I could be on the outside, breathing the warm steamy air, when they swung open and a tall man in black jeans walked in. My heart rose. Here at last was the kind of man I had dreamed of. He was dressed entirely in black, wearing an ordinary, rather crumpled black shirt with the sleeves rolled up and well-worn black jeans. His slightly long hair brushed his battered collar. He wore no jewellery except for a beautifully carved silver buckle on his belt. But it was the way he carried himself that made him stand out. He looked wary yet unashamed, like a creature that lived part way between the darkness of the jungle and the intimate darkness of the city night. His eyes moved restlessly over the room as if he was searching for someone. I tried to imagine the lucky woman but there was no one in the bar that could match him, except one. And that woman seemed lost in conversation with my father.

The stranger moved to the bar and squeezed himself onto a stool between two lumpy men in business suits. The barman came up to him, his face breaking into a smile. They shook hands over the counter and then the barman turned to the beer tap and filled a long glass with the frothy golden liquid. He handed it to the stranger who then swivelled around on his stool, beer in his hand as if it belonged there, and surveyed the room. His eyes came to our table eventually and I quickly looked away. But I wasn't quite quick enough and for a second our eyes touched and I had the strangest feeling of being looked at through a microscope.

I looked at Mandakini and my father. She was saying something to him, her eyes laughing into his. Then he was asking her, 'So why did your parents send you to St. Andrews?' She laughed as if he had asked the cleverest question. 'I think they wanted me to see what India was all about.' She rolled her eyes at the rest of the pub. They laughed together. I felt horrified. She was lying to my father, looking so beautiful as she did it! The conversation continued, with my father asking her what she wanted to do after she finished school and listening intently to her answer. She said she wanted to be a computer programmer and my father nodded, impressed. I shut my eyes, unable to bear the sight of them any longer.

In the middle of telling her how he could help her get a training job, I heard my father falter. I opened my eyes, and there, towering over me, was the man in the black jeans. But he wasn't looking at me. He was looking at Mandakini. She smiled at him, and then he was leaning across me to kiss her on both cheeks. She curled her arms around him in answer and even the air around them held its breath.

They hugged each other forever, he a tall Krishna, holding her like the clouds held the moon on monsoon nights. In their embrace the pub of my dreams suddenly revealed itself. I looked at my father, wondering if he could see it too. He had a sour expression on his face as if he smelled something rotten. Suddenly, Mandakini broke off the embrace. She turned to my father and introduced her friend. 'This is Mr Naren Nath. A friend of my family from Dubai,' she said prettily.

'I'm not in Dubai any more,' he corrected her, laughing. 'I live in good ol' Bangalore now.'

'What do you do here?' my father asked with a sneer. 'Computers?'

'Primarily I am a photographer, though I also design web pages,' he replied.

My father frowned. 'What do you photograph?'

'Fashion mainly, a little film stuff also.'

Mandakini sat up excitedly. 'Have you photographed Sushmita Sen or Aishwarya Rai?' she asked.

He smiled and flicked a careless finger across her cheek. 'Of course! Many times, before and after they became Miss Universe and Miss World respectively. But they're quite boring to photograph, their features are too perfect. I prefer real people.' His eyes flicked over me for a second. Then he turned to my father. 'Can I sit down?'

'Of course, make yourself comfortable,' my father offered reluctantly.

That only made the man smile. He sat down and gave Mandakini a long sexy look.

My father missed none of it, and a telltale muscle began to jump near his left temple. But he managed to pull his mouth into a semblance of a smile and say, 'What can I get you to drink, another beer?'

The two men began to speak to each other. First, the man asked my father what he did. My father brightened and began to talk happily about himself, his business, his interests. Then they began to search cautiously for people they might know in common. Each time they found someone they both knew, my father looked disappointed. This went on for a while until Mandakini cut in with a question of her own for the photographer. His eyes warmed as he answered her. The two of them began to talk excitedly about friends they had in common 'from the Dubai days' and they forgot all about us.

My father concentrated moodily on his drink. He ordered another whisky for himself and stared into the middle distance, pretending to ignore them. The talk shifted to the present and the photographer asked her what she was doing in Bangalore and why, with her beauty, she wasn't already in Paris. She laughed delightedly and told the photographer how and why her parents had sent her to our boarding school three months ago. I didn't dare to look at my father as Mandakini told the true story to the photographer. She ended by saying that she was staying with me for the school holidays because her parents were in Europe. He smiled sympathetically and then the talk shifted to their Dubai days and the parties they had been to at some disco called Blaze.

At last my father looked at his watch and seemed relieved.

'Eleven o'clock, time you girls were in bed.'

Mandakini's friend got up to leave as well. He thanked my father for the drinks and the company and said he hoped they would meet again. My father smiled politely but did not give the man his card. The photographer gave him a mocking smile as he handed my father his own. Then, he was looking at me, and the smile changed. Once again I felt the sensation of being looked at through a microscope. 'It was nice to meet you, Mandakini's friend.'

I racked my brains for something smart to say, something that would make him remember me. 'What do you like in Bangalore?' I blurted out.

He looked a little surprised. 'The trees,' he replied seriously. A different smile appeared on his face, making him look suddenly younger. 'I love the trees. They still dominate this city.'

'I love the trees too,' I said, delighted.

But he was no longer listening. Mandakini had claimed him, throwing herself into his arms in a clinging goodbye. My father and I stood side by side and watched them. Two beautiful things joined together. I looked up at my father. A light had gone out in his face and he looked old. I slipped my hand into his. 'Thanks for bringing us here, dad. It's been great.' He didn't notice.

In the house he made himself a whisky and retreated into his study. I showed Mandakini to the room.

'Why did you lie to my father?' I asked as soon as we were inside.

'What do you mean?' She didn't look at me, pretending to be absorbed in her nails.

'About why you came to school … why didn't you tell him the truth?'

Her face grew hard. She arched her eyebrows mockingly. 'Why should I have told him the truth? Only an idiot tells a stranger the truth.'

He's not a stranger, he's my father, I wanted to reply. And he welcomed you to his house and dropped his dinner for you. Suddenly, her face didn't look quite so beautiful any more.

But even as I was thinking that, it changed, wonder softening her features. I shut my eyes, feeling the goosebumps pebble my skin.

An awestruck silence pervaded the room. Mandakini was looking fixedly at a spot above eye level on the adjacent wall. Finally, her liquid voice broke the silence.

'That's a beautiful photograph. Who took it?' she asked softly.

With a woman's instinct I knew which one she was pointing at. 'That's my mother,' I replied guardedly.

'I know, silly, you look like her. But who took the picture?'

I looked like my mother? I stared at Mandakini unable to believe my ears.

'Who took it?' she repeated a shade impatiently.

I shook my head to get the ringing out of my ears. 'You … you think I look like her?' I asked again.

The Elephant and the Maruti

'Of course,' she snapped, 'it's obvious. But tell me, who took that picture? He must have been a professional.'

A smile plastered itself hugely across my face. She was my dearest friend again. 'I-I don't know his name,' I confessed. 'He died a few years ago. But I think he was quite famous. The photo won a prize in Japan.'

I lingered over the word 'prize'. My father always said it with such ownership in his voice, as if it was he who had won the prize. Now I felt it too. Mandakini walked up to the photo and stood in front of it for a while.

'Naren's won prizes too,' she said abruptly, facing me.

My face burst into flame. Mandakini saw it and laughed. 'You liked him, didn't you?' she teased.

I looked down at the flame-coloured counterpane. 'What's the point of my liking someone like him? He'll never notice me.'

Mandakini's arm came over my shoulder. 'Didn't you hear Naren say the best models are real people? A photographer is like a diamond cutter; he simply chisels away until he has let the light shine through. Just like that photographer did for your mother. She couldn't have been so beautiful in real life.'

'But she was, everyone says so,' I insisted. But for the first time I felt uncertain.

She laughed. 'They only say it because she's dead. Don't believe them.' Then she added coyly, 'Naren takes good photos. You could look as good as she does.'

'I couldn't!' I gasped, deaf to the voice inside that said she was lying.

'Of course you could. All you need is the right photographer.'

I stared at her, torn between guilt and hope. 'I think it's fate that we bumped into Naren again,' she continued. Her face became dreamy. 'You should see Naren's work. He can turn a girl into a piece of art, something no one would forget. I'll be in Paris by next year if he photographs me.'

'Of course you will,' I said warmly even though the thought of her leaving India filled me with dismay.

'I'm sick of this country. I want to go where I will be noticed.'

Mandakini walked to the mirror and began to pose in front of it. I went and stood behind her, trying to imagine what she was seeing, trying to imagine her as a series of pages in a magazine.

But all I could see was God winking at me.

That night I dreamt I was swimming. The sea took away my ungainliness and made me fast and sleek. I rode waves as big as buildings from the middle of the ocean all the way to the shore. As we got closer to the beach, the waves gathered speed and I fell from unimaginable heights onto the beach. My body shattered into a million pieces and then flowed back together again, whole and unharmed. And when I walked out of the water, God was looking at the world through *me*! This is what it must feel like to be beautiful, I thought.

I told Mandakini about the dream in the morning.

'My God, what a violent dream,' she said as she walked into the bathroom, slamming the door.

I stared at the door, confused. Didn't she understand that my dream was part of the spell she cast over all of us, that through her I too was being transformed.

When she came out of the bathroom she announced, 'I want to go where the artists hang out.'

My heart lurched. I had no idea where artists hung out. Finally, it was my grandmother who came to our rescue. 'Go to Koshy's. That's the place you want,' she said. How she knew remains a mystery to me.

I had never been to Koshy's because it looked so dingy from the outside. I preferred Coffee World or one of the new Internet cafes where beautiful young people were to be found sitting before the huge plate-glass windows, drinking real Italian coffee instead of Nescafe. But Mandakini was delighted with Koshy's.

The inside of the restaurant was done up in muddy old-fashioned colours. Low rexine sofas in brown and dark green lined the walls. The furniture was also painted dark brown. Wood panelling in the same dark brown lined the walls. The walls were painted a pistachio green slightly lighter than the sofas. Hardly any light filtered in through the bamboo blinds. The people inside didn't look anything like the people outside, for most of them wore strange prints in earth colours and tie-die markings. The men had long unkempt hair, and the women's clothes didn't quite match. Most of them were grey-haired and wrinkled. They blinked at us when we entered, their eyes magnified by their old-fashioned glasses. Then they went back to talking in important whispers. Huge ceiling fans, also painted brown, creaked loudly, sounding like frogs around a monsoon puddle.

'This is a wonderful place,' Mandakini whispered as soon as we sat down.

'What's so great about it?' I whispered back.

'It feels … artistic. Anything could happen in a place like this.' She waved her hands expressively.

A waiter in a curry-stained jacket walked up to us. 'What do you want?' He yawned as he slapped the menu down on the table.

'Can't you give us some time to look at the menu?' I snapped.

But Mandakini broke in and ordered a coffee. I tried to warn her, but she refused to listen. So I ordered a strawberry milkshake.

'We don't have that,' the waiter said.

'Vanilla then.'

'We don't have milkshakes.'

I was about to say something blistering but Mandakini got in before me. 'Get her a cold coffee,' she ordered, smiling at the waiter.

'But … it's Nescafe,' I tried to warn her.

She pretended not to hear.

'Sorry I cut you,' she said after the waiter had left, 'but real artists, people who come here every day, would know the menu.'

'What do you mean?' I was mystified.

'Trust me, I know artistic places,' she said.

'But how do you know this is one? Maybe they're all pretending too.' I refused to give in so easily.

She stopped her delicate scanning of the room to look briefly at me. 'It has an atmosphere,' she said authoritatively. 'Famous people have been here, and therefore others will come. Like temples. When good people go to a certain temple, others end up there too. That is what makes a temple a temple. Artists have their temples too. This is one of them. I can feel it.'

'Why?'

She raised her eyebrows. 'What do you mean *why*?'

'Why are you suddenly so interested in artists? Yesterday, on the way down from school, you said you wanted to go to pubs and go shopping.'

'Who's that man?' she asked, changing the subject.

'Which man?' My heart speeded up. I didn't dare turn around.

'He's wearing a hat and he has a long white beard and white hair.'

'He's probably some artist.'

'Of course, I can see that. But who is he?'

'I can't turn around, so I can't tell you,' I snapped, wishing we were at Coffee World, sipping real cappuccinos.

Mandakini looked at me coldly. 'Don't bother. You wouldn't know who he was anyway. I wish Naren was here.' She went back to silently scanning the room. I bit my lip, feeling miserable. She was right to have come here, I thought to myself. Beautiful girls also need temples.

The waiter returned with our order and plonked it down untidily before us. It was Nescafe, I noticed with some satisfaction. Mandakini wouldn't look at me. She busied herself with pouring the milk and adding sugar to her coffee. I noticed that she had painted her nails red, which was probably the reason why she had taken so long in the bathroom that morning. I watched the brown fans turn on the shiny red surface. Suddenly, the nails were withdrawn and I heard Mandakini say, 'Hello, Naren.' Her voice didn't sound at all surprised. My heart almost stopped in its tracks. I continued to stare steadfastly at the table. It trembled as a chair was pulled back and he sat down beside us.

'So, are you girls having a good time?' he asked.

The waiter came up to him immediately, a smile on his face, and asked him what he wanted.

'You know I want a beer. You're just curious about my two pretty companions,' he teased the waiter.

The waiter grinned. Mandakini and I both laughed simultaneously. Our eyes met and the discomfort of a moment earlier vanished. Attracted by the laughter, the other customers looked at us.

'I was asking Renuka here who that man in the safari hat is. But she doesn't know,' Mandakini said to Naren. 'Do you know him?'

'You don't know him?' he said, turning to me, eyebrows raised.

I wanted to disappear.

He gave a sudden smile. 'That old pretender will be shattered to hear it.'

Relieved, I smiled back. Once again I had that feeling of being examined under a microscope.

'That man is Keerath Kunnadi,' he said, still looking at me. 'He thinks he's an intellectual, an astrologer, a guru and a food critic. Oh ... and a gemmologist as well.'

I felt thrilled. He was talking to us like we were grown-ups.

'Oh,' Mandakini sounded disappointed, 'I thought he was a photographer or an artist.'

'Because he's surrounded by women?' Naren asked, a hint of mischief in his voice.

Mandakini blushed.

'Actually, he's probably a closet gay and now too old to do anything about it. Which is why he hangs out in this café, holding hands with every pretty woman he can get his hands on.'

'Wh-what do you mean?' I asked, shocked at the naked cruelty of the remark.

'It's all about the public eye. He has to be seen in public with girls, only then can he feel comfortable with who he is in private.'

'But why?' I was mystified. I imagined a huge eye, shaped like a camera, staring at us.

'He's like a vampire,' he explained, 'who loves humans and is almost human in public, but feels jealous of them in private.'

I nodded hesitantly, trying hard to picture it but not quite succeeding. Something seemed to have been left out.

'Now replace human with woman and you've got his story in a nutshell.'

Mandakini laughed and he fixed his eyes on her lips.

'He must be dying of jealousy right now, seeing me with two such pretty young girls,' he said to Mandakini, leaning closer.

She laughed even harder, throwing back her head, so her long throat was exposed. At last I could see it. I imagined the old man's head settling there as he drank her blood and felt an unfamiliar sensation spreading below my stomach.

'Why does he feel jealous of women?' I asked quickly, to shake off the feeling.

'Because he wants to steal what you have,' he answered glibly.

'What is it that we have?'

'Your femaleness—he wants it. But he is scared of it. And that's why he wants to steal it from you.'

'Why does he want to steal what he's scared of?' I asked sceptically, certain he was toying with us.

'That's an excellent question, little girl.' He seemed to read my mind, emphasizing the 'little girl' bit to put me in my place. 'It's called the war of the sexes. But the men are finally winning because they have at long last got the women convinced that it's better to be men.'

'Oh.' I became silent.

'Soon femaleness will be wiped out and all that will be left will be men making love to men. That's why I only photograph beautiful women. One day my photos will be the rarest things in the world. And I'll be the richest man in the world.'

Mandakini, who seemed to have been paying scant attention, sat up. 'So why don't you photograph me,' she asked directly. 'I am beautiful.'

I held my breath. Naren Nath looked hard at Mandakini. Then he shook his head. 'I can't. You're too young. I'll be thrown in jail.'

'No, I'm not. I am almost seventeen,' Mandakini lied, throwing her head back in a very adult way. 'We'll go and buy some sexy clothes and I know how to do really good make-up. You won't even have to call in a make-up artist.'

He laughed and shook his head. 'Now you've proved you are a child. I won't do it.'

Mandakini's face darkened. 'What do you mean? Do you want me to take my clothes off to show you I'm not a child?'

His eyes narrowed. He didn't like to be argued with. 'So you think you can show me what a real woman is just by taking off your clothes?' he sneered.

Mandakini didn't reply. They stared at each other, her eyes stormily beautiful, his cool.

Suddenly, she grabbed his hand. 'Look at me, Naren,' she commanded, her voice throbbing with urgency. 'I was made to be a model. Your photos will make me unforgettable.' She let go of him, and the light went out of her. 'Please, I'll do anything you want,' she mumbled.

I opened my mouth to protest. Why was she begging him like this? It didn't suit her.

For a second he remained absolutely still, his handsome face shuttered. His eyebrows rose uncertainly, then fell. He shook his head as if he was freeing himself of his doubts.

'All right,' he said, 'as you wish.'

He had told her to come around noon on Sunday. I knew I wasn't meant to be a part of such an event. But Mandakini insisted I go with her. 'You understand beauty,' she said, giving me her 'special friend' look. 'You have to be there.'

We got there closer to two o'clock because Mandakini spent ages getting dressed. But the final result, I had to admit, was worth it. Her eyes looked more doe-like than ever. Her lips seemed especially supple and velvety, and her skin had the look of a ripe peach. Her strong out-thrust chin was subtly highlighted so that it caught your eye and drew you in to her eyes.

Habbagouda was a labyrinth of mud roads hiding large fortified bungalows. It was a place where those who had something to hide lived. As we drove through deserted, winding lanes bounded by high blank walls topped with barbed wire, the air felt heavy with secrets.

Finally, the auto-rickshaw stopped before a huge wrought iron gate. It opened silently after we spoke our names into an intercom, into a jewel of a garden. We drove through an avenue of coconut palms to a low single-storeyed, terracotta-and-orange house. Magenta bougainvillea grew up the sides of the house and curled riotously over the flat roof. A riot of flowers I couldn't name, lilac, mauve, gold and orange grew on low bushes, spreading out like petals from the house. Vines curled around cunningly hidden bamboo trellises and in between them were pools of dark still shadow surrounded by interestingly shaped rocks. The city had vanished. All we could hear were the birds and the crickets, and somewhere in the distance, frogs calling to each other.

'This is like a dream—I never imagined anything so beautiful could exist!' I whispered to Mandakini as the three-wheeler set us down before the entrance.

Mandakini's eyes had widened in wonder. 'I never knew he was so rich,' she replied.

A huge purple-and-gold butterfly flew up in front of me. Dazzled, I followed it with my eyes. When I couldn't bear the beauty of its colours any more I let my eyes wander over the landscape and slowly became aware that the garden was filled with butterflies of every imaginable hue and size. All of a sudden I was seized by the feeling that this garden had been made especially for me.

'Oh, Mandakini,' I reached instinctively for her hand, 'how can I ever thank you for bringing me here?'

'Silly, you don't have to thank me,' she laughed, squeezing my hand in return, 'you brought me to Bangalore, remember?'

I squeezed her hand tightly, wanting, yet unable, to find the words with which to explain to her how much she meant to me.

'What a lovely photograph you two girls make,' a male voice remarked, laughing. We both turned around. He was standing in the flower-filled patio, framed by the darkness behind him, a camera in his hand. 'Welcome,' he said, opening his arms wide. Mandakini ran up to him and pressed herself boldly into his arms. I hung back awkwardly.

'Your garden is a dream,' Mandakini told him, echoing my words.

He looked pleased. 'Come, let me show you the inside,' he said hospitably, disentangling himself from her embrace.

We stepped through the veranda into an airy plant-filled room with turquoise and white and aquamarine tiles on the floors. But Mandakini wasn't interested in the house.

'Show me where you will photograph me,' she demanded, looking up at him coyly.

'Impatient little puss! I work upstairs where there's more light,' he answered, lightly touching her cheek. 'I'll take you there after brunch. Come, let's eat first, I'm hungry.'

He led us through the French windows on the far side of the room, past the sunken sofa sets, and onto a brick-paved terrace cocooned in vines covered with deep blue and purple bell-shaped flowers. In the centre was a small wicker table, laden with fruit, milk and a collection of mysterious earthenware dishes.

Naren turned out to be an easy companion. Over brunch he talked non-stop about himself, telling us of all the prizes he had won and the cities he had been to, the famous models he had met, the film stars he had photographed. There wasn't a celebrity he hadn't worked with. He told amusing stories about the ones we had heard of, making them seem just a little stupid, a little less than perfect. Mandakini drank it all in, 'oohing' and 'aahing' at every famous name, laughing at his stories. He used the word Paris at least once every three sentences. But I preferred his stories about himself, how he went off alone into dangerous jungles and filmed never-visited tribes with strange customs. Most of all I liked him when he spoke of his garden, how he had planned it all, supervising the workers himself and how he had come to know each plant's likes and dislikes the way he knew good friends.

At last, when he seemed to have exhausted himself, I asked, 'So why are you photographing Indian women? Isn't it rather boring after all your adventures?'

He gave a start as if he had only just remembered I was there and a flash of annoyance lit his eyes. But it was quickly extinguished. His mouth twisted into a wry smile. 'Full of good questions as usual,' he remarked, and turning towards Mandakini said pointedly, 'I am glad you brought her.'

I felt so small that if I had moved I think I would have disappeared into a crack in the floor.

Naren Nath continued to speak, his voice deepening as he caressed Mandakini with his eyes. 'All men are extremely sensitive to beauty. We can't help it. Women are smarter. They look for what they can get out of a man—they have the knack for digging inside. We men are different. We're poor, besotted creatures, worshippers of feminine beauty in spite of our better selves. Me, I use my camera to worship that beauty. But, as I said the other day, a truly beautiful woman is a creature on the verge of extinction. Modern women aren't women any more. They've had womanhood educated out of them.' Suddenly, his mask slipped and I felt the full force of his contempt. 'Only the poor and uneducated women of the East still retain their natural beauty. That's why I am here. To capture that beauty before development wipes it off the face of this earth.'

He stared at me searchingly, willing me to agree. But I knew he wasn't really seeing me, he was hypnotized by his own words, like an actor in a play. I nodded anyway, so he continued.

'Men cannot live without beauty. They are like butterflies, attracted to beautiful flowers, so that beauty can reproduce itself.'

'I know what you mean,' Mandakini whispered huskily. 'I believe beauty is God's way of telling us he exists. That's why men are attracted to beauty, that's why life depends upon it.' The words glided easily off her tongue, as if she owned them!

Naren looked surprised, then smiled at her in a genuine way. 'That's certainly the most original argument in favour of the existence of God I have ever heard. I wish someone had told me that twenty years ago, I might have become a believer.'

Feeling utterly depressed, I looked out at the rear garden. We were on a hill with the land sloping down to the right. Not an inch of it had been left bare. The garden had a bit of everything, all mixed up and growing into each other. To the right it ended in a tangle of jungle. On the left, closer to the house, a jumble of scarred marble rocks peeped out from under a fringe of feathery umbrella trees. A pebbled path wound down to the bottom of the garden between clumps of young bamboo and date palms. And in the centre there was a little sunken garden with an amphitheatre made of red sandstone. Beyond the garden, on the opposite hillside, coconut tree-lined rice fields rose upward in a series of gentle terraces till the horizon met the sky.

A thought struck me, making me smile. Women weren't the most beautiful things. He was wrong. Even if they all died, there would still be the trees. Their limbs wouldn't shrivel up or grow fat. Suddenly I heard a click. I looked around. He had the camera pointed at me. Click, click, click, it went, singing to me.

I stared at it curiously, seeing my face reflected in its rapidly blinking eye. I felt looked-at in a way I had never been looked at before, and it filled me with a joy so intense, it was painful. The camera came closer and I looked back at it more openly. When at last he stopped I just kept staring into the camera wanting more. He was about to reach for the camera again but Mandakini had had enough.

'But she's not beautiful,' she said, her voice rising shrilly, 'why are you wasting your time?'

I cringed.

'True, but her face is intense, and intensity can be sexy on film,' he replied seriously.

I felt dirty. Models were supposed to be beautiful, not sexy.

'Anyway, you can photograph me now. I'm ready.' Mandakini pushed her chair back and stood up.

But he wasn't watching her. 'What were you thinking of?' he asked me.

'When?' I asked, suddenly feeling shy.

'Just now when I photographed you.'

'I was looking at the trees,' I stammered.

'What about them?'

'I was thinking that the trees would still be there, even if all the beautiful women died.'

'What a stupid thing to say!' Mandakini snapped. 'C'mon, let's go, we're wasting time. Let her stay with her trees.'

He kept his eyes fixed on me, ignoring her. 'I'd like to photograph you properly someday.'

My heart missed a beat. 'Oh no, that … that just won't be possible.'

'Why?'

'Because … because I don't like being photographed,' I said.

'Really?' He stared hard at me. 'All women like to be photographed.'

Mandakini tried to reclaim his attention. 'Come on, Naren, quickly. She won't make you any money.'

He glanced up at Mandakini, a shadow crossing his face. Then he looked at me again. To my surprise, there was respect in his eyes.

Mandakini tried grabbing his attention again. 'What are we waiting for? Take my pictures before I get too educated.'

I shut my eyes, wishing I had never come. When I opened them, he was talking excitedly to Mandakini.

'Women and trees, women and water … why didn't I think of it before?'

He leapt up and grabbed the camera.

'Beautiful women in front of beautiful trees with sun-dappled rocks and crystal clear water behind them. It won't be just another sexy book for horny men, it'll be a sexy plea for saving the environment. Everybody will buy it, even the feminists. It'll be a best-seller.' He walked off in the direction of the rocks. 'Come, girls,' he ordered. We hung back, wondering if he was crazy. He stopped and gestured impatiently. 'Hurry up, we don't have all day.'

Obediently, we both began to run after him.

He led us down a tiny mud track around the side of the white rocks. We turned a corner and there it was: a miniature oasis, complete with waterfall and surrounded by flowering trees and purple bougainvillea, and behind it the jungle. I held my breath. It was almost too beautiful.

'All right, take off your clothes and go sit there by the magnolia tree.'

We looked at each other, stunned.

'Naren, this ... this is a joke, right?' Mandakini asked him hesitantly.

'Of course not, I am perfectly serious,' he replied, his face grim. 'Take them off. The light's perfect right now.'

'But I—'

'No buts,' he said cruelly. 'You wanted to be a model. This is lesson one. It's called losing your inhibitions.'

The blood slowly drained from Mandakini's face. I wanted to rush at him and hit him. And I wanted to cry. Because a part of me still thought he was beautiful and couldn't understand how anyone so beautiful could be so cruel.

'Don't do it, Mandakini,' I said urgently, grabbing her hand.

But she shook it off angrily. 'Don't try to get out of it like this, Naren. You promised you'd take my pictures,' she said in her best baby voice.

'All right.' He looked bored. 'Go stand by the tree.'

She went and stood under the champa tree.

'C'mon, show me something, little miss model,' he shouted, lifting his camera to his eye. Obediently, she flowed into one of the poses I'd seen her practise in front of the mirror. His hands didn't move. He screwed up his other eye and stared at her through the lens. Suddenly, he burst into laughter.

Mandakini froze. 'What's so funny?' she asked.

That made him laugh harder. 'Go on. Give me another pose. I haven't laughed so hard in years,' he said.

Mandakini covered her abdomen with one hand and her breasts with the other in a classic gesture of shame. Her face crumpled.

He brought the camera away from his eye.

'Hey, go on,' he ordered, 'real models don't stop because the photographer doesn't like their first few poses.'

'I-I can't.' Mandakini's lower lip trembled and her eyes filled with unshed tears.

At last Naren stopped laughing. 'Damn,' he swore, 'get out. I've wasted enough time with you. You're nothing but a child.'

'But you promised,' she whispered.

'I promised to take photographs of you, not your clothes.' He turned and began to walk uphill.

It took less than a minute for Mandakini's resistance to crumple. He had barely reached the crest of the hill when she began taking off her clothes. I looked away, too ashamed to watch.

'I'm ready,' she called when she got down to her bra and panties.

He turned around slowly. To my horror, he was smiling. He knew she would break down! He knew she would do it!

He began walking back down the hill. But I got to her first. She had a dumb smile plastered on her face and I didn't think she looked beautiful at all. I bent down to gather her clothes.

'Stop it. Let's go,' I told her.

She looked at me as though she didn't know me any more. I heard him come up behind me. 'Take the bra and panties off too,' he called over my shoulder. 'You've got a lovely body, don't be shy.'

Blindly obeying that coldly brisk voice, she reached behind her and unfastened her bra. In the same movement she stepped out of her panties, turning slightly sideways out of shyness.

I had never seen Mandakini completely naked before and so I couldn't help staring at her. To begin with, she didn't look naked. To my mind naked was something weak and small and easily destroyed. Naked was something fallen. But Mandakini's beauty, now no longer veiled by the everyday mystery of clothes, seemed indestructible, flawless. Thinking back on that moment I realize it was her remarkable skin that made her appear so. It was the colour of sunlight on new wheat and emitted a light of its own, shimmering like a fast-flowing river in places, shadowed and depthless in others. Since that day I have never seen skin like that. It was an invitation. It made you want to run your hands across her smoothly rounded belly, cup your palms under her plump high breasts and around her smooth rounded bums, then run them back up into the small of her back and up the delicate channel between her shoulder blades. There was nothing lumpy or out of place on her body. Everything fell together in perfect harmony.

Even the photographer was impressed. I heard his sharp intake of breath as he walked around me and stood close to her.

'Silly little kitten! Making such a fuss about nothing. You should be proud of your body. It's perfect. You're a photographer's dream. You've nothing to worry about,' he said, curling his arm around her waist familiarly.

I turned away.

'Now you'll do whatever I ask and no whining,' I heard him say more firmly as he led her away. 'This is adult stuff now, no little girl nonsense.'

'Of course,' Mandakini answered eagerly.

'No, Mandakini.' The words were torn out of me.

But she ignored me and he laughed in triumph. 'Good girl,' he told her.

Suddenly, he stopped and beckoned me. 'If you want to watch, you'd better shut up and make yourself useful,' he said coldly.

I should have walked away. But something stopped me. Perhaps it was the glint of sunlight on the camera lens, inviting me to pierce the veil along with it. Or perhaps it was because I thought I could save her by being there. Or maybe I knew that as the watcher I was a part of the picture too, and that Mandakini would never forgive me for walking away. From that moment on, I surrendered my will to him like she had and the afternoon took on a dreamy surreal feel. Afterwards I wondered where God had gone in those hours, and how he could so easily have abandoned his most beautiful creation.

Naren led Mandakini to a pretty little magnolia tree with deep pink flowers, just a little taller than she was.

'All right, my dear, stand under the tree, clasp your hands in front of you and look at me,' he told her in a businesslike way.

The sunlight played on her skin, which glowed even brighter against the dark leafy background. She put her hands modestly in front of her and looked up shyly. The thick clusters of magnolia made a halo around her head and cast a dull glow on her hair. Her face remained in shadow, just the whites of her eyes gleaming mysteriously.

I held my breath. He lifted the camera to his eye and began to shoot non-stop, circling her like a hunter, talking to her constantly like an animal tamer. Slowly she relaxed.

'There,' he murmured, 'that's much better. Doesn't the sun feel lovely on your skin? Can you feel the way it licks you?'

She giggled and nodded her head.

'Don't move,' he barked.

She froze.

He began shooting again, going closer little by little. 'Turn to the tree, press your breasts against that rough bark, feel it enter your skin. Good. Right, now curl one leg around the tree. Lean back. More, I say. Now lean back and look at me. Think of being famous, think of Paris. Yes, very good. That's very, very good. Now, just one more close-up. Yes.'

His voice went on endlessly, the clicking of his camera making a rhythmic counterpoint to his deep bass drone. My eyes began to close.

Suddenly, he leapt forward and pushed Mandakini down brutally.

'Ouch, my back,' Mandakini shouted.

I was wide awake.

'Shut up.' He grabbed her chin and made her look up at him. He stared at her for a long moment and then took a bit of mud and rubbed it onto her cheek. 'Open your mouth a little. Just slightly. Right. Now the legs. Stop.'

He removed his hand and began to take photographs.

I edged closer to see what he was doing and noticed that Mandakini was crying silently. But such was the photographer's spell that neither of us said anything.

When he stopped she said humbly, 'My back hurts.'

'All right, get up,' he ordered.

She stood up awkwardly. I caught sight of her back and gasped. It was scratched, and bleeding slightly in a few places.

'Oh, I guess we won't be able to do any more back shots then,' he remarked, unmoved. 'A pity. Never mind, there's lots of other options.'

I stared at him in horror. Mandakini, though, didn't seem to mind.

'Go wash it off,' he said, pointing to the pool.

'But that water is dirty. She needs medicine,' I said.

He screwed up his eyes, a gesture I was beginning to recognize. 'Go squat in the water like a washerwoman,' he ordered Mandakini. Hesitantly she obeyed. He took a few shots from a distance. Then he made her lie down in the water like the girl in the *Hamlet* story. He scattered crimson petals around her and spread her hair like a fan behind her. Next, he made her stand up and shake herself dry. He told her more funny stories about famous people so that she laughed and forgot to be self-conscious.

'You're superb,' he told her, 'just superb. You were born for the camera.'

Suddenly, a thought struck me and I felt as though someone was twisting a knife inside me. That's what the other photographer must have said about my mother. Did he make her take her clothes off too?

My blood went cold.

His mocking voice jerked me out of my nightmarish reverie. 'So, tree girl, where shall we go next?'

I shrugged.

'What's the matter?' he asked. 'You look unwell.'

'No, no, I'm fine,' I muttered. 'What about the coconut palm there?' I pointed to a strangely bent tree leaning over the tiny bit of sandy beach.

He nodded and began to walk towards it. I watched the two of them go, pleased to be left alone. But he wouldn't do that.

'Tree girl, come here,' he called.

With heavy steps I joined them. He had made her sit with her legs curled around the base of the tree and her arms wrapped around its smooth trunk. Her upturned face and back were striped with the spiky shadow of the palm leaves. He bent over her, arranging her legs in such a way that they looked almost like a pair of external roots. Distantly, I admired his little arrangement. He twisted Mandakini's body this way and that. He played with her arms and breasts. He pulled up her arms and fastened them to an overhanging branch. He whispered something into her ear and she laughed, her breasts shivering. He adjusted her hair and twitched a palm frond into place so that its pointed shadow fell on the base of her throat. He raised his camera and pointed. Later, he ran a careless hand across her belly and then took a leaf and stuck it between her lips.

The afternoon wore on with the slowness of a bad dream. To my utter amazement, Mandakini flowered. After she came out of her 'bath', she seemed to be completely at ease with her nakedness. She began to suggest poses on her own. He nodded or made little alterations. Every once in a while, when he was really, really pleased, he groaned, 'You're an excellent model.' He told Mandakini as he changed rolls, 'I promise you'll be a great success.'

'But … but Naren, you won't show these to anyone, will you?' she asked worriedly.

'Of course not! They're just for you and me,' he said reassuringly. Quickly, he grabbed a creeper hanging from a huge banyan tree and wound it around her arms and let it slide down like a snake's tail between her breasts. 'This tickles,' she giggled. He quickly shot a stream of pictures.

At last it grew too dark to photograph outdoors, so he took us indoors. There he made Mandakini wear barbaric tribal jewellery and pose in the antique bathtub with the velvet shower curtains. He made me help him adjust the lights. He made her play with the curtain rising up between her legs. Then he made her sit on top of the old-fashioned steel bucket and pour water on herself. He photographed her from the side, and the back and then took a few close-ups from the front. Then he made her play with the giant seashells he had in the corner. Mandakini no longer looked like a goddess. She looked tired, and closer to my idea of naked—though she looked beautiful still. And the same tiredness weighed down my arms as I strained to hold the lights steady.

At last he put his camera down. 'I've no more film. You've exhausted me,' he told Mandakini. 'Come back on Tuesday. I'll have developed these by then and seen your best angles. Then we'll do a portfolio.'

'Really?' Mandakini reached up and gave him a kiss. 'Thank you, Naren Uncle,' she said naughtily.

He gave her a light slap on her bottom. 'Watch your mouth, little girl, or I'll have to spank you.'

She giggled and ran off to get her clothes.

It was late when we returned. My grandmother was waiting for us. 'Your father's gone out for dinner,' she informed us.

We silently ate the sumptuous dinner she had cooked for us. Neither of us felt like speaking. My grandmother tried. 'How was your day? What did you do?' she asked.

Mandakini and I looked properly at each other for the first time that day. Then we both quickly looked away.

My grandmother scented a mystery. 'So where did you two girls go?' she asked, watching our faces closely.

'Nowhere,' I mumbled. 'We just went shopping.'

'What did you buy?'

'We window-shopped.'

The rest of the meal was cloaked in silence. Then Mandakini and I headed for the bedroom. As soon as we got inside, she went into the toilet with a magazine. I stood at the door and looked around the room.

My bedroom looked exactly the way it had that morning. My eyes were drawn like magnets to my mother's picture on the wall. Somehow it surprised me that it should still be there. I walked slowly around the bed and took it off its hook. I held the photo in my arms till they grew tired. Then I hung the photo back on the wall. She stared down at me, ageless and inscrutable. As I undressed, her beautiful almond eyes followed me around the room, as they always had. Suddenly, I could no longer bear her looking at me. I went up to the photograph, turned it around so she faced the wall, put my nightdress on, and switched off the light.

four
_____

the elephant and the maruti

*I*n Delhi freedom begins on the roads. Behind the wheel of a car, a man ceases to be the shackled, duty-bound creature he is and becomes God, untouchable, governed by rules of his own making. On the road it doesn't matter if one is a Brahmin, a Cabinet minister, a bureaucrat's wife or a sweeper. Four wheels come between a person and his social status. All drivers are not equal, of course. Size counts. As does speed and manoeuvrability. But only up to a point. In reality one advantage cancels out the other. Slim little scooters can manoeuvre themselves into the cracks between cars. Cars, using the strength of sheer numbers, close ranks till their mirrors and fenders touch, thereby squeezing the scooters out. Buses, on the other hand, rely upon their bulk and other drivers' survival instincts to forge ahead. Bus drivers swear that size beats manoeuvrability any day and they are usually right. Cows and elephants rely on the aura of the sacred that clings to them. Cyclists count upon their vulnerability, daring people to kill them in much the same way that buses dare people to come in their way and get killed. Taxis and chauffeur-driven cars are the only creatures that dare to respond to the cyclists' challenge. But even they don't dare hit a cyclist in broad daylight, because they know that the mob will not let them get away. The little 800 cc Marutis always give way to the cyclists, for they are the mobs' favourite car—so fragile, so easy to overturn. They make a weak man feel strong.

*

'Let us face facts. The Maruti is a woman's car. You know why?'

The listener would shake his head.

'Because in a Maruti, a lady can honk all she wants and no one will take any notice.'

Even after a gap of five years, Shweta could still hear her husband's voice quite distinctly as he chortled with glee at his own humour.

'Those damn Japanese,' he would continue, 'they really fooled us. For nine years they fooled us and look how much money they made! They and that Gandhi family—all crooks and foreigners.'

Her reverie was broken by a huge truck that tried to wedge itself into the sliver of space in front of her, forcing her to brake. The engine died. She honked furiously at the good-looking young Sardar driver. He looked into the rear-view mirror. Seeing that the woman driving was middle-aged, he pressed his foot on the accelerator, and covered her in a cloud of unburned diesel. She cursed and honked violently at the cyclist now cutting in on her stalled car, two schoolchildren perched in front and behind him.

The cycle wobbled dangerously, bringing her back to her senses. She counted to ten and restarted the car. It promptly came to life. Whatever had been blocking the traffic had cleared and the traffic had speeded up considerably, so that by the time she was moving again, the truck was long gone, and so were all those who had watched her humiliation. Roads have short memories.

The traffic remained light and friendly as she drove towards Delhi, and she cheered up. Nowhere, she decided, nowhere was she more aware of the Brave New India in the making than when she was on the roads of Delhi. Rudeness and aggression made a refreshing change from the obsequious attentions of her husband's juniors and their wives.

Shweta flew over the Japanese-built Nizamuddin Bridge across the Yamuna and turned right onto the Ring Road. Mercifully, it too was free of serious congestion. This happy state of affairs lasted till the turn from Bhairon Marg onto Mathura Road. The crossing was, as usual, jammed with cars crawling at a snail's pace towards Minto Bridge and Old Delhi.

Twelve minutes later she turned onto Tilak Marg. Almost there, she thought as she approached the ITO crossing and saw the buildings of Bahadur Shah Zafar Marg—India's own Fleet Street—rear up ahead on her left. The muscles in her shoulders eased in anticipation. Then the light turned red and she had to stamp on the brakes once more. This time her other foot was equally fast on the clutch and the engine didn't stall. She looked at the glowing traffic light that had thwarted her. It had been so close, she thought regretfully.

And then the light went out. Around her, the suddenly liberated drivers of other cars immediately revved their engines and began to bully their way into the middle of the crossing. But the lights had not changed: they had simply blinked out, so the river of cars, buses, motorcycles, scooters coming into the crossing at right angles from the ITO bridge and Deen Dayal Upadhyaya Marg continued to flow undaunted. Car, bus and scooter horns rent the air and a gridlock began to develop. Shweta found herself swearing once more.

The policeman assigned to ITO that morning was young and good looking. It was his first week of work and he had already controlled the dreaded crossing for three days. Full of a new-found self-confidence, he leapt into the road like a young bull, slapping the hoods of cars to make them stop, leaping in front of scooters and physically unseating unruly cyclists. But it was like damming a river. No matter how many he stopped, he had only to turn his head a fraction for them to sneak past again. He soldiered on bravely, getting more and more frustrated and only adding to the confusion. Until finally it dawned on him that the traffic had a life and will of its own and that all he actually had to do was to seem to be directing it. With studied nonchalance, he climbed back onto his traffic island and raised his arms languidly. The flow of traffic resumed, led by the biggest and most fearless. To the policeman on his island, it began to resemble an angry mountain river. He grew calm. There was a God looking after the traffic, after all.

At last the stream of traffic heading east towards the ITO

Bridge tapered off and the policeman came to life again. He waved his sticks with greater enthusiasm and stepped boldly in front of a horse-drawn tonga carrying a cargo of chickens that brought up the rear of the convoy. The horse, young and untrained, took fright and reared. The baskets of live chickens slid off the wagon and onto the road. The horse reared again. The policeman, feeling his manhood at stake, shouted to the driver to move his cart back. The driver ignored him, swearing in a dull monotone as he struggled to bring his horse under control.

'Go back, I tell you,' the policeman shouted, hitting the horse over the ears with one of his red sticks. The horse began to rear again, but this time the driver was ready for it and brought him back down.

'What's the matter with you, hitting a poor frightened animal,' he shouted.

'Didn't you hear me?' the policeman demanded. 'I said, go back.'

'What do you mean, go back? I have to go forward,' he shouted indignantly. 'I've work to do.'

'I say you have to go back. The light's changed.'

'What light? I don't see any light.'

For a second the policeman was confused. Then he remembered that it was because the lights had broken down that he was where he was. '*I* am the light, you fool. You should have stopped. Now I will have to ticket you.'

'Well, I never saw you,' the tongawala muttered. 'I was just following the man in front of me and he went right past you. How come you didn't ticket him?'

'*I* decide who gets tickets here. You better shut up if you don't want two.'

'Who is the second ticket for?' roared the tongawala, bridling. 'The horse? And what about my chickens? Who's going to pay for those? I will not move till my chickens are returned.'

The young policeman blanched. 'I'll help you with the chickens. As for the Maruti before you, since I couldn't catch him I let him go.'

Too late the policeman realized the price he would have to pay for his honesty. 'Now get back there and start collecting your chickens before I give you that ticket,' he said furiously, by now quite red in the face.

'Thank you. You're very kind.' The tongawala, all smiles, jumped off the cart and began to throw the chicken baskets back onto it. The policeman climbed onto the traffic island again. As if this was the signal they had been waiting for, the cars around Shweta revved their engines and surged forward.

The policeman turned around and faced the cars, an expression of utter loathing on his face. He raised his sticks and then suddenly let his arms drop. He was tired, too tired to pretend. The cars moved ahead. Nobody paid the slightest attention to the huge elephant, all painted and primped, with a mahout dressed in a smashing new green-and-red tracksuit on its back. The elephant was going to a wedding in south Delhi. And the mahout knew they were going to be late. So he forced the elephant into the traffic regardless.

The sudden onrush of cars and buses was too much for the nerves of the tongawala's horse. It reared again and then again. The chicken baskets went flying into the face of the beautifully painted elephant. The elephant didn't take well to such disrespect and let out a squeal of rage and reared, towering high over the traffic around him. Immediately, what had been a sea of motion became still as a picture. In slow motion the powerful front legs of the elephant descended upon the cart. There came the terrible sound of wood splintering and the cart split into three. A wheel detached itself from the wreck and rolled away to the west. Freed of its burden and happy to be alive, the horse dashed away in the opposite direction.

The tonga driver, who had been catapulted off the tonga, landed unhurt right beside the traffic island. But the elephant, not content with the damage it had wrought, reared again. This time the mahout raised his iron stick, a heavy black thing with four sharp prongs on one end, and brought it down hard on the elephant's head. The elephant let out another squeal, this time of pain, and landed with far less elegance and planning than the last time while the mahout rained blows upon its head and ears.

The elephant stood still for a few seconds, twitching its ears. All of a sudden it lifted its trunk and trumpeted long and loud. This time the sound was quite different. It was no squeal of protest and pain. It was a blast of steely intent that cut through the car horns and the general cacophony like a knife through butter. Then it grabbed the axle of the cart, one wheel still stuck to it, and swung its muscular trunk left and right, using the axle like a battering ram. Shweta heard the sound of glass shattering as a semi-circular bit of wheel went through someone's windscreen. She looked around to see if she could spot the car that had been hit. Just then the elephant started trumpeting again. That heart-stopping sound was followed by the scrunch thud of metal folding in on itself, and glass exploding. That was when the screaming began.

Afterwards, Shweta could never reconstruct precisely what had happened. It seemed to her that the elephant had finally heeded the goading of its mahout and begun to back away from the scene of its crime. But in doing so, it had backed into an intrepid little red Maruti that had been trying to edge around it. Somehow, the fact that its retreat was blocked enraged it even more than the beating from the young mahout. It ploughed into the red Maruti, rearing up and stamping down upon it till it became a flattened piece of metal the size of a carpet. The person inside never had a chance.

It was close to half past eleven when Shweta arrived in the car park. Her usual spot was taken so she parked in front of the urinal, beside the aloopuriwala. She was still shaken by what she had seen but fear of her boss was slowly beginning to take precedence. By now the super-important meeting with the Koreans would be coming to an end. She couldn't walk in there and say that she was late because an elephant went mad and killed a man. Her boss would think she was making fun of him, taking full advantage of her position as the wife of the secretary of mines.

She got out of the car, and locked it carefully. She looked around for the car-park boy. He usually hovered around like an anxious bee, insisting he be paid straight away. But this time he was nowhere in sight. She frowned. Her lips became a straight line. So this was the way he looked after the cars, disappearing god alone knew where the moment he had been paid. He could pay for the parking ticket himself this time, she decided. That would teach him responsibility. Holding her bag like a shield, she made her way along the crowded pavement to the BHEL office.

Under the Iceberg advertisement, the aloopuriwala was chopping onions and dhaniya, their fragrance masking the ever-present smell of the urinal. He saw the angry-looking memsahib walk past but hardly glanced at her. She was the kind that always carried home-made lunches in her bag.

At the other end of the lot, in the shade of a giant peepul tree, the parking-lot attendant was dreaming of his wife. He was barely seventeen and hadn't even finished class twelve. But school felt far away now. He had been a working man for a month, a married one for a little longer. He hadn't wanted to get married, but his parents had forced the marriage on him. He had been furious. Until he saw his wife. Sushila was tiny and shy and scared, with shining blue-black hair to her knees. She had driven all thoughts of flight from his head. As he sat under the peepul tree, the fragrant April breeze caressing his face stoked his longing for her. Today he would be paid. He would take his fifteen hundred rupees to his wife, make her undress and bury her in the money. Then they would make love. Later, he would give half to Sushila for the house, give five hundred rupees to his parents and use the rest to buy his wife presents. His first salary. He looked around the full parking lot and could hardly believe his luck.

A parking lot was a place full of opportunities. One got to rub shoulders with important sahibs and with their drivers. The latter were a storehouse of knowledge. They knew how to cheat at cards, and how to fix cars so that they consumed less petrol. They would sit around talking about the lives of their sahibs and memsahibs, or just read the newspapers and make sage comments on what was happening in the world. Then there were the cars themselves. Each car was an opportunity to learn. He wanted to learn to drive. Drivers earned unimaginable salaries. They dressed well, lived well, and listened to music all the time on their employers' car stereos. Some even had mobile phones. Kishore had got to know some of the drivers who came there each day. One had already offered to teach him how to drive but he had recognized the moist look in the man's eyes and politely refused. But there were others. He had already identified one, a dark quiet man who spent all his time inside his car reading, as a possible teacher. Then there were the mechanics on the western edge of the parking lot. He could ask them to teach him their trade. But he would much rather be a driver. A driver was the master of the car while the mechanic was only its caretaker.

His eyes moved over the cars again. The driver he liked had the hood up and was washing the car's engine. As the clear transparent water gushed over the darkly shining curves of the radiator he saw Sushila as she had looked that morning, her face and breasts shining with perspiration, all of her so round and firm and inviting. Like a car, she felt curved everywhere.

A gust of wind brought the scent of flowers to him. The parking lot was lined with golden amaltas and red gulmohur trees in full flower. Above them, the sky seemed deeper and clearer than ever before, brimming with hope. His head swam. Everything seemed to be collaborating to make this, his first payday, the most perfect day of his life. Through his haze of happiness he thought he heard a car come into the lot. But another gust of wind brought the scent of spring and took him back to Sushila. He closed his eyes and saw the little house with a garden he would one day buy for her. He would plant trees and scented flowers in the earth so that his Sushila would never have to smell the stench of garbage, the smell he was so familiar with but she, fresh from the village, wasn't.

'Hey dreamer, the fat memsahib in the blue Maruti already parked and left,' Pappu from the adjacent lot shouted to him. He curled his fingers together and moved his hand up and down. 'This is going to cost you five rupees. You could have got one of the junkies to suck you off for that amount.'

'Shut up,' Kishore growled, standing up hastily, his eyes immediately spotting the new car. Sure enough, the memsahib had already left. 'Why didn't you tell me earlier?' he demanded of Pappu.

'It's not my job to tell you when cars come into your lot, your highness.'

Kishore contemplated beating him up. But the boy was already halfway across the parking lot. So he decided to stay and look after the cars instead. After all, he was a married man now.

The meeting was almost over when Shweta arrived in the office. So she waited for the guests to leave before she went to her boss. As soon as she saw his face she realized she had made a terrible mistake.

'I don't care if your husband is a bureaucrat, this kind of negligence I won't tolerate,' he thundered.

Shweta stared at him, thinking for the thousandth time how like her husband he was.

'What? Have you run out of excuses?' he said nastily. 'No more baby sick, mother-in-law dying, husband—' He stopped. There were some lines he wouldn't cross, no matter how angry he felt. Her husband was a secretary to the government, after all, even though the whole world knew he had been living with a well-known singer for the last five years.

On the other side of the plate-glass doors, Shweta felt the entire office listening. She decided to tell the truth.

When she finished her story the director just laughed. 'If this were a private company, I would sack you for daring to make up such a wild story. You think I am such a fool?'

'But it's true. I am not lying,' Shweta protested.

'Really? No sane person would wait around to see an elephant kill a man. Especially if they had an important meeting to attend and they were the one with the all-important file.'

'I didn't see the elephant kill him,' Shweta corrected, 'I saw what was left of the car. The man never had a chance.'

'What kind of a woman would wait around to look at a dead body?' He eyed her disgustedly.

'I was stuck in the traffic jam, what else could I do?' Shweta tried to defend herself.

'Shut up! I don't want to hear any more lies. I'm making a report of this to the ministry. Get your husband to come and fight for you.' The chairman turned away, satisfied.

Shweta backed out of the office. Everyone else immediately pretended to be busy. She went to the corner she shared with a fat and inefficient widow, the charity case and butt of all office jokes, and sat down. She looked at her watch. It was 11:52. For the rest of the morning she struggled with her work. But the image of the flattened Maruti kept returning. She turned the image over and over in her mind, hoping to find a way in which the person inside could have somehow survived. That gave her a headache. So, at a quarter to three she packed her bags.

'I am going home. I'm not feeling well,' she told the fat widow. 'This morning my husband told me he was divorcing me.' She didn't wait to see the look on the other woman's face. Within an hour, she knew, it would be all over the office. By tomorrow the chairman would know, too, and maybe he would let her stay on in the job, out of pity, like he had the widow sitting next to her.

A parking ticket was the last thing on her mind when she found the parking-lot boy barring her way. At first she thought he was a sex maniac or drug addict. Then she recognized him.

'What do you want?' she said coldly.

'You forgot to pay for your ticket,' he said, holding out the pink stub.

The stub brushed her breast and she trembled. This was not about the ticket at all, the boy was trying to harass her, using his superior strength to put her in her place. Well, this time she was going to stand up for herself.

'How dare you touch me?' she spat.

He jumped back immediately. 'Madam, I—'

'How dare you? Who do you think you are?' she shouted. 'Do you know who you are talking to?' How many times she had heard her husband use those words. It felt good to be finally using them herself.

'You still have to pay for your ticket,' Kishore insisted.

Shweta swelled with indignation. 'I paid already,' she said calmly. 'How dare you try to make me pay again!'

'You haven't paid. You came late today and you forgot.'

'Are you accusing me of lying?' The lie tripped easily off her tongue. She turned away and began to unlock the car door. He would be all right without the five rupees. Anyway, it all went to some filthy paan-chewing seth.

She felt a tentative tap on her shoulder. 'Madam, you must pay me now, or I … I won't let you park here tomorrow,' Kishore said.

She whirled around. He had actually dared to touch her!

'What! Now you're trying to threaten me as well. Just who do you think you are? Get your hands off me. I'm going to call the police.'

'You have to pay. I cannot let you go like this.'

But Shweta was already walking away.

Luckily, she didn't have to go far. Attracted by her angry shouts, a crowd had formed, a respectful distance away.

The moment they heard the magic word 'police', two policemen stepped forward, detaching themselves from the crowd. Shweta eyed them with misgiving. One was as fat as a water buffalo, the other looked like a skeleton with rotten teeth.

'What's the problem, memsahib?' the thin one asked.

'This man threatened me.'

He immediately grabbed Kishore by the arms. 'Why did you threaten the madam?'

'I did nothing,' Kishore answered. 'I just asked her to pay for her parking ticket.'

That made Shweta feel small, so she said, 'How dare you lie like that?' Then, turning to the crowd, she asked, 'You think I look like someone who would not pay a measly five rupees for a ticket? The boy is trying to cheat me because I am a poor, defenceless woman.'

The crowd remained silent and staring, but the policemen nodded in agreement, smiling ingratiatingly. Of course, it was unthinkable that a memsahib would cheat a parking attendant of five rupees. 'Is that any way to talk to a memsahib?' they told Kishore sternly. Then they turned to Shweta. 'What would you like us to do with him? Shall we take him to jail? They'll teach him manners there. If you'd like to make an FIR right now, we'll be happy to call a police van straightaway.' And the policeman pulled out a walkie-talkie and waved it proudly before her.

All of a sudden, Shweta felt trapped. She didn't want the boy beaten for no reason. Yet, how could she stop it without losing face? The expression on the boy's face was eloquent. He knew she wasn't going to do anything. Suddenly, she couldn't look at him any more.

On his part, Kishore could hardly believe what was happening: a memsahib with her own car, and working in an air-conditioned office, lying about five rupees? It didn't make sense. But now there seemed only one way out, and that was to pretend he was guilty. He turned to the policemen and fell at their feet.

'I made a mistake. Please let me go,' he pleaded. 'I swear I'll never trouble a lady again. Please let me go.'

The two policemen ignored him. They were waiting to know the wishes of the memsahib.

'Let him go. I don't have the time to fill out an FIR,' she said grandly.

The two policemen nodded, looking pleased. They would administer justice then. 'Of course, madam, you are right. We will take care of him. We know exactly what to do with troublemakers like him. We'll teach him respect for his superiors.'

Shweta stared at them helplessly. Then she turned away. But before she could take a step, the boy had caught hold of her feet.

'Please memsahib, I am sorry, let me go,' he begged. The fear in his voice was palpable.

'I can't help you,' she said coldly. 'You will get what you deserve.' He was almost a man after all and would one day certainly beat his wife.

'Madam, don't listen to him. He is a rascal. I know him,' the fat policeman said. 'Boys like him are lower-caste criminal types. They belong in jail. The jails are full of them.'

Their words salved her conscience and she suddenly remembered she was a mother and a married lady, in short, a woman worthy of respect. 'No, I don't want to ruin the boy's life. He's young and hopefully he'll learn.'

The policemen looked disappointed.

'He was wrong to threaten me,' she amended quickly. 'Maybe you can explain that to him. But don't beat him too much, he is young.'

They brightened immediately. 'Don't worry. We'll give him something to help him learn.'

Shweta smiled gratefully at them. They weren't half as bad as they had seemed when they first appeared. The police force was obviously improving—becoming more helpful, less corrupt. Perhaps those gender sensitization workshops her friend Mahima from the Ford Foundation organized were having some effect. India was changing for the better, she decided. She got into the car and the crowd watched in silence. She stared at the sea of faces. Even the crowd seemed more controlled, less stupidly savage. As she backed out of her space and drove out, the policemen saluted her. She nodded at them, and thought about the day her Brave New India would rise and sweep men like her husband and her boss out of power. And as a liberated woman, she would be a part of it. She would join an NGO and work in the slums. She would tell her boss to take his job and stuff it! She would be poor but she would be happy. Caught up in her plans for the future, she never looked in the rear-view mirror as she drove away.

Kishore had never been beaten before. He had been in plenty of fights. But this was different. Because this time his hands were tied behind him with a handkerchief and he was unable to give back what he got. It was the humiliation of his helplessness that really hurt. The beating itself wasn't so bad until the thin one kicked him in the groin. Then excruciating pain exploded upwards into his stomach, and down into his legs. They buckled instantly under him. Once on the ground, the policemen kicked him in the ribs and on the back. But since he had instinctively curled himself into an unprotesting ball, they soon got bored. After a while they lit their beedis, and waited for him to get up.

Kishore realized the blows had stopped only when he smelt the beedi. He began to cough and tasted blood. His eyes focussed on their shoes, black and shiny with a zigzag pattern of dust. A half-smoked beedi lay smouldering beside the toe of one of the shoes. How did this happen, he wondered, dazed. Suddenly, one of the shoes moved, prodding him in the chest. 'Eh, you made us do a lot of work to save you,' a voice said. He looked up. His vision grew blurred so he focussed on the shoes again.

'That fat old bitch would have taken you to the police station if we hadn't got here first. You're lucky we were drinking chai and saw what happened.'

'But I didn't do anything wrong,' Kishore said.

'Doesn't matter. Once you get put on a sheet, it follows you around. Your life is ruined, no one will give you a job. The police will be onto you every time anything big happens.'

'Yeah, we certainly saved your life.' The fat policeman held out a hand and helped him sit up. 'I have a relative who had that happen to him through no fault of his. They had to sell their house and go back to the village. The family committed suicide in the end.'

Kishore shuddered.

'You okay? We can give you a lift to the hospital if you want.'

'No, no.' Kishore shook his head, and then groaned as a fresh wave of pain shot through his skull. 'I have to look after my cars.'

'Poor you ... these old bitches ... they'll steal the last bite from a poor man's mouth.'

'Dried-up whores! That's why their men prefer our women. Which is why those old bitches are so hungry.'

The other policeman laughed. 'Who'd ever want a rotten fruit like that one?'

Kishore tried to stand up. His legs shook like leaves and he would have fallen on all fours if it weren't for the policemen. They grabbed him under the arms and pulled him upright.

They walked him gently to the peepul tree. 'Hope she gets a disease,' the thin one said sympathetically. 'Look what she made us do to you.'

'It won't be a sexual one for sure,' the other pointed out.

'Cancer then.'

'Maybe she's already got it.'

They both laughed. Kishore felt uncomfortable.

They put him down gently and towered over him. Kishore didn't look up. 'Hey, you know, because of you we never finished our tea,' one said.

'It must have gone cold by now,' the other added, poking Kishore in the chest. Kishore looked up.

'Aren't you going to give us anything for our trouble?' the first one demanded.

'Wh-what do you want? I have nothing,' Kishore replied.

'At least give us a little something for chai-paani, boy,' the thin one said.

At last Kishore understood. He fumbled in his shirt pocket, feeling relieved. He had twenty-five rupees of his own for tea and the bus home. He took it out and offered it gratefully to them.

'Is this how you show your gratitude?' the fat policeman snarled, knocking Kishore's hand away. 'We should have let her take you to the police station. You're not worth saving.'

'Hold on,' the thin one said, laying a restraining hand on his colleague's beefy arm. 'He's young, he doesn't understand what would have happened to him in prison.' He turned to Kishore. 'They would make a hijra out of you, you're so young and pretty. Do you want to be a woman?'

Kishore went cold. 'What do you want, that's all the money I have,' he quavered. All he wanted was to be left alone.

'Two days inside and your backside will be so sore you won't be able to sit comfortably ever again.'

'What can I do for you?' Kishore asked, his mouth dry.

'You married?'

'Yes, in February,' Kishore answered without thinking.

'And when did you get this job?'

'In March.'

'You're a lucky man—a wife and an excellent job all in one month.'

Kishore nodded, licking his lips worriedly. Suddenly, the thin policeman's hands shot towards him. He raised his arms to ward off the blow. But it never came. Instead, he felt his inside pocket—the one in which he kept the earnings from the parking lot—being emptied.

'Hey, that's not mine, that's the seth's money.'

'Who says? It was in your pocket, wasn't it?'

'Yes, but I have to give it to him this evening.'

'If it belongs to the seth but is in your pocket, you must have stolen it. We'll return it to him. Don't worry.' The fat policeman laughed.

'Please give it back,' Kishore begged, fear reducing his voice to a whisper. 'What will I say to the seth?'

The two men began to walk away. 'Tell him no one came to his filthy parking lot today because there was a dead rat that stank up the place,' the thin one said over his shoulder.

Kishore stared after them dully. He knew it was useless to follow them. After a while he went back to his place under the peepul tree. The billboards glittered in the sun, and the trees swayed in the spring breeze, bringing with them the scent of flowers. But Kishore couldn't smell them any more. How would he face his parents, his neighbours? The parking lot—with its cars, and dogs panting in the shade, its trees and buildings and billboards—seemed suddenly hateful.

'At least they didn't take you to jail.'

He looked up—he knew the face.

'What?' he shouted. 'Go away.'

'You don't have to shout at me. I was only trying to make you feel better,' Pappu answered.

'I wasn't shouting. I couldn't hear what you said. My ears are still ringing.'

'What do you mean you didn't hear me? How come you hear me quite clearly now?'

'You want to say something, say it, or get out,' Kishore said harshly.

'You hardly cried when they beat you,' Pappu said. 'Just like heroes in the movies.'

The roaring inside Kishore subsided somewhat. 'It wasn't too bad,' he replied.

Pappu nodded, shifting from one foot to the other.

Kishore got fed up of waiting. 'What is it? Say it and get out.'

Pappu looked relieved. 'I was wondering if ... well, I see you haven't eaten your lunch yet and it's almost four o'clock, and I was wondering if you were hungry.'

Kishore laughed in spite of himself. 'Here, you can take it.'

Pappu grabbed the packet and retreated a little. He sat down on the edge of the pavement and began to eat. Kishore watched him distantly.

'You know,' Pappu's mouth was full of food, 'I also didn't feel hungry when it happened to me.'

Kishore stared at him. 'When did it happen to you? Where?' Hope flared briefly within him. 'Was it with the same woman?'

'No, bhai, it was in Noida. The police there beat me up just like they beat you. And they took my money.'

Kishore moaned. He'd forgotten about the money. 'Tell me about it. What did you do?'

'I ran away,' Pappu said simply. 'I even left my food behind.'

Kishore shuddered. 'I don't want to run away.'

Pappu belched loudly in response. 'Lucky you, your mother is a good cook. Mine's dead.'

'My wife made that,' Kishore said dully.

Pappu's eyes became saucers. 'Your wife? You have a wife?'

Kishore nodded wearily. 'Tell me Pappu, what shall I do?'

Pappu stood up and came over. 'If I were you I'd piss on a car.'

'What?' Kishore was shocked. 'Don't make stupid jokes, I'm serious.'

'I am not joking,' Pappu replied. 'I'm telling you, when I get so angry I can't hold it inside any more, I pee on a car. Then I feel better. You should try it. My water comes out as strong as the Ganga. Earlier, I was always angry. Now I can't wait to get angry.'

'No wonder you're such a fool,' Kishore said disgustedly. All of a sudden an idea struck him. He grabbed Pappu's shoulders. 'Listen, the seth will be here at seven. You still have your money, don't you?'

Pappu nodded dubiously.

'Can you give me half?'

'Half? Are you crazy?' Pappu leapt back. 'And what will I tell the seth about where the other half went?'

'Tell him that fewer cars came today. I'll tell him the same thing. He'll have to believe us if we both say it.'

'Nahi bhai, I can't. You think the seth doesn't know exactly how many cars come every day? He's smarter than us. He went to school. That's why he's the seth.'

'Don't be such a fool,' Kishore said urgently. 'He's the seth because he has money to pay policemen, money we earn for him. Come on. Don't be scared. He can't do anything to us. Who'll look after his lot without us?'

Pappu was quiet for a while. Then he shook his head. 'There are lots of boys like us.'

They were both quiet.

Suddenly, Pappu brightened. 'Why don't you tell the seth the policemen took the money, then he can take it back from them.'

'Don't be stupid. He will never believe it. He'll think I am lying and throw me out.'

'Then why don't you try borrowing money from one of the drivers?' Pappu asked.

'And how will I return it?' Kishore replied sarcastically.

'You could give it back slowly ... say ten rupees a day. No ticket for a year.'

Kishore stared at Pappu with new eyes. Of course! The driver he had marked out for lessons would help! He had a regular job; he must have lots of money. Kishore stood up and looked around. But there was an empty space where the car normally stood. Kishore cursed.

'What did you say?' Pappu asked.

'Nothing. I was talking to myself.'

'You are always doing something to yourself,' Pappu giggled.

Kishore ignored him. He scanned the parking lot again, his eyes coming to rest on the tea stall. The other drivers were all there in a group under the other peepul tree. He got up and began walking towards them.

'Where are you going?' Pappu asked.

But Kishore wasn't listening.

The drivers were all laughing about something when he arrived.

'How come you're looking so handsome, Kishore? A car run you over or something?' one of the drivers asked him.

'I need seven hundred rupees,' he replied, ignoring the question.

They all stared at him.

'What do you want so much money for, boy? To gamble it away? Or to start a business?'

Kishore frowned at the man who had spoken. 'I'm a married man,' he replied with dignity.

'Then what do you want money for? Go play with your doll.'

Kishore glared at the speaker. It was the driver with the moist eyes who was always offering to teach him to drive.

'The police took my money and I have to pay the seth.'

The drivers looked at each other. It was as if each was waiting for the other to speak. At last one of the card players, a man with a scar on his left cheek, put down his hand of cards and spoke, 'You want us to give you money? What will you give us in exchange?'

'I'll work off the debt by letting you park free. And … and I'll pay half back in two weeks.' Quickly he calculated that if he collected garbage till midnight, Sushila could sort it by four in the morning and he could sell it off on the way to work.

The thin man smiled. 'What guarantees do we have that you won't just take the money and run away?'

'Why would I run away? I like this job, I want to be a driver like you one day.'

They all roared with laughter. He joined them, thinking he had won. When the laughter died down, one of them said, 'You want to be a driver? And you let a woman defeat you? Forget it. You can't be a driver. You're not even a man.'

'It wasn't my fault,' Kishore protested angrily. 'I'd have got my money out of her if the police hadn't interfered.'

'That's your story. How do we know you didn't steal her money in the first place? You're probably a smack addict. Why else would the police beat you up so badly? You want money? Go to the public toilets, girl. You're so pretty, you'll soon be rich.'

Kishore didn't need to look at the man to know which one he was. His hands curled into fists, he took a step towards the man and swung a punch at his face. But that was what the man had been waiting for. With lightning speed, the man grabbed his wrist and twisted it, throwing Kishore to the floor.

The other drivers clapped and laughed triumphantly.

'Look at the sissy. He can't even fight. And he says he has a wife. What a liar.'

Kishore lay there and wished the earth would swallow him. At last he got up with as much dignity as he could muster. 'Don't make the mistake of trying to park without paying,' he said to the man who had hit him.

The man didn't even look at him. 'I'll be dead before I pay a good-for-nothing like you for a ticket again,' he said calmly. 'Go take off your pants and put on a petticoat.'

Far away in east Delhi, Kishore's wife Sushila was picking her way through the mountain of rubbish her mother-in-law had collected early that morning. With infinite care she separated the plastics from the paper, the coloured from the uncoloured. From a single mountain of garbage she made four neat piles—one of cardboard, one of plastic bags, one of shiny aluminium foil that glittered in the sun, and one of coloured paper and newsprint. She sang a little as she worked. A gust of wind, maybe the same wind that had beguiled her husband into dreaming of her, filled a shiny blue-and-red-and-green foil packet and lifted it up into the air like a sail. The bag sparkled like a droplet of water caught in the sun and Sushila's heart lifted. The wind vanished as suddenly as it had come and the bag fell to the earth. Suddenly sadness stabbed her. She rescued the little bag, smoothed it out lovingly and placed it along with the others.

The dun-coloured mountain of unsorted rubbish grew rapidly smaller. In its place four little hills emerged, covered in multicoloured vegetation. In the centre was a little village of cardboard boxes. They were the most highly valued of her wares; each was worth almost as much as an entire hill of paper. One of the boxes had a little boy with bright red lips and round cheeks on its top. The boy was dressed in a shining white shirt and khaki shorts with a striped scarf around his neck. Candles danced around his head and at his feet. As she stared at the picture, the breath slowly left Sushila's body. She thought of the child that would grow in her belly one day, filling it the way the wind had filled the packet. Would a child born in a world of such brightness and colour look like the boy on the box or would it look like babies in the village, all shrivelled up and dark?

She touched a little scrap of pale blue, a colour like the evening sky in winter. Four months ago she could never have imagined that there existed so many shades of a single colour. Or that there were so many colours in the world. In the beginning she had wanted to hide away each new colour she discovered. But there would have been no room for all of them. So she learned to restrict herself to one new colour a day, carefully stealing it off the pile and hiding it in her clothing so her mother-in-law wouldn't notice. In the evening, in the light of the street lamp that crept through the crack in the wall, she would show it to Kishore and ask him to name it for her.

The sky colour she chose as the colour for today was wrapped around a beautiful fair-skinned girl with light green eyes and straight hair. Were there really girls with skin that colour? Kishore insisted that all rich Delhi girls were like that. But she couldn't quite believe him. He had said he would take her to see them as soon as he got his first month's pay. Her heart missed a beat. Today was that day. She stared at the woman in the picture and wondered if she was a movie star as well. Kishore could tell her, but he would only be back at night, by which time their piles of glorious coloured paper would have been sold. She took a rusty blade she kept especially for this and carefully cut around the edges of the picture.

The charas smokers' corner was a rectangle of pavement, three feet by seven, in the southwest corner of the parking lot between the electricity pylons and the public toilet. It stood underneath a hoarding showing a woman's stomach and a bottle of beer. The charasis (charas smokers) were very proud of their corner. A long time ago someone had played Holi there and coloured the pavement pink and green. Now of course, much of the colour had faded. Oil stains and paan spit had added their own colours to the pavement, but enough of the Holi colours remained for the charasis to see heaven's designs in them.

One famous charasi used to tell people's futures so accurately that there was always a line of people waiting to pay him his five-rupee bullet of charas. Kishore wished the man was still around. Anyway, Kishore had a pretty good idea of what his immediate future held. All he wanted was to make things the way they had been at eleven o'clock that morning. But he wasn't going to sell himself. And if those who called themselves respectable would not help him, why shouldn't he go to the criminals?

The charas smokers' corner was empty, except for one lone occupant sitting on a heap of rags, surprisingly neatly dressed for a charasi. Kishore had never seen him before.

'Why are women like beer bottles? Answer me and I'll share my last packet with you,' the old man asked, addressing him straightaway.

Kishore looked at him in disgust. 'I don't know and I don't want any. I just want to see your seth.'

The man looked amused. 'In every man, there is a charasi. It's just a question of when the moment of enlightenment finally arrives. Show me your hand. I'll tell you if your time has come.'

Kishore crossed his arms across his chest and stared down at the man. 'You don't seem to know a charasi from a non-charasi then,' he said.

The man laughed with his teeth, the knowing look in his eyes deepening.

Kishore was in no mood to talk. 'If you want to sell here, you'd better pay me, this is my parking lot.'

The man ignored him. 'I can see the desperation in you. Give me your hand and I will see if you are ready to have it taken away.'

'I don't want any charas. I want money.'

'Blasphemy! You compare water with alcohol, a prostitute with a film star?'

Kishore held out his hand. 'Just give me money.'

'Charas is better than money. And she is choosy. She likes some, is faithful to even fewer. But if you happen to be one of those she loves, there is nowhere she won't take you. Beside her, even a woman is bland. Me, I was just a simple man when she found me. I didn't want to live but I was too lazy to die. Now look at me. I have something to look forward to every day.'

This was the way they lured newcomers, thought Kishore. This had to be the right man. He decided to ask for the money directly.

'Can you lend me some money?'

The man looked shocked. 'Never sell your soul for money. Then there is no place for love. I gave my soul to love a long time ago and I am always faithful.'

Suddenly, an incredible idea seized Kishore. 'You're not the fortune-telling baba?' he cried,

The man nodded, 'I am.'

'But ... but they say a seth took you away in his car.'

The man snorted disgustedly.

'Why did you come back?' Kishore asked.

'It's a long story.' The old man refused to meet his eyes. He looked up at the hoarding instead. 'When I was here I had no future and so I could tell other people's futures. When I went with him the future made me its prisoner. It wouldn't let me go. The more money I made for it, the tighter the future held me. Then I realized that freedom is not having a future. So I am back.'

Kishore sat down beside him. 'Can you change my future for me?'

'Of course.' The man laughed, showing all his teeth again.

'I don't want a different future, I don't want money or a house or ... or a new job. I just want the past back. Can you put the past in the place of the future?'

The old man looked at him strangely. 'Easy.'

'What do I have to do? I have no money now, but I'll let you stay here for free for the rest of your life if you want. I'll get you food. Home-made food. My wife is a great cook.'

'Food? Who needs food when one has the Goddess Lakshmi on one's side?' he said scornfully. 'Not good enough. You will fail because you don't know how to insure the beginning. You have to give before you can get. That's the secret of success.'

'But I am just a poor car-park attendant, what have I to give?'

'If you go to the doctor and he tells you that you are ill, you pay him, don't you? You must do the same for me. It is a question of respect.'

'Of course I respect you,' Kishore replied. 'But first you must give me back my future the way it was this morning. I was going to be paid today. Then things happened. Right now my future spells death. So give me back the past and I will pay you.'

'Show me your hand.'

The baba looked at his hand for what felt like an age. He

shook his head and frowned. Then he let go of Kishore's hand. 'I was wrong. Yours is a very difficult case. In most people's lives past and future are not so different. In your case, there is a clean break.'

'Wh-what does that mean?' Kishore's blood ran cold.

'It means that you will have to sacrifice something to the goddess in order to get your past back. Only Kali mata is strong enough to do what you ask. But first you will have to give her an offering.'

'What kind of an offering? And how do I give it to her? Is there a temple close by? I have to be quick.'

'Oh, you can just give it to me. I am her priest.'

'What will she want from me in return?' Kishore asked suspiciously.

'Smack,' the man replied promptly. 'Just one hit will do. The rest you can give later.'

'Then you can't be the fortune-telling baba!' Kishore exclaimed. He tried to get up. But the old man was quicker. He threw Kishore to the ground and sat on him. Kishore struggled to get the man off, but he was surprisingly heavy for someone so skinny. So Kishore lay still. Once more I find myself eating the dust of this wretched parking lot, he thought.

'Get me some smack and I'll show you how to change your future, I'll even share it with you. That's what you want, isn't it?' the old man whispered in Kishore's ear.

'I don't take smack,' Kishore replied through clenched teeth.

'You lie.' The smack addict twisted his arm ferociously.

Desperate fingers probed his pockets. When they found nothing, self-pity overcame the old man. 'Oh devi, why are you doing this to me?' he cried. 'First you send him to me and then you trick me. Haven't I worshipped you faithfully, haven't I? Why are you abandoning me now?' Hot tears rolled down his cheeks and fell on Kishore's back. He rolled off Kishore who sat up cautiously. The addict was standing beneath the beer advertisement looking up at it, his face alight.

So that was his devi. All of a sudden, Kishore felt very, very tired. He looked at the smack addict one last time. The man was pleading with his goddess to come and save him like she had all those other times. 'I forgive you for tricking your servant,' he was saying, 'now come and save him.' The image of the man talking to the advertisement burned itself into Kishore's brain. Never again, he vowed to himself, would he look to someone else to come and save him.

When Kishore returned to his peepul tree, shadows had spread themselves over three-quarters of the parking lot. The few cars that remained seemed like guests. Even Pappu had disappeared. Kishore cursed himself for having listened to Pappu about collecting the money as the cars came in, rather than when they went out. He should have listened to his father. Short cuts were trouble. Always. The police would have found nothing if he had done as he had been told and collected the money from the cars in the evening as they were leaving. He stared out over the empty parking lot and a wave of love engulfed him. The parking lot was his home. The parking lot was his future. How could he leave it? He decided to wait for the seth. Even if the seth decided to kill him, at least he would die like a man. Not like the other boy who ran away and was caught and killed in Ghaziabad.

After she had finished sorting the last of the garbage, Sushila took the pile of rags she had rescued and soaked them in water. Then she dropped the syringes and other metal bits into a plastic bag. She packed each pile of paper into a separate jute bag and loaded them onto the cart, ready for her father-in-law to take away. Then she went inside, ate a little cold rice and watery dal, got out her only other sari and her soap, and set off for the tap. Mercifully, there was only one small girl at the tap. She sat down, her back to the little girl.

Sushila still hadn't got used to bathing in public. She hated having to push her way through the circle of leering men to get to the tap in the mornings. The tap was always crowded, the women jockeying for a place closest to the nozzle. Once they had filled their buckets, they sat to one side and began to wash, casting sidelong glances at their male audience. It was like a play whose plot remained the same but whose script changed each day in little ways. For the spectators, the interest lay in the ever-expanding encyclopaedia of erotic detail the women offered them. They would applaud a subtle new move by one of the women and censure those who got carried away and did something that was deemed too provocative. Sushila refused to join the game. She tried to hide herself instead. But that only made the men watch her more carefully. Inadvertently, she had opened up a new chapter in the game, combining modesty and provocation in a single set of gestures. And for that she became a minor celebrity. As a result the other women grew to hate her and made no secret of it, accidentally kicking over her bucket, dropping her precious soap in the mud or rubbing their dirty feet on her washed sari.

Free of the staring eyes and tormenting hands, Sushila washed herself leisurely. The little girl beside her sang snatches of Hindi film songs in a sweet and surprisingly tuneful voice, the running water giving the song an unexpected depth. Sushila poured mug after mug of cool, clean water over herself, washing away the accumulated layers of invisible filth that being watched had generated inside her. Then she undid the knot of thick black hair at the nape of her neck and washed that too. When she finished, the light had softened and the shadows had begun to lengthen. She got up. The little girl was gone. Sushila hadn't even noticed when she had left. Soon, Kishore would be back with his salary. She walked quickly back to the jhuggi to get dressed for him, humming little bits of song under her breath.

In Kishore and Sushila's half of the room they shared with his parents, tucked into a corner, was a little plastic suitcase. Inside it, Sushila kept the few things she possessed: her bindis, her wedding sari, a few glass bangles, a blouse, a framed photograph of herself and Kishore standing before a freshly painted sunset, and her collection of coloured paper cuttings. To the bundle she added her newest one. On an impulse, she spread them all over the bedding. The dull grey mattress came alive. Sushila stared.

The coloured foil caught the last rays of the sun coming through the crack in the wall and their colours caught fire. An idea took hold of her. She thought of the village she had so recently left but which already felt far away, separated from the city by a giant river of colour. She thought of the city and the light that shone there all the time—even in the night. It was the same light, she felt sure, that the movie girls wore in their faces. She looked down at the river of colour on the mattress and the thought came to her that if she could only somehow surround herself with them, her baby would be a bright city baby, plump and pink-skinned, rather than a dark, wrinkled country baby.

Quickly she rummaged through her box for the thread and needle. She pierced a hole through the cardboard lady in the blue and put the needle through it. She tied the thread into a knot and, standing up, reached up to the ceiling and pierced the plastic roofing with her needle. She knotted it and then stood back to survey her handiwork. The little figure was alive now. A gust of spring wind blew in and the lady pirouetted wildly. The blue sari seemed to balloon around her as if it too were real. An unknown emotion entered her: pride. Within seconds it had taken possession of her completely. Next, she put up the stars around the lady and then the little red cardboard boy she had found that morning, and then more shining women with big smiles.

Soon the ceiling was crowded with them and she could hardly see where to put the next one. They kissed her face as she moved amongst them, making her feel full of light. At last she was done and lay down on the floor. Her arms and back ached. But when she looked up, her breath caught in her throat. Though the light was almost gone, the ceiling glowed and writhed with life. The river of colour she had seen in her mind was alive.

'Sushila, have you gone mad?'

Sushila's mother-in-law was a tiny, wizened creature, gone prematurely grey. Life had bleached the colour out of her skin and hair and now only her eyes remained their original shade.

Sushila sat up hurriedly, her hand flying to her chest. To her horror, and utter humiliation, she realized that she was still wearing only her petticoat and blouse.

'Shameless girl, what are you doing?' her mother-in-law cried, coming into the room. She pushed a hanging star away from her head. It swung back, hitting her in the eye. She grabbed it and pulled angrily. There came a ripping sound and a section of the roof came away, letting in the light. They both stared at the gap in horror. Her mother-in-law was the first to recover.

'What is all this? Have you gone mad? We came home to find the food cold and no fish bought for the evening. Don't you know what day it is?'

Sushila refused to meet her mother-in-law's eyes. She groped in the darkness for her sari.

'Is this the kind of wife you are? Wasting your time with rubbish instead of looking after your husband?' her mother-in-law cried, coming up to her.

Sushila looked up at last. 'Ma, I'm sorry. I'll go right away, as soon as I put on my sari.'

The mention of the sari seemed to further inflame her mother-in-law.

'What were you doing, prancing around half naked?' she asked. 'Have you already found a lover? Was he in here with you?' She grabbed the terrified Sushila by the shoulders.

'N-no one was here,' Sushila stammered, blushing guiltily. 'I did this for Kishore.'

'Liar! How dare you try to use Kishore's name against me? He is my son. He would never have dreamed of asking you to do this.'

She grabbed Sushila's long wet hair and pulled.

'It was my idea,' Sushila confessed, adding hurriedly, 'but I did it for him, I swear.'

Sushila screamed as her mother-in-law pulled again. The pain made unknown colours dance in front of her eyes, moving like lightning through her forehead and neck. Her mother-in-law kept talking but Sushila no longer understood what was being said. Numbness had succeeded the pain and now a fog had blanketed the colours in her brain. Suddenly, her mother-in-law let her go.

'We have been cheated. I will send you back. They never told us there was madness in your blood. Your parents have cheated us!'

'No-o-o,' Sushila wailed, grabbing her mother-in-law's legs.

The old woman didn't soften. She began to hit Sushila again.

Head between her knees, Sushila waited for the storm to abate. She knew her mother-in-law's rages never lasted long. A bangle broke. And then a second one. Then, all of a sudden, the blows stopped. She waited, not daring to raise her head out of the safety of her knees.

'What is going on here?' a foreign voice asked in clipped accents.

Sushila looked up quickly. A tall woman in a white sari stood in the doorway.

'Why are you torturing that poor girl? We could hear you screaming all the way to the school. Do you want to kill her? What could she possibly have done to you to make you hate her so much?'

Sushila stared in wonder at the woman's face. It was so pale and so beautiful—even in anger. She looked like a devi come to protect her. Sushila's mother-in-law glared at the intruder but didn't answer. She too was cowed by the tall lady's presence.

Then the lady entered, coming straight over to Sushila. 'Oh, you poor child, you're bleeding,' she exclaimed in English. She bent down and put a gentle hand on Sushila's nose.

Sushila flinched, more out of surprise than pain.

'There, I won't hurt you,' the woman murmured. 'I just need to see if there are any bones broken.'

At first, Sushila let the woman feel her face. Suddenly, she was overwhelmed by shyness and retreated into a corner.

'You poor child,' the woman said in English, remaining where she was. Then she turned to someone in the doorway and said in a very different tone, 'I need an interpreter, please.'

From her corner Sushila stared curiously at the strange woman. Everything about her was different. Her skin was rosy, like the girls in the pictures she collected. At the same time, she was taller than a man, and seemed to be stronger too. Her voice also switched from being commanding like a man's to gentle like a woman's. Maybe she was a hijra? Kishore had told her about them. The thought made her smile.

The woman smiled back delightedly and sat down on her haunches in front of Sushila.

'How old are you?' she asked in heavily accented Hindi.

'Sixteen,' Sushila replied. She didn't know her age but Kishore had told her he was sixteen so she decided that she must be sixteen too. He had asked her the same question right after they had met, and she had giggled, not understanding what he meant. He had explained what a birthday was to her and she had listened to him, enchanted by the serious way in which he talked to her.

'Sixteen? You don't look more than twelve, you're so small,' the woman exclaimed.

'Child malnutrition makes them small. She is probably telling the truth,' another voice replied from the doorway.

Sushila suddenly felt self-conscious, remembering that she still wasn't wearing a sari. With a little cry she turned away and scrambled among the bedclothes for it. The tall lady put a hand on her shoulder.

'Wait, I must examine you properly,' she ordered.

Sushila froze.

'Can you tell her, Margaret, that I must examine her?' the lady called over her shoulder.

'Don't be frightened. This lady is a nurse, she just wants to make sure you are all right,' the beautiful voice said in chaste Hindi. Sushila understood little of it as she herself spoke only Bhojpuri. But she let the nurse run her soft cool hands over her face anyway, drinking in the unfamiliar scents of rose and sandalwood. Before this magic lady, even the all-pervasive smell of garbage acknowledged defeat.

The English nurse suddenly spotted a bit of broken bangle and her expression changed. 'That bitch,' she spat. Sushila instinctively raised her hands to protect her face. The nurse's face softened immediately. 'Here, let me look at those cuts again,

I have to make sure no glass got stuck in them.' She leaned down and, with gentle hands, pulled Sushila up so she could examine her hands and face in the light pouring in through the tear in the roof. As she straightened, her head knocked against the hanging papers, making them dance. Looking up, she laughed.

'See, I told you the girl is mad. See what she has done?' Sushila's mother-in-law said loudly. 'She's even torn the roof so badly we won't be able to fix it, and the monsoon is only months away.'

'You mean this little girl did all this?' the nurse asked, looking oddly at Sushila.

'Yes, just this afternoon,' her mother-in-law explained triumphantly. 'I can't leave her alone for a minute, what will I do? I'm a working woman, I have to go and collect garbage with my husband or we won't survive. His eyes are bad.'

'But it's wonderful. She's an artist. You should be proud of her,' the lady said in English, looking at the mother-in-law and smiling while the other lady translated her words.

Then the nurse approached Sushila. 'You did this?' she said in broken Hindi.

'But I'm not mad.' All of a sudden Sushila found her tongue. 'It was for the baby. I wanted to have a bright, shining city baby like you. That's why I put them up there. Babies look up all the time. I thought perhaps the colours would enter my child and it would be fair, not dark like me!' After she had said it, Sushila stared defiantly at her mother-in-law. She didn't even look at the Englishwoman and her companion who were whispering together. All she could feel was the older woman's jealousy. Then the Englishwoman came between them.

'I want to talk to your daughter in private, please.'

'She's not my daughter, she is my son's wife,' the older woman snapped. 'You can take her with you if you want.'

'And will *you* take those ladies with you,' the nurse replied, pointing at the mohalla women who had crowded in on the translator's heels. The translator immediately began to shoo them out, speaking in a tone they couldn't fail to understand. When at last there was no one left, Sushila felt nervous. She stared apprehensively at the English nurse. How could anyone have such pale skin, she wondered. It was not pink like the girls in her cuttings. It had a cold flat light like the light from a TV screen. Her eyes were so light they seemed almost invisible; her hair was grey and pale brown, the colour of dust. Then it struck her. The city's lights had in fact bleached the lady. That's why she was so lacking in colour!

'Are you happy?' the lady asked her in broken Hindi.

Sushila nodded uncertainly.

'They aren't trying to harass you for dowry?' she continued.

Sushila felt even more puzzled. 'What dowry?'

The woman sighed. 'You won't talk, will you?' she said in English.

Sushila pointed to the roof. Then she let fly a stream of words in her own dialect. For, her bewildered mind had suddenly remembered Kishore telling her that city ladies were rich and though she couldn't understand why such an obviously rich lady was visiting a jhuggi, she decided to ask the lady for money to repair the roof. That would make her mother-in-law happy and then Kishore would not be angry with her.

'Yes, yes, it's beautiful, what you did. That's why they're jealous,' the nurse agreed. She asked the interpreter rather peremptorily to translate quickly.

'She's asking for money to fix the roof so her mother-in-law will be happy, ma'am,' the interpreter replied in a colourless voice.

'Oh, the roof.' The nurse gave an embarrassed laugh. 'I suppose it always comes down to money in the end, doesn't it, Margaret?'

The interpreter said nothing.

The Englishwoman then turned to Sushila and was all bright and smiling again. 'I'll help you, don't worry,' she said. Then she asked in Hindi, pointing at the ceiling, 'Can you do more of these for me?'

Sushila looked at her worriedly. Then she looked at the translator who obligingly repeated what the Englishwoman had said. Sushila's face cleared and she nodded enthusiastically.

The Englishwoman thought for a while. Then she turned to the interpreter. 'Maybe we could organize an exhibition for her. Something nice and unpretentious. What do you think, Margaret?'

The other woman nodded but didn't reply.

'We could organize it through the diplomatic wives' association. I'll introduce our little artist by describing how I found her being tortured by her awful mother-in-law.' She gave a musical little laugh. 'I'm sure that'll make them loosen their purse strings. What do you think, Margaret?'

'I don't know, ma'am, if she will be able to make these things again,' the interpreter, Margaret, replied, looking at Sushila.

'I'm sure she will. Ask her, Margaret, ask her if she can make more.'

So Margaret the translator translated the nurse's question into good Hindi. Sushila didn't understand all the words, but she understood that it had to do with her cuttings, and that the lady wanted her to make more of them. So she nodded. Tears of excitement filled her eyes and flowed down her cheeks.

'There, there, don't cry,' the nurse said, looking uncomfortable. 'Everything will be fine.'

Sushila leaned down and clasped the hem of the lady's sari. It felt wonderfully soft, unlike anything she had ever touched before. She kissed the cloth, letting the scent of roses and sandalwood overwhelm her.

At seven o'clock, the monstrous black Mercedes of chhota seth pulled into the parking lot. Night had fallen and all that was left in the parking lot were the shells of abandoned cars. Then, from all four sides, shadows detached themselves from the walls and headed for the lamp post beneath which the seth always parked. They all had the same slightly stooped loping walk, for they carried their day's earnings, mostly in heavy five-rupee coins in a plastic bag under their shirts. Quickly, a noisy line formed.

Kishore watched them enviously. How he wished he could be in that line too. A thought struck him. He could have lain in wait in the shadows and jumped on one of the boys as he made his way over. Then some other boy would have been staring enviously out of the darkness at the line under the lamp post. He discarded the idea immediately—he couldn't make some other innocent bear the burden of his misfortune.

The car parked under the usual lamp post, the only one that worked in the lot, and the tall, muscular driver got out. He went to the paan stand and picked up chhota seth's daily Banarasi paan and his boss' share of the paanwala's earnings. This was the signal for the boys to count their earnings one last time and make sure they tallied with the number of ticket stubs. Anyone whose earnings and stubs didn't tally was immediately sacked. Chhota seth didn't wait for explanations. Nor did he give second chances. All the boys knew that.

The driver returned to the car. The boys watched expectantly. Most of the time chhota seth didn't come and the driver collected the money for him. But today the careful way in which the driver ignored them had alerted them already. Immediately, all the boys had stopped fidgeting and stood at attention. The driver went to the back door and opened it ceremoniously. After a few seconds, a pair of shining black-and-white zebra-striped leather shoes emerged and planted themselves on the ground. The white pyjamas that went with them were crisp and well cared for. The rest of chhota seth remained in the darkness. The driver handed chhota seth his paan. Fat pink fingers ringed with gold and diamonds touched the paan and the notes to his forehead and then the shoes retreated. One by one, the boys began to approach the car.

Those in line went silent as they all watched the first boy getting paid. Kishore counted eighteen boys in the line. There were twenty altogether and they accounted for all the parking lots in Rajiv Chowk. Chhota seth had other businesses too—car dealerships, petrol pumps, shops, moneylending, security agencies. The boys knew they had a future with chhota seth, and that, more than anything else, was what kept them honest.

Then Kishore spotted Pappu. He was third in line. Every few seconds, he would look towards Kishore's peepul tree. Kishore pressed his body into the trunk of the tree. Eventually, it was Pappu's turn to kneel beside the car and hand in his earnings. As soon as he got paid, he scampered off without looking back. At last all the boys had been paid and there was no one left in line. Kishore felt tempted to just let chhota seth drive away. But he knew that was not possible. It would be a short escape followed by a more permanent one. He remembered the story of Shekhar and shuddered. So, as the last boy handed in his earnings, Kishore detached himself from the shadows and approached the black Mercedes.

He peered through the passenger window of the car and was blinded by the darkness.

'Hey, you beggar, what are you doing? Get out,' the driver shouted.

'I'm not a beggar, sahib, it's me, Kishore, of lot 461,' he replied.

Silence followed this revelation. Kishore waited, peering into the darkness. When at last his eyes got used to it, the only thing he could see clearly was the illuminated miniature temple on the dashboard. Then he noticed the space. It was so big that the light didn't penetrate very far. Somewhere in the back he could hear chhota seth chewing his paan.

'Been a good day, huh?' whispered a voice that sounded like a body being dragged over a pile of dead leaves.

Kishore shivered. 'Sahib—' he began.

'You've been in some trouble, I hear,' the voice continued.

Kishore's legs went weak. 'It w-was ... an accident,' he stammered.

'I'm sure it was an accident,' the voice interrupted again. 'No sane man gives his employer's hard-earned money to the police. But I am curious, how did such an "accident" happen?'

'I didn't give it, sahib,' Kishore protested, 'they stole it from me. I would rather die than give your money away.'

'Wrong. The police can't steal from you, child. They're the ones who punish those who steal. Therefore, by definition, they cannot steal ... they can only take. Like Brahmins, you give and they take.'

Kishore didn't understand what Brahmins had to do with the police. He felt sure chhota seth was making fun of him. 'But I swear I never gave it to them, sethji. They took it from me. They beat me first. Look.' He tried to push his face further into the darkness, but the driver shoved him back.

'You didn't have to give it,' the same implacable voice continued. 'Even when they take it, it means you have given. That is why they are not stealing ... you are—from me. And I don't like that.'

'B-but ... ' Kishore felt as if he was fast drowning. He clung to the windowpane. The glass squeaked in protest.

'Hey, don't ruin that window,' the driver shouted.

Suddenly, the window began to move under Kishore's fingers. He clutched it even harder. The motor made a horrible grinding sound. 'Let go, you fool,' the driver shouted. But panic had overtaken Kishore and he had only one thought in his head: to be heard by chhota seth.

The window stopped moving.

'Seth sahib, seth sahib,' Kishore panted, peering into the darkness, 'you're a big man. Everyone listens to you. You can get it back from them. They'd have to give it to you.'

'Why should I?' the voice replied. 'I never gave them the money in the first place. It was you who gave it to them. They would never take my money. Now give me my money and get away from my car.'

'But, sahib, I have no money. Today is the last day of the month,' Kishore cried.

'No money?' the voice hissed. 'Then why are you here? Run away and hide so I can catch and kill you.'

Kishore moistened his suddenly dry lips. 'Please sethji, I have a wife and two old parents to look after ... and ... and I love my job, sahib.' Suddenly, the engine was turned off. In the silence Kishore once again tried to peer into the darkness. He wondered what chhota seth looked like. In all their conversations, none of the boys had ever described him. His facelessness had made him seem even more frightening.

'Ah, so you're a responsible married man. You look rather young to be married,' the inhuman voice said.

'I just got married, sethji. She came from the village only two months ago. I'll pay you back, sethji, just let me work for you,' Kishore pleaded.

'I'm not the government—I am a businessman. I don't let people who steal from me keep their jobs!' the chilling voice replied.

'I am not a thief,' Kishore snapped, forgetting himself. 'I cannot get your money back. But I will work hard for you and pay it back. You could cut a little each month.'

There was a long silence. Then the voice asked, 'What guarantee do I have that you won't cheat me?'

Kishore felt confused, and so he said the first thing that came to his mind. 'I love my wife, seth sahib. I will work hard. One day, I hope to be a driver.'

'Huh, a driver, an ambitious boy.'

All of a sudden Kishore heard the springs squeak and a hideous pink face appeared. Chhota seth's albino blonde eyelashes sparkled in the tungsten lamp light.

'Get in,' he ordered and retreated just as quickly into the darkness.

Kishore blinked. Never had he seen such a terrifying face, all pink and flat and featureless. There was not a hair on it and it had no eyebrows.

'Hey, stop staring and get in.' The driver leaned over and opened the door. Kishore drew back fearfully.

'No one's going to eat you,' the driver snapped.

Terrified but hopeful, Kishore got in.

As soon as he was in, the driver started the engine and the car began to pull out of the parking lot.

'We're moving!' Kishore squeaked in terror. He turned to the seth in alarm. 'Seth sahib, where are you taking me? Please don't give me to the police. I'm not a thief, I'll pay you back.'

Chhota seth gave him a smile that was all teeth and shadows. 'Don't worry. We're not going to the police.'

The car moved into the traffic. Kishore stared at the faces in the cars. He had never seen such important faces so close, some just inches away, separated only by a thin wall of glass. Yet each face looked as if it was unwatched: safe, protected, unconnected to any other. Slowly, despite his fear, Kishore began to feel the same. This is what it is like to ride in a car, he told himself. He leaned back against the padded seat, enjoying his proximity to the sahibs.

The car picked up speed suddenly. In a fraction of a second the other cars were left behind.

'It is so fast,' Kishore couldn't restrain his admiration any longer, 'and so silent.'

'This is the best engine in the world,' the driver answered, his silence abandoned in the face of Kishore's enthusiasm.

'Engines are like dogs, as long as you feed them, they stay loyal to you,' chhota seth remarked from behind.

The driver laughed. Kishore, following the driver's lead, laughed too.

Suddenly, chhota seth's jewelled fingers were patting his shoulder 'You're an intelligent boy. I don't like to lose intelligent boys.'

The car stopped before a block of flats with big black gates. It was guarded by men in black-and-red uniforms. The gates opened smoothly and the guards saluted smartly as the car went through. In the marble entranceway the car stopped and the driver leapt out to open the door for chhota seth.

But Kishore was there before him.

'You learn quick, I like that.' Chhota seth laughed and patted Kishore's arm as he got out. He handed him two plastic bags of money. The driver gave him a strange look and moved away to get more bags out of the back. Together the three of them walked into the marble foyer. Kishore was struck by its cleanliness. The security guard in the foyer, dressed in blue to distinguish him from the guards outside, saluted smartly. They got into the automatic lift.

'This building is owned by sethji. Even the security company,' the driver whispered proprietorily to Kishore. They got out on the first floor.

They were in a long corridor with spotless marble floors. Four doors opened from it. The driver led the way to a black steel door at the far end of the corridor. He took his time unlocking the door which had three locks and so Kishore had time to wonder where they were taking him, and whether he would be killed there on the spotless marble floor.

It was a corner flat. The marble corridor continued into the flat itself. Inside the main hall, the walls at the back and to the sides were covered from floor to ceiling with mirrors. Heavy maroon velvet curtains, with gold satin roses embroidered on them, masked the windows that made up the far wall. Slightly in front of the curtains, with its back to the windows, there stood the most enormous television screen Kishore had ever seen. On either side of it were statues of naked women. One statue was black and the other was white. On either side of them were giant potted plants with fan-shaped leaves of purple and green, like giant hands. On the right-hand side, covering an entire wall, was a huge bar made entirely of glass and chrome. Bottles of every sort decorated the bar and beneath them, exquisitely cut glasses were arranged in a double row. Cunningly concealed lights, set into the glass bar itself, made it glow like an iceberg on fire. The tables were of glass, and glass shelves crammed with porcelain knick-knacks lined the walls. In front of the television was a black leather sofa and behind it, a glass dining table with chrome and velvet chairs. Kishore's senses reeled. He had never seen colours like these before. He wished Sushila could have seen it too.

'Put the bags on the table there,' chhota seth ordered. He sat down on the leather sofa and began to count his money. The driver went to the bar and poured a glass full of golden-coloured whisky. This he brought to the seth.

The seth took a sip and made a face. 'More ice, you fool. How many times have I told you that?'

He turned to Kishore, his face mottled with rage. 'Drivers are fools. Their brains go into their pants. You shouldn't become a driver. Become something else instead.'

'Whatever you decide, sahib. My life depends upon you,' Kishore replied humbly.

The anger faded from chhota seth's face. 'Good boy. I like you.'

The driver returned with the whisky glass filled with ice cubes, his face blank. 'I'll go and park the car, sethji,' he said woodenly.

Chhota seth took a sip and nodded. He went back to counting the money. Silence enveloped the room, except for the rustle of money. Kishore began to feel drowsy. When will he tell me what to do, he wondered. Just then the seth began to speak.

'I am a lonely man,' he said, taking a stack of notes and putting it into a white envelope. 'I have many responsibilities ... many people depend on me. But no one looks after me. You are lucky. You have parents, a wife to look after you. You are rich. I am the poor one.'

'Seth sahib, how can you say that!' Kishore protested. 'You have so much. No one can touch you.'

Chhota seth laughed grimly. 'This world is an illusion. None of it is real.'

Kishore felt confused. Why was a man as rich as chhota seth unhappy? Chhota seth put another bundle of notes into an envelope, ticked it off in his register and looked up at Kishore. 'Everything in life boils down to just two things in the end, money and friendship. You know why?'

Kishore shook his head.

'Because money is life, you have to have money to live.' He took another noisy gulp of his drink. 'So, in order to live, you make the money. But you also need friends. People you can trust. You need someone with you to make you feel alive. Otherwise you may as well be dead. The problem arises when you have lots of money. Then everyone wants to take it away from you, even your friends.'

In the mirrored wall Kishore saw their reflections. Chhota seth's face looked like the wall of a public building, stained and peeling in places. He felt suddenly, inexplicably, sorry for the seth. This could not be the face of a man who killed boys who owed him money. There was some mistake.

Suddenly, chhota seth held a sheaf of notes out to Kishore. 'Can you tell me what this is?' he asked.

Kishore's heart clenched at the sight of all that money.

'You don't know, do you? If you did, you wouldn't be sitting here with me.' Chhota seth looked over Kishore's head at something far away that only he could see. He emptied his whisky glass and signalled for another. 'Money is a hunger,' he continued. 'It is the best measure of life, the most efficient. Everybody is hungry for life.'

Kishore looked again at their reflections. He looked at the glittering silver ornaments, the porcelain figures of squirrels and swans and naked children. Life felt very unreal to him just then.

'Sahib, I want to make money. Tell me what I can do.'

'Come here.' Chhota seth looked at him sternly. 'Kneel down so I can look at you properly,' he commanded. Kishore knelt before him, feeling strangely shy. Chhota seth put a fat pink hand under his chin and tilted his face up. Kishore looked up at him and tried to see only Sushila. Chhota seth's white-lashed eyes stared into his. 'How hungry are you? Are you prepared to give up your friends?'

Kishore didn't move. He felt hypnotized by chhota seth's pink-rimmed eyes.

'All right then, keep the picture of these notes in front of your eyes,' chhota seth said, waving another bundle of money in front of his eyes. 'Now I'm going to teach you some magic. Shut your eyes.' Chhota seth gave Kishore's cheek a quick pinch. 'Now imagine that every person in the world is a petrol pump and you are a car. You need their petrol to live, so your objective is to pump as much petrol out of them as possible while paying as little as possible for it. Can you see that?'

Kishore couldn't but he didn't want to offend chhota seth, so he nodded enthusiastically.

'Good.' He went back to his counting. Kishore remained where he was, afraid that if he moved away he would be forgotten.

Silence descended on the room once more. Kishore waited. The bundles before the seth grew fatter and taller. At last he could bear it no more.

'Sethji,' he said.

Chhota seth ignored him.

'Sethji, what about my salary?'

A fat pink hand came at his face. He ducked a little too late and it got his ear instead.

'I'm counting, fool. Shut up,' chhota seth growled.

At last the seth shut his red-cloth-bound register and tied it up with a string. He put the envelopes into his briefcase and the rest of the money into another bag. Suddenly he asked, 'You know why this world is hell, and why we yearn for freedom from it?'

Kishore shook his head but kept his eyes firmly on chhota seth's shiny black leather shoes. Privately he decided that chhota seth was even madder than the charasis. 'Money and friendship, the only two things that are alive in this world, are at war with each other because they are opposites, constantly fighting each other. That is why there is no peace in this world. To live, you need money. To live, you need friendship. That is why I am a lonely rich man and not a poor happy man like you. Only Krishna is my friend. And he waits for me in the world after life. But what about this life, I tell him. Do you know how much I gave to the temple fund last year? Forty lakhs! Yes, forty lakhs, and what do I get? Did he come down to this world and even kiss me 'thank you' for building his temple? Instead, he makes the sun jealous of me and so he gave me this disease that forces me to come out only at night, when all decent people are asleep with their wives. I hate the sun. He hates me. Can you imagine a more powerful enemy than that?'

Kishore stared nervously at chhota seth. All he wanted now was to get out of the flat. Chhota seth had stopped speaking and was staring moodily at the television screen. He turned to Kishore, abruptly.

'So, young Kishore, I have made it easy for you. Tell me,

what guarantee can you give me that this will not make me your enemy?'

Kishore struggled to think of something that would please chhota seth. He felt afraid.

'Come, I will make it easier still for you,' chhota seth growled. 'I want your friendship. Give me a sign of your friendship and that is all the guarantee I need for the two years it will take you to repay me.'

Kishore's heart leapt. 'Of course, sethji, I am your faithful friend. What can I do to show you?'

Suddenly, Kishore was catapulted forward and landed on his knees. He felt hands grab him from behind and tear at his pants. 'Sahib, what—' Something hard crashed into the back of his skull and he sank into darkness.

The black Mercedes stopped on an unlit stretch of the Ring Road. The door opened and a large inert bundle was tossed out. The door closed and the car drove off in a little puff of diesel smoke. Kishore lay on the still warm asphalt, praying that it would open and swallow him. He had no clear recollection of what had happened to him. There was fire and pain between his legs. He had a hazy recollection of pink groping hands. He knew what had happened to him but in a dim and detached way, almost as if it had happened to someone else.

He turned slowly till he lay on his back, and looked up at the sky. It was a remarkably clear night—the kind of night that only came occasionally, in spring, when the winds were blowing. Kishore looked up at the millions of stars carpeting the sky. Soon, he knew, a car would come along and crush the life out of him. He hoped it wouldn't take too long. He heard the tinkling of a bell. Suddenly, an enormous jet-black head blocked the stars. 'Oh, my God, no!' Kishore shouted, his desire to live coming back with a fierceness that surprised him. He rolled over, barely escaping the huge paw that was bearing down on him.

The elephant came to a halt.

'Hey you, are you mad? What are you doing sleeping on the

road?' a furious voice called down. 'My poor Rani has had enough shocks for one day.'

Kishore didn't reply. He was listening to the drumming of his heart.

'Are you hurt?' the mahout asked, peering over the head of the elephant.

'No, I'm all right, go away,' Kishore replied.

'Don't you have some place to go? If not, at least go sleep on the pavement like a human being.'

This was too much for Kishore. 'You—you swine, I have a place to go. But I have been robbed, assaulted, and have no money to get me home. I have lost my month's pay and maybe my job also. I do not know how I will tell my wi—family.' He stopped abruptly.

The mahout's voice softened. 'If you live on the other side of the Yamuna, I can give you a lift till Patparganj. That's where Rani and I live. You're too young to be alone in this city. Bad things can happen to boys here.'

'My family lives in Nand Nagri,' Kishore mumbled, after a minute's silence.

'Nand Nagri!' The mahout whistled. 'That's a long way away. You'd better come with us. My Rani may not be a Maruti but she can move quickly when she wants to.'

Kishore stared up at the elephant, seeing it properly for the first time. He had never seen one so close before.

'She's so bulky, can she really go fast?' he asked the mahout.

'Just you wait and see how fast she'll go. It's been a long day for her and she almost got put into prison!' He laughed.

Kishore laughed too, imagining sharing a cell with the elephant. He almost told the mahout how he, too, had almost got put into prison. But that would have led to other questions and things he did not want to talk about, so he kept quiet.

'Hai … Rani … Hai … we're taking him with us,' the mahout told the elephant.

Obediently, the elephant wrapped her trunk around Kishore's waist and lifted the boy easily onto her back. Together, the three of them left the streets of New Delhi behind.

sleepers

My first posting as a servant of the state was to Mangladi. It was a peaceful little place, lying half-forgotten on the border of Karnataka and Kerala. No VIPs ever passed through it. But VIPs mattered little to me. My interest lay in making sure that things were done in the proper way and order was maintained. The key to maintaining order was good governance. And that is what I concentrated on.

I had few illusions about my job. My fellow citizens were a ramshackle, superstitious bunch. But I believed that a rational, enlightened state could eventually wean them away from their dark and chaotic ways. Then India would become the great country it was meant to be and take its rightful place as a leader of nations.

Mangladi taught me otherwise.

On 13 May 1998, I was on a routine inspection of flood control systems and irrigation canals in the coastal part of the district, in preparation for the rains. It was the last day of the tour and I was looking forward to my return to civilization, but a complicated land dispute in a neighbouring village forced me to decide on an unscheduled night halt in a village I had previously never visited. The name of the village was Purandaru.

An assiduous reader of files, I knew that the village had not been visited in the last ten years. As far as the state was concerned, the village didn't exist except as a part of the larger theoretical village, Daaru, which was itself not a real village but a group of ten hamlets housing different castes. I found out the name of the village by asking a man chopping coconuts on its outskirts that evening. Luckily, the files had thought fit to mention that the village possessed a disused forest bungalow at its edge and I decided to put up there for the night.

It was close to sunset when I entered the village. There was a great deal of activity on the streets. The villagers, it seemed, were out in full force. That in itself was unusual for that time of day. And they all seemed very busy. They hurried past without acknowledging me, barely suppressed excitement visible on their faces. Even the little children of the village hardly blinked when they realized there was a sahib in their midst. The women were out too, flocks of them, all wearing their finest saris, with flowers in their freshly oiled hair. I assumed the reason for this was a visiting theatre party that would perform the Mahabharata or Ramayana, interspersed with film songs and bawdy skits, through the night.

So the sahib's arrival had been eclipsed by a two-bit travelling theatre! I smiled to myself. Then I noticed that the women were all wearing their mangalsutras and bangles, had sindoor in their hair and were carrying trays laden with coconuts, fruits and flowers, topped with freshly made garlands. I realized that more likely, there was a community function that night—a puja to honour the local deity. But unlike their menfolk, there was nothing joyous in the way the women moved, and I saw in their faces none of the eager anticipation that heralds a night of celebrating the goddess. Instead, their faces were curiously blank. And their shining finery was dimmed by neglect. Dust streaked the clothes that the women and children were wearing, and some even had bits of food clinging to the brightly coloured cloth.

The village bore signs of dreadful neglect too. The thatch of the houses was untidily repaired and certainly not capable of facing the onslaught of the coming monsoon. And I was ready to bet that the flood tanks and irrigation canals were in a similar state. I had already noted with disapproval that half the fields surrounding the village were lying fallow. The remainder, including the fields to which the rice seedlings would be transplanted, were badly prepared, the furrows crooked and ending abruptly, with bald bits of land, like islands in an unruly sea. Leaves had not been swept off the state highway into the village, many of the drains were choked, and garbage lay everywhere. Even inside the courtyards of the houses, it lay piled in unsightly heaps or just left where it had fallen, to decompose at leisure.

At last a dirty little girl noticed me and tugged at her mother's hand. The mother stopped, twisted the poor child's arm and began to hit her. There wasn't much strength in the blows but the arm must have hurt. The child looked up at her mother dully, not a single cry escaping her lips. The mother continued to hit the child, unable to stop, while the others either stood around or continued on their way.

For a few moments I watched the little tableau in horror. Then I acted. I strode up to the woman and caught hold of her hand. 'Get a hold of yourself. Can't you see you'll hurt her?' I shouted. Immediately, her hand went slack and she stared up at me wearily, her eyes ringed in darkness. I let go. Then she took her daughter's hand and went on her way as if nothing had happened. Mystified, I caught hold of a villager.

'What is happening here?' I asked. He shied away from me like a startled horse. I grabbed him before he could run away and repeated the question. He looked down at his feet and muttered something incomprehensible, then literally tore himself out of my grasp and dashed away.

I wondered whether I had chanced upon the local madman. But when the next two men I asked behaved in much the same way, I decided that there was something seriously wrong with Purandaru, and that I would have to stay put for as long as it took to unravel what. Next, I noticed a man sitting before his house, chewing a piece of sugarcane. He seemed to be deliberately ignoring the bustle around him. I walked up to him and asked for the forest bungalow. He turned swollen, bloodshot eyes on me and gave me precise directions on how to get there.

Encouraged by the normality of the man, though he had the eyes of an alcoholic, I ventured another question.

'What is the occasion? Why is everyone in such a hurry?'

In the middle I cleverly inserted an unspoken third question: Why was he not part of it?

His eyes flashed, hatred animating them for a moment. 'The same occasion as every night,' he replied laconically, ignoring the important third question.

'What do you mean?' I asked warily.

'They have all-night prayers, these Hindus. And so the rest of us can't sleep,' he told me, generously including me in the 'us'.

'The rest of you?'

'Us Christians of course.' He looked at me as if I were stupid. Suddenly, he seemed to realize that I was a stranger. His eyes became wary. I quickly thanked him for his trouble and continued on my way. The caretaker at the forest bungalow should be able to tell me what I needed to know. Tomorrow I would visit the headman.

As I walked through the village, I noticed the islands of silence in the midst of all that activity, the darkened windows and tight-shut doors. I came to the centre of the village and saw a tall, splendid church, pristine and stately, in the midst of a colourful chaos. Right next to the church, spread over what must have been a cricket field, was the hub of activity.

People were running in every direction, fetching, carrying and calling to each other. Children and dogs chased each other between and around the grown-ups' legs, dashing away before they got a clout on the head or a kick in the side. Cows solemnly munched used banana-leaf plates and other rubbish. Loudspeakers crackled, and an insistent voice rattled off the programme of events, interrupting itself every now and then to shout urgent instructions at the people running across the field. Here and there, like eyes in the night, I saw sadhus, solitary and arrogant in their orange robes.

The crowd was thickest by the squat little temple at the other end of the field. A makeshift stage protruded from between the red-and-gold canvas walls of a half-erected tent. A third of the way across the field, a much larger tent in pink, blue and yellow pastels—looking somewhere between a pastry and a castle—was being decorated with tinsel streamers and Christmas lights. Behind the tent, like abandoned weapons, enormous cauldrons lay upside down or on their sides on the fire-scarred earth. A pack of dogs clustered around them, eating the remains of a meal. All around the edge of the field were smaller tents made of bits of tin, plastic and rags. In these sat a variety of hard-faced traders, selling everything from bindis to household implements. A Ferris wheel and a merry-go-round at one corner of the field, to the right of the temple, blared its own version of popular film music and drew ragged children like a magnet. Already, the noise emanating from the field was cacophonous, and the bhajans hadn't even started. Knowing the noise would only grow with the night, I couldn't help pitying the Christians.

Then I heard the church bells, their low, sweet sound sweeping over the field. I looked up, and saw them silhouetted against the red sky. The sound transported me back to my school years with the Jesuit fathers at St. George's in Patna, where each day was ushered in by the bells and the same sound bid the day goodnight. I wondered suddenly whether they were what had awakened my love of Western classical music. But even as I was thinking this, the bells interfered, becoming noisier and more frenzied, shedding their music with every toll.

A white-haired old man walking beside me began to curse loudly and fluently in a rich baritone. My shocked expression made him hasten to explain as soon as the bells had grown silent.

'They do it all day, on the hour, sometimes even on the half hour, just to torment us.'

I stared at him in sheer astonishment. 'What do you mean?'

But before he could answer, the bhajans came on from the other end of the field, so loud that all further conversation became impossible.

I decided to add a visit to the church to my agenda for the morrow.

The houses ended and the road dwindled into a simple forest track, surrounded on both sides by trees. I arrived at last at the bungalow. It looked as if it had been abandoned years ago. A huge spider's web substituted for hinges, uniting the gate to the gatepost. There was no bulb in the lamp post. Leaves and broken branches were strewn across the drive. In the fading light I could see that a carpet of dust covered the porch, making it glow palely. To my not-very-great surprise, my car, which I had left at the entrance to the village in order to enter its narrow mud streets on foot, was nowhere in sight. Neither was my driver or any representative of the local administration. I shouted for the chowkidar but only silence answered.

Logic told me that no government property was ever abandoned without it being laid out in writing. I tried again, shouting for the caretaker this time. A gust of hot wind answered, bringing with it snatches of an old film song. I pushed open the gate, breaking the cobweb. Bits of it clung to my shirt and I brushed them off superstitiously. It was bad luck to break a cobweb. I went to the front door and banged on it loudly. There was no response. I waited and tried again, but had no better luck. Desperate, I went around to the back of the bungalow in search of the transistor radio.

Hacking away at the undergrowth with my cane to make sure there were no snakes, I came eventually to the servant's quarters and banged on the door. After a rather long wait, I heard scuffling and footsteps. The door opened and a bleary face looked out.

'I am the assistant district magistrate and I want a room prepared for me at once,' I told the man icily.

He didn't move, disbelief spreading slowly across his features.

'My car broke down so I walked,' I found myself saying shamefacedly. 'It will be here shortly.'

'But I am not the caretaker, sir, I am only the chowkidar.' He began to shut the door.

'I don't care who you are,' I snapped, losing patience. 'Just get out here now.'

He understood that tone of voice. His face cleared. 'Of course, sir, one moment, please.' He retreated and emerged a few minutes later in a lungi and a crumpled white undershirt. I wrinkled my nose in distaste. He smelled of sleep.

I made him follow me to the front of the house.

'So you are the chowkidar?' I said finally.

'Yes, sir.'

'And where is the caretaker of the rest house?'

'He is not here, sir.'

'What do you mean, he is not here? Is he not a government servant?'

'He went back to his village, sir.'

'And did he take permission?' Of course I knew the answer, but felt impelled to ask anyway.

'I don't know, sahib.'

'And you let him leave, you said nothing?'

He stared at me stone-faced. Suddenly, I became conscious of how big and strong he was. I couldn't afford to make him angry, not without the full paraphernalia of the state.

I thought quickly. 'All right then, you come and show me my room and then you can get me some tea.'

At first he seemed reluctant to move, then the stubborn look retreated. He bobbed his head and disappeared. He came back a scant five minutes later with the keys. This time he was wearing his forest-green chowkidar's shirt.

Like the outside, the room he showed me was covered in dust. Cobwebs hung like exotic ferns from the walls. I was tempted at that point to return to the village and ask the Christian to whom I had first spoken to give me a bed for the night. Then the weight of my office settled upon me. I squared my shoulders and prepared resolutely to face the night in the forest bungalow.

'Send someone to clean this room immediately,' I ordered. 'I will have tea in the veranda, meanwhile.'

I walked onto the veranda, carefully dusted a chair, and sat down. I looked at the unkempt, leaf-strewn garden and wondered how long this state of affairs had existed. More importantly, I wondered how long it would take me to sort out whatever had caused it and leave the village behind me forever. I had already conceived a grave dislike of Purandaru.

A slovenly woman brought me tea in a cup with old tea stains decorating the cracks on it. I was tempted to order her to clean the cup and make me some fresh tea, but knew from experience just how far one could push illiterate villagers before they rebelled and refused to follow orders. So I took the cup from her and pretended to be blind to its filthy exterior. At least what was inside had been boiled to annihilation. Right after her came the chowkidar with an even filthier duster. He began to swat at the furniture as though he were driving away flies, creating veritable clouds of dust everywhere. I began to cough instantly.

'Stop,' I commanded. 'Forget the dusting, just get me clean sheets.'

He looked confused.

'Sheets,' I said, miming the gestures of making up a bed.

His grey face brightened for a second, then dulled again. 'No sheets,' he muttered, staring at the floor.

'What do you mean, no sheets?'

'No keys,' he said, mimicking the sound of keys jangling. I understood that the caretaker had either hidden the keys or gone off with them.

'All right then, what about dinner?'

'Dinner?' He looked even more uncertain than before.

'Yes. Dinner. Food,' I said, thinking that maybe he didn't understand my north Indian accent.

'Oh, food.' He nodded. 'Glucose biscuits?'

'No, I don't want biscuits with my tea. I want to know what you can give me for dinner tonight,' I replied, enunciating each word carefully.

'Yes, yes.' He pointed at the darkening sky to show he had understood. 'Only biscuits for dinner,' he said in English.

My mind went into semi-paralysis at the idea of biscuits for an assistant district magistrate's dinner. 'I don't think I can eat biscuits for dinner,' I said as calmly as I could. 'I need proper food. Rice, sambar, vegetables.'

'Yes, yes, sir. But no food in market many days now,' he replied in Hindi, obviously feeling I hadn't understood him.

'What do you mean?'

'Ration shop shut. Many, many days, sir.'

'The man at the ration shop is a government employee, he cannot shut his shop whenever he feels like it!' I exclaimed.

'The shop is closed for many days now,' he repeated, sounding distressed.

'Then tell him to go and open it,' I snapped.

'I cannot, sir, he is at the puja.'

I began to feel seriously concerned about the state of the village.

'Is everyone at the puja then?'

'Yes, sir, it will begin at sunset. Big puja tonight.' He switched back to pidgin English, obviously feeling it was easier to play dumb in.

'But why is there no food in the guest house? Surely you know that you are expected to be able to provide food for an officer at a moment's notice,' I said impatiently in Kannada.

He shifted uncomfortably from one foot to the other. 'But we are always getting advance notice, sir.' His stance implied that I couldn't be a real government sahib for I had come alone and unannounced, without even my official car with its red light.

I cursed myself for having let go of my car. I had grown so used to being surrounded by the trappings of my position that I had forgotten what it was like to be without them. I felt absurd, a soldier without weapons.

'What about your food? You can bring me a little of that, surely?' I could hear a conciliatory note creeping into my voice.

'No food. I have to go,' he said firmly.

'What do you mean, you have to go? Surely you will eat first.'

'No. I go to the temple.'

'I'll wait till you return.'

'I come back in the morning. We all do.'

'Then let your wife come back and serve me.'

He looked shocked. 'But she must be there, too. Everyone must be there tonight.'

I grew tired of trying to reason with an illiterate. 'I forbid you to go anywhere. Or I will have you sacked.'

His eyes widened in horror. 'Sir, the pujari, the village ... I cannot!'

'I don't want to hear those words,' I told him sternly, feeling the situation come under control at last. 'If you go to that stupid feast, I will make sure no child of yours ever gets a government job.'

'Sir,' the poor man fell to his knees, all traces of defiance gone, 'please, sir, have pity. Don't punish my children. I am a poor man.'

I relented a little. 'All right, but get me something to eat.'

He burst into a torrent of impassioned Kannada. 'Sir, I have to go, please. I beg you, let me go, the pujari will be very angry. Big devi puja tonight.'

'No.' I frowned fiercely, hoping I looked angrier than the pujari. 'This is your job.'

'But the devi can only be brought back today. Sir, I must go.'

'I don't care about your devi. I want my food.'

He gave me a look that told me exactly what he thought of my blasphemous point of view. Then, cleverly, he changed tactics. 'But everyone in the village will be there. They will know that I have not come.'

'So what? They all saw me walk through the village. They will know that you are doing your job and looking after your sahib.'

His face became a mask. 'But sir, I am just the chowkidar, it is not my job to look after you.'

Anger burnt away any inhibitions I might have had on the use and abuse of power.

'And I can get you thrown out of your job tonight,' I snapped.

To my horror the man lunged at my legs and buried his face in my trousers. I tried to get him off me, but he only held on tighter.

'Please, I have to go, sir. Or they will say I am a bad Hindu, sir.'

Trying to detach him from my legs and console him at the same time, I said, 'You don't become a bad Hindu just because you miss one visit to the temple. And you can go tomorrow after I am gone.'

For a second his arms loosened their pincer-like grip. Then they tightened again. 'I have to go, sir, I have to,' the man began to whimper, 'or they will say that I have become one of them. And then, sir, I don't know what they will do to me. I am a good Hindu ... I don't want to become Christian, sir. What will my father say? And my children, sir, I will never see them again.'

I stared at him. For a second, time seemed to stop. Then my heart began to beat very fast. I tried to think intelligently. 'Here, stop crying, you can go if you want to.' The mewling stopped. 'But tell me first what is going on in this village.'

The man sat up and rubbed his face with the end of his filthy lungi. 'I will tell you everything,' he said eagerly, his face transformed.

As I waited on the veranda for the chowkidar to change into his dhoti, I thought of what the files had to say on Purandaru.

It was a fairly typical Kannada village. The villagers grew rice and vegetables and fruit—mainly mango and coconut. Betel-nut trees provided them with a stable cash income. Their ponds were full of fish. The reason the name had stuck in my memory was because of a curious letter written nearly two years ago by someone who claimed to be the pujari of the temple, begging the government to send them a teacher for their school. The letter claimed that the government-appointed schoolmaster had not visited the school for over three months and no replacement had been sent either.

I had called the superintendent of schools and told him about the letter, explaining that there was no follow-up letter from our side in the file. He couldn't remember the case but promised to look into the matter. A few weeks later, at the inauguration of his wife's school, I brought up the case again.

'Did you check what action was taken then?'

'Just the usual, sir,' he replied, not meeting my eyes, 'villagers trying to use the state to settle personal vendettas. I checked the files. The teacher had been attending school every day.'

'Oh. All right, send me a copy of our reply—I'll need it for the files.'

And Purandaru had slipped from my mind.

But the village pujari, I now knew, hadn't been trying to settle scores.

'Because the government teacher never came, we had no choice but to put our children into their school,' the chowkidar said, not looking at me.

'What school?'

'The Christian school ... by the church ... The Christian pujari teaches in English there.'

'But what does that have to do with the devi puja?' I asked impatiently.

The chowkidar's face filled with shame. 'It is because some of us sent our children to *that* school, that the devi became angry and left us.'

'That's ridiculous!' I exploded. 'You call yourself a government servant and believe such rubbish. Devis can't walk away. They aren't human.'

He waited patiently for my anger to dissipate. 'Last year, our crops failed. First, she took away the rain, then the fish died, so we lost our only other source of food. If the rains don't come this year, we will all die.'

'What rubbish, the rain was fine last year.'

'But not here.'

'That's impossible—' I spluttered, then came to an abrupt halt, remembering reading about a similar case that had taken place twenty years ago.

'Then, when the fish in the pond died, too, we had to do something. We went to the pujari and he advised us to do a devi mahayagna. At first we were reluctant. Mahayagnas cost a lot and no one had very much left. But in the end Rajamma convinced us.'

'Who is Rajamma?' I asked.

'She is a widow, sir, with one son, Raju, who is a little mad. He is a very good boy though, and loved by the devi. He would sit with the devi, all day sometimes, singing to her. He was also very friendly with the Christian priest. Since Rajamma worked all day, Raju would often go to the school.'

'So what does Raju have to do with the church?' I asked impatiently.

'Well, after the priest got the bells for his church, Raju disappeared. Someone said they saw the priest taking Raju away in his car. Then the ration shop owner saw Raju in the convent school, sir, in the town.'

Rumours. Every village was a hotbed of rumours.

'Then what happened?'

'Rajamma went to the local oracle and begged him to ask the devi where her son was. He told her that Raju had indeed become a Christian. But not of his free will. He had been bewitched. Rajamma was very sad. So our pujari told her that he would do a special puja to the devi to set the boy free and bring him back to his senses. All the villagers were asked to attend the puja. Rajamma sold her land and used the money to pay for it. The puja took all night. The pujari hired loudspeakers. A special group of sadhus came to sing bhajans all night.'

'And did Raju come back?' I asked sarcastically. He was probably a shoeshine boy in Bombay by now.

'Yes, sir.'

'What!'

'He came back, sir, but he couldn't say where he had been. He hasn't spoken since he came back. It was the devi's price for returning him. After that, the village decided to do a puja for her. The priest hired a group of singers and they came and made their home in the coconut grove behind the temple. He hired painters from Kavallur and while they painted, temple musicians, also brought in from Kavallur, sang. Then he called the Brahmin cooks from Kokinallam and while the statue of the devi was washed and repainted, they sang and recited shlokas and cooked.'

I couldn't follow his logic, but I'd heard enough. Things would come to a boiling point soon if nothing was done.

'How long has this been going on?' I interrupted him.

'How long since what has been going on?'

'Since the all-night jagrans began?'

He looked vague. 'I don't remember, maybe a month? Two weeks? It's hard to tell, it's been so long ...' he yawned.

'So long since what?'

'Since we slept,' he said matter-of-factly.

He stopped and wiped a tear from his eye.

'Each night we have gathered at the temple and prayed and sung to the devi till dawn, begging her to come back. But still she does not come. Our children are weak from lack of sleep, our eyes are dry and we cannot cry, our feet ache, and our throats are raw from calling out to her. But still she does not come, sir.'

'Why don't you stop and let the pujari take over? Maybe the devi will listen to him better than she listens to you. He is, after all, a professional.'

The irony missed its mark. 'Oh no, sir, a single voice is not strong enough to call back the devi once she has gone away, even though our priest is a great man. It's the bells, sir.' All of a sudden his face became unrecognizable. 'If you could only stop the bells of the church,' he cried, 'I am sure the devi will come back.'

'Why? What is wrong with the bells?'

'They ring all day so we cannot sleep, stealing our shakti so we cannot pray properly to the devi. We fear that already the devi may be too far away.'

I remained silent, appalled at the complexity of the problem before me.

'Sir, can you not speak to the priest, tell him that the government has ordered the removal of the bells?' the chowkidar asked.

'Of course not.' I cut him off before the idea could take hold.

If the villagers came to see me in a group, the state would get dragged in, the media would find out and splash it all over the front page, and the problem would become political. Only blood would resolve it then.

'I will meet your pujari and theirs together and order them to stop this madness right now,' I announced.

The chowkidar's eyes grew huge. He clutched my feet wildly. 'No sir, please sir. They will kill me if they know that I have told you. Please, sir.'

I looked down at the man. His face was bathed in sweat and he was trembling. 'All right, all right, I won't say anything. Take me with you, I need to eat at least,' I lied.

'Then you will come back to the rest house and sleep?' he asked worriedly.

'Yes. I promise. Shall we go?'

Night transformed the road to the village, turning it into a pale silver stream slicing through a dense unified mass of black that rustled and shivered like a creature alive but asleep, dreaming strange and restless dreams. Soon we were part of a group of ragged, wild-eyed men and women shuffling along slowly towards the temple. They walked carefully, as if the mere task of putting one foot before the other was fraught with danger. An exhausted silence hung over all of them. Only when we came into the lighted part of the village did they become animated, pulling their shawl-like upper garments over their heads and sinking their necks into their chests.

We came up to the church. In the moonlight, it glowed serenely. Someone spat.

'He used our money—collected from all the children in his school, our village children, sir, Hindu and Christian—to buy those bells,' a plump man who had the look of a barber explained. The others mumbled their assent. All of a sudden their shuffling feet became infused with a spurt of energy and we entered the field in a rush.

The cricket ground was ablaze with halogen lights. Bhajans,

bursting from speakers tied to the coconut trees, waged a not entirely successful war on film music coming out of the radios of the many vendors of bindis and cheap face powder. Odorous clouds of sweat, rancid ghee, incense and rotting food, urine and freshly frying ghee rushed to greet us. Yet, the field itself was unnaturally free of people.

The others melted away with breathtaking suddenness, leaving only the chowkidar, who guided me to the little tent in front of the temple that I had seen earlier in the day. We entered the tent and were confronted by a living wall of flesh. Miraculously, a crack appeared in it as soon as we stepped inside, one that was just wide enough for a single man to pass through. The chowkidar urged me forward.

'Sir, what is the matter? They are waiting for you,' he whispered.

Years of practice in the exercise of power came to my rescue. For, though I had no desire whatsoever to go to the front of that smelly crowded tent, I knew that as the sole representative of the state, I had no choice. God and the government had to share the same stage, or else we civil servants would never be able to function. The robes of power are seldom of one's choosing; yet never, till that night, had they felt so uncomfortable.

There was a murmur of approval as I took my place in the front. I tried to make myself tall, feeling like an ant with his back to a cyclone. Something demonic had been set in motion. I could feel it making its way through the crowd, boring into my back. Would I be able to control it? Or was it too late already? I stared straight ahead and tried to seem absorbed in the proceedings.

The stage itself looked rather demure, with orange and white flowers hanging down the sides and garlanding the walls, and four deepa stambhas, multi-wicked floor lamps, at the four corners. In the centre, in front of the red-and-gold curtain, was a single silver microphone. Behind it, in a curtained alcove, priests could be heard chanting. The heat was terrible. The smoke from the burning lamps stung my eyes, making them water. The smell of flowers and incense and ghee was quite overpowering. My lungs began to crave fresh air. Fearing I would be overcome, I put a hand out and leaned on the edge of the stage.

The chanting stopped and a man appeared in front of the curtain. He was not tall, but of an ascetic thinness that bordered on the skeletal. He walked languidly to the front of the stage. Yet, he carried with him such an aura of tightly controlled energy that he seemed to grow as he approached the front. His face was practically devoid of flesh. Thin blue veins criss-crossed his forehead. Empty skin stretched tightly between jaw and cheekbone. But his most striking feature was his eyes. Protruding and practically lidless, with beady black pupils that swam in a large surface of startling blue-white, his eyes seemed to see what no one else could. He came up to the microphone and stared into the assembly, picking out faces from the crowd. A tremor ran through them. I felt it, too, and knew with absolute certainty that I was looking at the village pujari, the selfsame one who had had the courage to write to us.

He was no ordinary village pujari, looking after the daily rituals of the temple, weddings and deaths, and minding his business. I understood why the chowkidar was so scared of him. There seemed nothing this man with the searing eyes didn't know about the unseen. Even when his eyes weren't upon you, his emaciated form was like some awful reminder of the essential weakness of the flesh. But more than his thinness, it was his skin that seemed to attest to his inner purity, for it glowed like burnished copper, more alive than a flame. Never in my life had I seen skin like that! As if aware of the magic of his skin, the priest was naked to his waist except for the sacred thread glowing white on his chest and the rudraksha beads around his neck. The saffron lungi he was wearing added fire to the colour of his skin, so that he seemed to burn in eternal penance for the weakness of us lesser mortals.

The pujari waited till the shuffling and whispering in the hall died down. It seemed to me to take an absurdly short time. Then he began to speak.

'I see you are all here. That is good.'

His voice was a delight to listen to, cultured and beautifully modulated, yet rich in the drama of emotion. No actor could have spoken like that.

'Today is the thirteenth day of our worship and amma still won't come to us. Do you know why that is?' A collective moan arose, like the wind of loss, from the assembly.

He shut his eyes and listened to it with satisfaction. His flesh quivered like the surface of a lake touched by the barest hint of a breeze.

'I will never forget …' he began. 'Today I saw her so clearly.' He paused, a sob in his voice. Then, just when the tension grew almost unbearable, he opened his eyes and let us feel their full effect. 'More clearly than I can see you with whom I have lived and eaten all my life and who are before me now.' His eyes shifted to an indeterminate spot above our heads. 'She was just there, at the edge of the village, outlined against the bamboo groves. She didn't look at me … her eyes were focussed on something far away that I could not see. I went closer. She ignored me. I wanted to cry, she was in such a terrible condition. She looked like a widow who had lost her way in the forest for many nights. Her beautiful red sari, the one I put on her with my own hands, was gone'—he lifted his hands as he said this, their emptiness emphasizing his message—'and the white widow's sari she now wears was streaked with grey and brown and torn in places. I could see evil-looking thorns clinging to the cloth in other places. Her lotus feet were so torn that they resembled the half-eaten remains of a tiger's meal. Her long black hair was caked with the dust and dead leaves of the forest. An earring was missing, and her belt had fallen off. Her bangles lay broken at her feet and her crown hung drunkenly down the side of her head, caught on her matted locks. Her face, her beautiful moonlike face, was lifeless and wan. Dark circles ringed her eyes and her lips were dull and cracked. Her bride's bindi was gone and there was no sindoor in the parting of her hair and dead flowers lay across her shrivelled breasts.

'"Amma, what has happened to you?" I cried, falling at her feet. "Why are you like this?"

'"My children have forgotten me. They do not remember me any more," she replied sadly.

'"That is not true, ma. They made a mistake, but now that they have seen the error of their ways, they are calling to you, amma. Can you not hear them?"

'She said nothing and started to walk away from me, towards the forest.

'"Oh, fish-eyed one, why do you persist in ignoring your children?" I called after her. "Have they not done enough yet? Are you not satisfied with their repentance? What more must your children do?" In my despair I fell to the ground. At last she turned her head and looked at me. Her hair caught on a bamboo frond and revealed her other ear. I thought I would die of shame. For amma's beautiful shell-shaped ear was bleeding. As I watched, the blood poured down like rain and soaked her white sari.

'"Oh, amma, what has happened?" I cried in alarm.

'"You have done this to me," she replied. "Save me."

'And she vanished.'

The priest stopped. People in the audience were sobbing loudly, some crying out, 'no, oh no', their bodies swaying back and forth.

'What can we do for amma?' they cried in unison.

He surveyed them in silence and a satisfied smile spread across his thin lips. 'We must continue to pray.' Suddenly, the heat and the smoke and the smell of so many bodies became too much for me. I turned and tried to push my way through the wall of bodies, heedless of the angry shouts that arose.

I must have fainted because the next thing I knew I was sitting on the floor at the edge of the hall, close to the entrance. I was a child again and someone was cradling my head in his lap, fanning me.

'Anna,' he said respectfully, the moment he saw my eyes open, 'are you feeling better? Can I get you some water?'

'How ... What ha-happened?' I tried to sit up.

'Hush, lie still, give them time to forget you,' he whispered as he fanned my face. His voice was unemphatic, with a curious lack of inflection.

'What do you mean?' I asked, trying to get a look at the man's face. But the darkness made it impossible to see anything more than the whites of his eyes.

'Anna, you have upset them. They're in a funny mood tonight, I can feel it.'

I could sense the truth underpinning his words, and so I obeyed him, wondering where my unknown benefactor belonged in the political mosaic of the village. I sat up suddenly, remembering who I was. His lips lifted briefly in acknowledgement, but his eyes never left the stage. The stillness of his body as he watched the proceedings, and the utter concentration that stillness implied, both impressed and disturbed me.

Suddenly, the hall was plunged in darkness and, as if that was the cue they had been waiting for, six priests appeared from behind the curtain that hid the sanctum sanctorum from the eyes of the spectators. They walked solemnly to the front of the stage. One carried a shallow tin box and a broom. The second and third carried the wood and the oil respectively. The fourth, fifth, and sixth were musicians who immediately began to play while the fire was prepared. Behind the curtain, meanwhile, lamps were lit and a play of shadows began. One pair of shadows with elongated arms bathed the idol. Another waved elaborately carved silver fly whisks. The third lifted two multi-pronged lamps and moved them in slow circles to the rhythm of the music, throwing grotesque many-armed shadows on the curtain. I glanced at my companion. His chest heaved with emotion, his eyes, moist and shining, were glued to the stage.

After the fire was lit and the music ceased, the pujari reappeared and took possession of the mike.

'The evening's programme will be the same as yesterday's. The only change is that today the abhishek will be followed by the kirtanam and then the distribution of prasadam,' he said.

A few groans escaped the crowd, and the woman in front of us clutched her children.

'Impressive, isn't he, our pujari?' the man beside me asked.

I said nothing.

'You don't agree?'

'It is not my place to agree or disagree,' I said carefully.

On stage, the pujari continued to speak. 'I would like to add that we have been forced to do this because some of the sub-cooks did not arrive on time. This is what happens when some of you do not take your responsibilities seriously. Everyone suffers—especially the children who are the devi's favourites and most likely to get her to respond to their call. If the children don't get their food on time, the devi will be angry.'

A collective moan went through the crowd.

'After prasadam, there will be the special pujas for those who have requested them and those who have been polluted by the touch of the enemies. I will call out their names and they can come and collect their baskets of offerings. Then the singing will resume and I want you all to be there. Tonight is ekadasi and the devi is most susceptible to your call. No one is to go to sleep.' He stared threateningly at several people. 'Especially you, Chinnakutty,' he called, 'I will be watching you.' His eyes pierced the black mass of bodies in the centre of the tent. 'And you, Gauriamma, no taking your children home early.'

I looked around to see who he was talking to and saw a woman with unhealthy, greyish skin and wide, staring eyes. She hung her head and clutched four scared-looking children to her.

'Poor children, can't he see he's making them suffer? They're dying of fatigue,' muttered the man beside me.

My ears pricked up. 'Has this been going on for long?'

He looked at me intently. 'Eighteen days, if we count today,' came the prompt reply. 'I wonder how much longer the village will last.'

I felt greatly encouraged. Here was someone intelligent and educated who could help me understand what was happening and perhaps help me put a stop to it.

The hypnotic voice of the pujari continued to flow through the public address system. 'I hope you have all left your donations in the donation box at the side of the hall. If you haven't, please do it now. There are some of you who came too late to do so, I know who you are.' He paused and looked searchingly at the audience. 'There has been a marked drop in the collections as well as the food. I was angry at the selfishness of some of us, but I realize that it must be the will of the devi that we purify our minds further. From now on, only rice payasam will be served.'

A ripple went through the audience and many hung their heads.

A sudden flurry of activity drew my eyes to the stage again. More pujaris, this time dressed like sadhus in saffron, and beating on drums and cymbals of all sizes, and blowing on horns and conches, swarmed all over the stage. They all looked fierce and devoted. The curtains flew back, revealing the idol at last. A sigh of relief rose from the crowd. For there, in the inner sanctum of the temple, bathed in a warm halo of light, was the devi herself.

I am not, by nature, superstitious. An agnostic father and an atheist mother had made me a worshipper of the rational world. But a shiver ran through me all the same, for in spite of what I had been brought up to believe, I felt the devi come alive. I felt it as surely as did every person there. I saw her hair move in the gentle lotus-perfumed breeze that suddenly invaded the tent, and I felt an inexplicable lightening of my heart, a silent invasion of joy in that dark, hot, smelly space. A joyous shout burst from my throat and I felt spontaneous tears wet my cheeks. I wiped them surreptitiously, glancing self-consciously at my neighbour. To my relief there were tears rolling down his cheeks too.

'She's beautiful, isn't she? It is hard not to be moved,' I said.

He turned his head and brushed away his tears. 'Idol worship is not a good thing,' he growled thickly. 'Come, let us go outside.'

I should have felt grateful. The man had saved me from becoming as superstitious as the villagers. Instead, I felt resentful, as if I had been unjustly rebuked.

The man stood up and gave me his hand. Somewhat reluctantly, I let him help me up and together we crept out of the tent into the deserted cricket ground.

A slight wind that smelled of the sea blew across the field, carrying the garbage with it. As I sucked the cooler air into my lungs, rationality took possession of me once more. The rains were coming. Would my car make it out of the village? Had it even arrived? What had happened to it?

The wind woke a dog lying asleep on a garbage heap. The dog opened his mouth wide and howled. An answering screech rent the peace of the night. The dog leapt high in the air and ran away.

'What was that?' I asked my companion.

He looked unperturbed. There came another shriek, but this time the static that followed made the cause of the sound clearly discernible. The loudspeakers had just been switched on.

'Are you hungry?' my companion asked.

Of course I was hungry, but first I wanted to know who my mysterious benefactor was. 'Not very,' I lied. 'Tell me, who are you? How is it you know English?'

The man laughed, showing even white teeth. 'First eat. You must be hungry.'

'No, I'm fine. I can eat later,' I told him impatiently.

'My mother always said one shouldn't talk on an empty stomach.' He laughed oddly.

I had to agree. The smell of the temple food being cooked in coconut oil was making my stomach rumble. I gave in.

'What about you? Will you eat with me?'

He shook his head. 'Later. I will wait for you by that tree over there.'

I ducked into the tent. A slovenly cook filled a leaf plate with lemon rice and watery curd. The filth was unbelievable. But I was too hungry to care. I helped myself to some chillies and walked out. The cooks watched me leave without stopping their work. Even they seemed to know who I was, which is why they let me eat before the gods.

When I stepped out of the tent the man was waiting for me beneath the tree, exactly where he had said he would be. He stood up and formally offered me a seat on a branch that curved like a swing just a few feet from the ground. Then he sat down on the floor before me.

'So, who are you? What do you do here?' I asked immediately. His answer astonished me. 'I came to meet you,' he said.

'Why? Are you a government employee, or a member of the panchayat?' I tried to read the expression on his face, but either by chance or by design, it was once more in shadow, whereas the lights strung on top of the huge tent practically blinded me.

'You are from the government—of the government,' he corrected himself. 'It is rare for a government official, even a minor one, to visit a village as tiny as this. What has brought someone as important as yourself here?'

The man had a natural authority that made one want to answer, but I held back, remembering my position. 'Word gets around quickly, does it not? Tell me, how is it that a man of your talents is content to remain here?'

'Because I know the world is nothing but a big village.' He laughed briefly, his eyes not leaving my face for an instant. I found his regard distinctly unsettling, but couldn't pull my own away. 'The people here are quite easy to manage. Except when they have been scared by something quite out of the ordinary … like your sudden arrival, for example. That's why I had to come.'

'How do you know English so well?' I asked, my curiosity getting the better of me.

'I wanted to be a bureaucrat like you,' he answered bluntly.

'Why didn't you?' I asked when I'd recovered from my surprise.

'You believe that life can be planned?' he asked.

Unprepared, I gave a stupid reply. 'Of course it can. If one is careful and prudent.'

'Careful. Prudent.' He smiled in a way that made me feel young and foolish. 'What lovely words! So vague and so comforting! And what if you were born in a pit? What would you plan then?'

'I would plan to climb out of the pit,' I replied patiently.

'You think I haven't tried?' my companion asked, his voice becoming thin with suppressed emotion.

'How do I know when you refuse to tell me anything about

yourself?' I replied. The opening I had been waiting for had finally arrived.

*

'I come from a Brahmin village hidden in a fold of the high Himalayas. My father was the village priest. He looked after the temple of the goddess Chamundi. In those days there was no road to get to the village and one had to walk the last ten kilometres up a narrow footpath. So no government teacher ever came to our school. As such, my father was the teacher too. He was a very good teacher and after the children of the village were finished with him, many went on to get government jobs.

'Though my father was highly educated and could teach all subjects, his great love was our sacred texts. He knew Sanskrit, as do I. I can still remember the glow on his face as he sat down on his mat in the morning and began to recite his prayers. So, though the village was poor and he was highly educated, he was content to remain there as its priest. He fed himself on the respect the villagers showered on him. When he was thirty, he married the thin, half-starved daughter of a Brahmin too poor to give a dowry. I was their first child and they were so proud that I was a boy, it took them almost three years to realize that I had been born deaf.

'After me, there came a girl and then another and another and another. My father was furious. Who would say his beloved mantras for him when he died and was laid on the funeral pyre? How would his soul reach heaven? Who would perform the rites that protected his soul while it wandered for one year and thirteen days before it reached heaven?

'I grew up to be strong and quick. I was never ill. My mother kept me beside her as much as she could, out of the way of my father. I helped her cook and clean and tend the animals. She loved me dearly. I could feel it in the way she held me close, the way she looked at me when my father was not there. But my father, he could hardly bear to look at me. All he could think of was the shame I'd brought on him. He felt certain the entire village was laughing at him—schoolteacher, pundit, the most learned man in the village, yet with an illiterate deaf-mute of a son. The older I got, and the stronger my body became, the more he hated me. I remember watching him shout at me. I couldn't hear him, but I felt the words hit me and I'd cry even before he touched me.

'When I was nine, my mother had another son. My father was overjoyed. However, when my little brother was three, a snake bit him and my father couldn't get him to the hospital in time. So he died. After that my father went mad. He took out his sorrow on me. I was a big boy by then and I hit him back, just once. But that was enough for him. He beat me with an iron rod till I was bleeding so badly that my mother and the other villagers had to drag him off me. The week after that we boarded a bus and then a train. In Lucknow, he left me in a small wayside tea stall. I never saw him again.'

'How ... how awful,' I gasped, scarcely able to believe my ears.

He continued as if he hadn't heard me. 'To begin with, I was overjoyed. It was like being thrust into a beautiful dream. Only when I grew hungry did I realize that I was alone; that I'd been abandoned.'

The memory of abandonment was like a wound on his face.

'I don't know how I managed not to get killed that first day. I couldn't hear the cars honking at me to get out of the way. Eventually, a scooter hit me and I awoke in the hospital. As they couldn't find my parents, they shifted me to the government boys' home. There, we were kept in cells like animals, woken up in the morning, fed something disgusting and then made to sit idle for hours in a classroom with steel bars on the doors and windows. A man would occasionally look inside and shout at us if we made too much noise. The boys ... well, I won't describe what I went through there, but it was horrible.

'Only, my own nightmare was worse. I knew people communicated with each other in some mysterious way that was related to the mouth. But when I opened my mouth, whatever sounds I made seemed to provoke reactions similar to that of my father's. I thought words were shadow equivalents of the expressions on a person's face. I felt them stir inside me, too. I would open my mouth, think of the feeling and make a sound. But then the person's face would turn away and I would know that I had failed to communicate. I tried again and again, growing more and more violent as the desperation built up inside me. At last they decided that I was too dangerous to be kept with the other boys. I was given to the Christian missionaries in Lucknow.'

'The Christian fathers!' I exclaimed. Suddenly, a terrible suspicion struck me. 'You're not ...'

He smiled grimly and nodded. 'I was little better than an animal when they found me. I trusted no one. I did not even know my name. I didn't, and still don't, know the name of my village. I can never go back to where I came from. The fathers called me John. They taught me to lip-read, to write and speak.'

I couldn't contain myself any longer and turned to face him fully. 'You're ... you're the priest?'

'At last you've guessed it,' he said sarcastically. 'After all the hints I gave you, I'd have thought you'd catch on much faster. Why else can I speak English as well as you?'

'I ... I never thought, never expected to find—' I stammered, uncomfortably aware that he was lip-reading. What else could he read in my body language, I wondered.

'—a priest here? Why not? I wanted to talk to a real sahib. And I knew you'd be brought here first.'

'I was coming to meet you tomorrow,' I explained quickly, guiltily.

He frowned. 'Tomorrow? Tomorrow may have been too late. Anyway, I wanted to talk to you to learn if you were really a better person than me.'

'Why should I be better than you?'

'Because you rule this great country ... I only take care of its soul,' he replied, not sparing the irony.

'From all I hear, you are the Pied Piper of this village,' I said dryly. 'You've taken away all the children.'

He gave me a strange look, not unmixed with respect. 'I am no Pied Piper. I never told the government to refuse to educate its people.'

We were fencing with each other, I realized, and to my surprise, I found that I was enjoying it.

'You hate the Hindus, don't you? Because of your father.'

He laughed cynically. 'My father was nothing—an unthinking animal with pretty words in his mouth. What did he know about God when he knew nothing of morality?' He looked towards the tent and his face twisted with bitterness. 'Why should I hate these people? They are not people—they are a single, undefined mass. They ooze over the earth unthinkingly. They can be stamped upon, and they won't react, because they have no mind, only feelings. And feelings without a mind to direct them are powerless. But touch their symbols, and they go wild with rage. My only regret is that my father's Hindu blood is in me and will one day betray me.'

'Touch any group's symbols and they will riot,' I said coldly. Then something made me add, 'And yet, I will bet that Hindus are by far the most tolerant group. Take this, your own district. Christians and Muslims live happily in a Hindu-majority state. There has never been a riot here.'

'Because Christians and Muslims know better than to try to wake the sleepers.'

'Or is it because Hindus tolerate you that you persist with your intolerable arrogance!' I snapped.

He just looked at me. Then his face split in a smile that had nothing spontaneous in it. All at once, I had a premonition of disaster.

The priest stood up. 'All right, let's find out how tolerant these people of yours are,' he said and ran towards the temple.

'Hey, you! Stop!' I shouted after him. 'What are you going to do?'

I was talking to the wind. He kept running. I ran after him. People were streaming out of the tent. I pushed my way through them. They didn't even react. Their eyes were dull and they fell away at the touch of my hand, their bodies crumpling like paper.

I rushed into the empty tent. It was dark and silent. The priest was nowhere to be seen. Then I heard the sound of feet on wooden floorboards. The priest was on the stage. I rushed up to the front of the tent and clambered onto the stage. In front of me, the devi was unveiled and smiled intimately at me, her glassy eyes serene, reflecting the scores of tiny lamps beneath her. I couldn't help staring at that face. Like a lake in the middle of a firestorm, I thought, deeply moved in spite of myself. Suddenly, I sensed a presence behind me.

The priest stood there, his arms filled with garbage.

'Why ...' Then a terrible thought struck. 'Why have you brought that here?'

He grinned sardonically. 'Wait and see.'

'What are you going to do?' My voice was a terrified squeak.

He leapt forward, pushing me aside. I fell heavily to the floor and lay there, stunned. He put one foot upon my neck and kept me pinned to the floor. I didn't need to look at him to know what he was doing. I could hear him whistling tunelessly. In the tiny pocket of my brain where my rationality had gone into hiding, I wondered how he had taught himself to whistle. Suddenly, a hand was pulling me up. 'Come on, get up, take a look at what you've done,' he whispered.

I turned towards the devi. Horror welled up in my heart. Around her the curtains were on fire, bathing her in an ugly orange light. Her face was covered with clumps of half-eaten rice and vegetables, plastic bags, peels, and something brown and lumpy which I didn't dare name. Her golden crown was ripped and fluttered like a moth in the current of air caused by the flames. Her sari had more brown stuff and food and leaf plates clinging to it, and her feet were completely hidden by more garbage. The lamps were upturned, and the prasadam of rice and laddoos was scattered amongst the flowers at her feet.

I turned to the priest. 'You bastard,' I screamed.

'Clean it up,' he ordered, laughing maniacally. 'I'll call the others to help you.'

He reached up and began to ring the temple bells. My fist wavered between his face and my duty. I stepped towards the desecrated idol. But it was too late. I heard the sound of many running feet, and shouts. The villagers were running towards their beloved temple.

The priest stopped laughing. He grabbed my hand. 'Come on, we must get out of here.'

'No, you clean this up before they come. I'll help. It's not right.' I brushed the filth off the devi's clothes, leaving streaks of brown on my fingers.

He pulled me away. 'They'll kill you if they find you here. They won't stop to ask questions.'

I looked through the gap in the back of the tent. The crowd had grown as the news spread and now it was a huge mass, a black wall of destruction, unstoppable as a tidal wave.

He pulled me down the steps alongside the wings of the stage and we stumbled through the garbage dump from where he had collected his offerings for the devi. As soon as we were through, we began running, him in the lead. We leapt over the low wall that separated the temple from the churchyard, we ran across the graveyard, dodging tombstones, and around the corner of the building to the front of the church. The priest struggled with the heavy wooden doors and I waited tensely beside him.

At last he got the door open and we dashed inside. He locked and bolted the door after us.

'It won't hold long,' I said grimly, feeling vaguely satisfied at the thought.

'You're right.' He frowned and was silent for a moment. Then he looked up and smiled. 'Follow me,' he ordered, pointing to some stairs at the side of the altar.

I hesitated. 'Is that the other way out of this church?'

His eyebrows went up. 'Out? There's nowhere we can hide in this village. They'll hunt us down like rats. We're safer here.'

'My God!' The dire nature of our predicament dawned upon me. 'Do you have a phone in here? I can call police headquarters.'

He gave a bitter laugh. 'What would a deaf man do with a phone?'

I looked away, embarrassed. The silence was broken by the sound of fists banging on the door.

'Come on,' he said brusquely. 'We can't wait here any longer, I know a place where we can hide.'

He dashed to the stairs and began climbing. I followed him, panting a little, for the stairs were steep. Only then did I realize what we were climbing towards. The breath caught in my throat, for he was leading me into a trap. The steps led up the church tower. Once we were up there, we would be stuck. I hesitated. He turned around as if he had read my mind.

'Don't worry, I know what I am doing.' Such was the power of the man that I believed him.

The stairs opened onto a little platform. Directly above us, within touching distance, were the bells. Below us, the entire village and the surrounding countryside spread out like a black mantle gashed with colour. Beneath us, in the bright glow of the floodlights, were the crazy reds and purples and pinks of the temple and fairground. Faintly visible around it, in the reflected light, were the white and burnt orange of nearby roofs and walls. Beyond them, the countryside was draped in the veil of night. From where we stood, I could clearly see spreading across the fairground, like a tattered cloak, the villagers who had stood aside so docilely for me to pass through, a bare three hours ago. Their anger was palpable, made more fearsome by its silence and its apparent lack of emotion. They moved across the field like a wave, crowned by a bright saffron dot brandishing a trident. Suddenly, from the cook's tent, torches appeared and rushed to join the main body of people massed at the entrance of the maidan. As the torches joined them, the others cheered once and then they swarmed forward. Every once in a while I heard a voice calling to the devi, calling to Mahadev, swearing to bring victory or die. The words seemed to belong to no one—they simply rose out of the mass of bodies streaming down the main street to the church doors.

'They're not going to stop till they've burnt your precious church down,' I told the priest.

'But I'll have won my bet,' he crowed.

'What bet? What are you talking about? You're sick!' I cried.

He didn't answer, he just looked at me and I felt every word that had passed between us come alive.

A cool wind cut through the heat and dried the sweat on my body, making me feel suddenly cold. 'Please, you've made your point, now put a stop to this madness.'

I looked down at the villagers massed at the foot of the church.

The priest reached up and grabbed the ropes that hung from the crossbeam supporting the bells down the middle of the tower. He began to pull on them.

'What, what are you doing?' I shouted, terrified. 'They'll be up here in a second.'

When he didn't answer, I tried to pull the ropes away from him. But he was at least one-and-a-half times my size and twice as strong. He shrugged me off like I was a blade of grass. I landed with a thud on the paving stones. For a second I felt nothing. Then I felt a burning in the base of my spine and my legs felt numb. I lay there and stared impotently up into the huge mouths of the bells.

At first the bells didn't seem to respond. Then, slowly, they began to move, just a few inches this way and that to start with, the arc increasing a little with each rotation. But still the movement had not reached the cavernous centre and no sound emerged. The priest looked up at them and pulled harder. Suddenly, the bells found their rhythm and began to swing backwards and forwards, ringing out across the countryside, calling out for help, and at the same time singing out their anger and defiance.

I struggled up into a semi-crouch and looked down over the edge of the parapet. Men and women were massed in front of the church doors for at least a quarter of a mile down the road. Their flaming torches illuminated their upturned faces. They were all looking at the bells, fear and wonder on their faces.

Then all I could feel were the bells. Like a million tiny arrows passing through my body, the sound of the bells drowned out all other sensation. I looked at the priest. He was clinging to the ropes, swinging on them with all the transparent delight of a little boy. His eyes were shut, an expression of blissful concentration on his face. He was far away from this world, in a world of his own where nothing could touch him. And I was all alone.

I looked down. The crowd seemed to have thinned. They've gone away, I thought bitterly, the bells have scared them away. Or maybe word had got around that I was in the tower with the priest. I regretted the unhappy coincidence that had brought me to this place. The next moment, however, I realized the villagers hadn't gone away. They had only retreated to the edge of the circle of light and were getting ready to beat down the front doors of the church with a wooden battering ram.

The breeze grew stronger, whipping through my hair and fear-soaked shirt. And then, I smelt it, that first whiff of dampness mixed with dust that is the messenger of the rain.

'They're going to break down the doors of your church,' I shouted to the priest.

'Don't worry, my people will be here soon,' he shouted back through the freshening wind. 'They won't let the church burn.' He pulled at the ropes even more fiercely as he said this. The wooden platform on which we stood shook with the force of it. I looked up at the bells. They were swinging wildly back and forth, the beam on which they hung creaking ominously.

'Stop. The beam will break and the bells will crush us,' I yelled.

Suddenly, I heard a tremendous crash. I looked down. The battering ram had begun its work.

'You see, they'll be in here very soon,' I told the priest with gloomy delight.

'So will my people,' the priest answered.

'Your people are cowards,' I spat.

But the priest didn't respond. He was swinging on the ropes, his eyes closed, lips moving wordlessly in prayer.

Another crash shook the building, this time accompanied by the breaking of glass. I leaned over the parapet. On the ground below, they were cheering wildly, scenting victory. Another cry to the devi rent the air and they moved back for the third and last strike.

Suddenly, the sky was rent by roll upon roll of thunder. But so intent were the people on the ground on what they were about to accomplish that they paid no attention. My ears seemed to be the only ones listening to God's warning.

'Did you hear that thunder?' I shouted at the priest. 'That's God's way of telling you to stop this madness now, before it's too late. If you won't listen to me, at least listen to him.'

The priest's rapt expression never changed. His eyes were glazed.

'I heard them,' he muttered blissfully. 'I heard the bells.'

'That wasn't bells you heard, that was thunder,' I cried.

He looked at me pityingly. 'You don't understand. God has given me his reward,' he said. 'This was meant to be.'

I stared at him with revulsion. 'Go down and apologize before it's too late,' I begged. 'Or you will have blood spilt in God's house tonight.'

'I did nothing wrong,' he said calmly. 'You did this.'

'This is the work of your hatred,' I said, 'and it's going to get us killed.'

'You shouldn't have come here,' he said in reply. 'You set this off.'

I hung my head. Somewhere inside me a voice whispered that the priest was right. Violence needs a spectator, someone who is outside it and can appreciate its horror. Then my ears distinguished thin cries, women's voices screaming in warning, coming from the back of the crowd. A bolt of lightning flooded the village in momentary daylight and I saw an armed group of villagers running down the main street of the village towards the church. They had torches and farming implements as weapons.

The group by the church split down the middle, half of them turning to face the oncoming group and the other half continuing to slam the battering ram into the church doors.

I lunged at the priest and pulled him to the parapet. 'Look, the bloodshed is about to begin. Look!' I screamed into his face.

But the priest pulled away from me, and grabbed the ropes again. The bells began to toll, and his face took on the same rapt, faraway look.

In the next instant, two completely separate events merged. The church door split wide open and two warring groups, one Hindu and one Christian, melted into each other with a roar. And in the bell tower, the priest knelt down and began to pray, thanking God for his personal miracle.

I tore my eyes away from the spectacle of the mad priest and watched in horror as below us, the bloodshed continued. 'No, no, no,' I moaned, 'please, God, no.' But even as I did so, a part of me was already removing my mind to that safe place in the future, seeing how all this would look in cold, permanent ink, in the words of the report I would have to file later. I felt something cold and wet on my cheeks. I reached up to wipe them away, thinking they were tears. But there were too many of them. I became aware of the drops hitting my head and shoulders as well. I looked up. The bells had stilled. Their rounded surfaces were dark grey, slick and shining like the skin of wild elephants. The rain cast a blanket of silence over the sounds of battle. I watched it fall on those hot sweating bodies, on the still-warm stilled ones, on the shining grey blades and sharpened sticks and the red-brown mud. All I could hear was the sound of the rain, the hiss of the raindrops falling on leaves and the wind that whipped them off the leaves.

I don't know how long I stood there, too afraid to go down. Finally, the rain petered out. The few survivors dropped their weapons and started helping the wounded and getting them onto their feet.

I heard the priest move. I looked around. 'It's over,' I told him.

He got to his feet at last and peered over the parapet expressionlessly.

'There! Are you happy with your work?' I cried.

He stared at the carnage below us and to my horror, his mouth split into a huge yawn. It closed slowly. Then he turned and, without looking at me, began to descend the stairs.

'What are you doing?' I called after him. 'Where are you going?'

We reached the bottom of the stairs and stumbled into a nightmare. The battle had spilled into the church. Small, evil-smelling bonfires revealed the remains of burnt individuals. Others lay in pools of blood on the stone floor, many missing arms, legs, and head. The priest wove drunkenly through the bodies. Some were still alive and calling weakly for help. He stumbled down the aisle, splashing through puddles of blood, ignoring the calls for help.

'My God! What have you done, what have you done?' I moaned, unable to tear my eyes away from those astonished dying faces. Then I followed him down the aisle.

Near the door I caught up with him and forced him to turn around.

'Where are you going?' I asked.

He looked at me as if I were a stupid child.

'To sleep,' he replied casually, 'to sleep, of course.'

the cook

Soup is the crowning glory of good cooking. It is the trumpet call of victory, signalling the triumph of taste over substance, love over life. Made up of the ends of great meals and served in lieu of a beginning, a good soup is a meal in itself, not because it is the essence of an entire meal, but because it brings alive to the senses the memory of a previous meal, and the promise, veiled and mysterious, of future ones. Thus a good soup cannot be dissected. For it most closely mirrors life.

—Le Chauldron d'Or

Lunch at the restaurant ended earlier than usual. So after wiping off his workstation, Marcello Tocinelli washed his hands, hurried onto the terrace and looked up. It was a glorious day. The sky was a blazing blue, unmarred by clouds. The sun had finally acquired the promise of summer, its gentle warmth entering his flesh like butter. A delicate wind teased the curtain of lavender-coloured wisteria separating the terrace from the pantry. Beyond the patio, their little vineyard stretched in arrow-straight lines down to the lake, the new leaves a tender green against the rich black earth.

He sat down against the sun-baked pantry wall, took out a cigar from his trouser pocket and sniffed it critically. Not as good as the Davidoff but adequate, reliable. From his other pocket he took out his Swiss knife and trimmed the end. Then he lit the corona and sat back, letting the taste of Cuban earth flood his mouth. It had been a good day, he reflected. A chef's job was like a general's. He led an army of mercenaries, all of whom were highly skilled with knives. To command their respect he had to be a few steps ahead of them at all times. And he had to be able to smell trouble when it was still in the making. This wasn't difficult, provided he kept the master plan fixed firmly in his head. The plan was what regulated the life of the restaurant. It was enshrined each day in the menu. For a cook or an experienced kitchen-hand, the menu read like a diagram of battle positions and commands. With a well-formulated and carefully worked out master plan, a meal was like an intricate dance, each dancer having his or her particular set of moves. The most important thing for a chef was to be able, come what may, to keep the rhythm going. Rhythm was what regulated the flow of food from raw to cooked. If that went awry, things spun into chaos very quickly. Then the army, feeling betrayed, would run amok.

But today, all had gone well. The morning had begun, as most mornings did, with him dreaming of food. At the crucial moment, when he was about to taste the manna he had created, his eyes opened. They adjusted effortlessly to the pre-dawn grey, his heart quickening as he thought of the surprises lying in wait at the market.

Dawn had broken as he arrived, but he was blind to its beauty. His mind was intent upon what might be waiting for him inside the labyrinth of stalls. The farmers at the entrance had set up their counters in the usual way, putting the flashier vegetables, fruit and cuts of meat and game on top and the less appetizing ones at the bottom. They all recognized him and several called out to him to come and take a look at what they had. But the chef paid little heed to their cries. He knew that, as with women, the best-looking vegetables were never the most satisfying. He searched instead for the unexpected—tomatoes with the scent of rich damp earth gentling their citrus tang, or carrots of an unusually deep, almost blood-red hue. These were what inspired his most successful dishes.

But that morning his senses had remained unmoved as he searched amongst the long-armed cucumbers and violet aubergines. In the end he had been forced to buy expensive wild morels instead. Nothing smelt right any more. What were the farmers doing, he thought in mild irritation as he puffed at his cigar. Had they exhausted the earth, leached it of creativity? His eyes plunged into the trenches between the vines, seeking an answer. It must be all those chemical fertilizers they were using now.

The restless wind ruffled the surface of the lake, breaking up the reflection of the pines. No one was sailing on the lake today. It was too windy. But as always, the sight of the water calmed him. The tension eased out of his muscles and was replaced by a gentle tiredness. Another battle had been won. He took a puff of the cigar and watched idly as the smoke draped itself around his head like a scarf. Slowly his mind emptied itself.

On the other side of the curtain of wisteria, under Madame Tocinelli's eagle eye, the last few guests lingered over their dessert. Most were regulars, retired bankers with their wives and grandchildren. Only one table, a very young couple, caught her attention. They were holding hands and the man was whispering something into the young woman's ear. As she listened, her face became a picture of embarrassed delight. Then her lips quivered and her Adam's apple jumped as she burst into sudden laughter. She had a beautiful laugh, deep and unafraid, youthful and sweetly seductive. The young man sat back satisfied and took another sip of the fine dessert wine.

Behind the trellis the chef's ears pricked up. He tried to picture what kind of woman the owner of such a laugh could be. Probably in her early twenties, he decided, beautiful, sexy, eager to be corrupted. What had she eaten, he wondered. Venison, or maybe the duck. No diets for a laugh like that. Just lots of firm young flesh that sprang to the touch. Long ago he had classified women into three basic kinds: appetizers, main courses and desserts. The hors d'oeuvre was the first love, a bitter-sweet affair, destined to end before it had really begun, and to whet the appetite only. Then there was the main course, the one that nourished a man, made him comfortable. And finally, when he was ready, came the dessert, the fantasy bride, all sweetness and light, an easy conquest lacking complexity, yet such a delight for those aging hunters.

Excited, he was about to get up and take a peek, when he heard his wife saying goodbye to a guest right next to the wisteria. 'Thank you for coming, Monsieur Flavius, I hope you enjoyed the meal,' she was saying.

'Of course we did. The soup, especially, was divine. It hasn't changed a bit since I first tasted it.'

'Twenty-eight years ago ... that's when you first came here,' Madame Tocinelli volunteered. How did she remember such things, the chef wondered.

'As long as that?' the regular sounded a little embarrassed.

'Indeed it is, though recently we haven't had the pleasure of your company quite so much.'

'The loss is all mine, I confess. We'd heard ...' There was a long pause. 'Tell me, Madame, does your husband have any enemies?'

Enemies? Marcello's ears pricked up.

'Enemies? He is only a chef. Why should he have enemies?' His wife sounded nervous.

'I am afraid he does, Madame,' the man continued gravely. 'I don't want to pry into your affairs, but please think hard, it is always better to know one's enemies.'

'But even my husband's rivals are old and doing very well. People have money to eat out but no new restaurants have opened here. Young people these days are not so willing to work hard.'

The man laughed in agreement. 'Yet, someone has been spreading rumours in Geneva about your food, that it is no longer what it used to be. Those who spread these stories are so highly respected that we bankers believed them.' A dry laugh followed. 'I am happy to discover that the rumours were baseless. Yet, I am mystified, too. A baseless rumour has a source and a motive, and I cannot fathom either in this case.'

Behind the trellis, Marcello ground his teeth in frustration. He listened even more carefully.

'I am not aware of such rumours,' he heard her say calmly. 'Of course, the chef is no longer young, but his age and experience aid him in his cooking, not take away from it.'

Marcello stiffened. What had *age* to do with it? Why was Marie being defensive? He was cooking better than ever.

'Nothing can replace experience,' the man agreed. 'I promise you, my wife and I will do our best to correct the impression with our friends and colleagues. Please congratulate your husband for us. Perhaps we could invite him to share a glass of wine with us the next time.'

Behind the trellis Marcello got up to confront his wife. But just as he was about to turn the corner, he heard panicky footsteps approaching at a run. Instinctively, he pulled back.

'Mother, we have to finish this,' he heard their elder daughter, Graciella, say in a rush. 'I can't concentrate on my work any more.'

Finish what, he wondered and began to listen more carefully.

'We can't,' he heard his wife say. 'You have to watch him when he isn't looking. That way he won't suspect a thing.'

'That's easy for you to say,' Graciella answered hotly. 'You're in the front with the customers. I have to stand beside him. You know he has the eyes of a hawk where his food is concerned. He almost caught me twice.' His daughter's voice rose, filling with panic, 'I can't go on much longer. I know he's going to catch me soon. We have to find another way.'

Another way to do what, he wondered.

'There is no other way,' he heard his wife say sharply. 'If anyone finds out, we shall be finished.'

Finished? The chef's puzzlement began to turn into alarm.

'Does Amanita know?' Graciella asked sharply.

'Not yet, I wasn't expecting her to come home this month. You know how fond she is of your father.'

'You'll have to explain the plan to her and force her to keep quiet. She is such a sentimental goose.'

'But we'll need her on our side if this continues.'

'Talk to him, mama.'

'I can't.'

There was a silence. Then his wife said, 'He'll be coming out for his cigar soon. Let's discuss this inside.'

Their footsteps receded, a door banged and the chef was left alone with his thoughts. For several minutes he sat smoking and staring unseeingly at the view. His mind was in a turmoil. He didn't know where to begin, which thread to pull, to untangle the chaos of thoughts and emotions that filled his mind. All of a sudden he felt an overpowering urge to hide.

'Lunch is getting cold, papa,' his younger daughter's voice jerked him out of his troubled reverie. He looked at her blindly.

'What's the matter?' she asked, shocked by the look on his face. 'Are you not feeling well?'

'I'm fine,' he answered gruffly. 'Why are you here? Surely the food here can't be better than your highly paid mentor's works of art? You haven't been thrown out, have you?'

She looked hurt. 'That's not fair.'

She was right and he knew it. She had an Hercule Poirot of a nose, just as he did. She could tell precisely which ingredient was missing in a dish, and to what extent, simply by sniffing it. She couldn't have made a mistake if she had wanted to. Which is why it had hurt so much when she left to become a sous-chef in a hotel whose chef cared more about the way food looked than the way it tasted. Grumpily, he levered himself off the bench and followed her inside.

Over lunch, the chef was unusually quiet, taking no part in the family conversation. Talk centred on the much-awaited first grandchild.

'You have to give me at least three weeks' notice or I won't be able to come to the hospital for the delivery. They're very strict in school,' Amanita was saying seriously. The two other women burst into laughter.

'You can't plan when the baby arrives. It's the baby who will decide,' Madame Tocinelli replied, with a twinkle in her eye.

'You, for example, came three weeks late.' She tried to catch her husband's eye as she said this, but he was staring at the wall, a little frown between his eyes. 'Marcello, are you all right? Do you have a headache?' she asked.

'Why? Why do you ask?' he asked belligerently. 'I'm cooking better than ever.'

'You … you seemed in another world, that's all,' she replied, looking hurt. 'We weren't talking about your cooking.'

'Do you think it will rain again this evening?' Graciella asked hurriedly, changing the subject. 'I'm so sick of rain. Why is the summer teasing us like this? We'll have to shorten the menu for this evening if it rains.'

The chef ignored his daughter's remark. 'Lunch finished early today,' he said deliberately, closely watching his wife's face.

'It's the beginning of summer, that's all. Not your fault at all,' she stammered, a telltale blush staining her neck.

Before he could ask her what she meant by 'his fault', their younger daughter broke in. 'Does the baby also decide how much Graciella eats?' she asked, pointing at her sister's plate.

'I can't help it. It's for the baby. Besides, this salad is different today, I can't stop myself, it's so good,' Graciella replied, stealing a look at her father.

They're trying to flatter me, the chef thought. He had done nothing unusual to the salad. He was certain of that. It was one of his favourite recipes. Simple and well structured, each ingredient fit together like bits of a jigsaw puzzle. First, he had sautéed the wild mushrooms with a little parsley and butter. Then, on a separate burner, he had cooked a little ham in cream and honey and butter. He had moistened the mushrooms with vermouth while he fried paper-thin slices of kidney and a little parsley. When all the ingredients were ready, he had arranged layer upon layer as if he were building a forest temple, starting with the salad leaves, then the kidney, a slice of preserved pear, then the ham and finally the mushroom. The result was perfection. How could one improve on that?

He got up abruptly. Outside, the first few drops of rain were flattening themselves against the French windows.

'There goes our evening menu,' Graciella remarked. 'Does it rain like this on the other side of the lake too?'

'I don't know,' her sister replied, poker-faced. 'I never see the sky.'

As he shut the door he heard their laughter ring out in concert.

All of a sudden he recognized the feeling that gripped his heart. It was the feeling of being shut out.

Marcello groaned aloud. He had been too confident, he had never suspected. His mind lurched. He thought back carefully over the last few weeks. Slowly, little details, things noticed and immediately buried in the everyday rush of emergencies, began to rise to the surface of his consciousness. A knife he had just used, not quite straight. A spoon at not quite the angle he always left it.

There was the time when he returned from a trip to the ovens to find Graciella hurriedly walking away from his stoves. When he questioned her about it later, she said that she had smelt something burning and had come to check. Of course she had been wrong. Graciella didn't have the nose. But he had let it go. Pregnant women were known to be extra-sensitive to smells.

Then there was the time eight days ago when an entire dish he had prepared simply disappeared. He had sent off the first course of a complicated order for twelve and set off to fetch the partly cooked duck and the veal for the second course. When he returned, he hadn't noticed anything amiss at first. He had busied himself with the meats and only when they were cooking did he check the two burners farthest away from him, which he reserved for the fish. But the two meunières that had been ordered weren't there!

'Where are my two meunières?' he had roared.

'What fish?' Immediately, his wife had been at his elbow, looking guilty and anxious.

'The fish on two.' He looked for the pink slip that had been sitting to the right of his right eye. 'It was almost ready to go and … and it's gone.'

'How can that be so? Are you sure you didn't send it off already? I'll go look.' And she had rushed away.

He had been about to start all over again when she came back looking relieved. 'Graciella had them. She finished the plates and sent them off already. You must have forgotten.'

But Marcello knew he had never sent them to her.

It had happened again a week later. This time it was the *magrets* of duck that disappeared. And even after he shouted for them, they refused to return. So he began the process of making them all over again. When the meat was almost ready, he bent down to put the *magrets* inside the heating chamber while he finished off the sauce. And there, sitting innocently on the shelf, were the *magrets*.

He had chalked it up to forgetfulness. For none of the incidents had been serious, and they had had no visible consequences. So how was he to blame for not realizing that something strange was happening under his very nose?

Midnight was Marcello's favourite time of day. Every night after the garbage had been cleared and everyone had gone home, he would let himself out into the yard, sit on his favourite chair, an old kitchen stool, his back propped against the garbage vat, and look at the stars. The stars inspired him to do things he rarely did: remember stray lines of poetry or think about the meaning of life. Or just sit still and inhale the sweet night air.

It was a full moon night. A light breeze, the sister of the one that had lured him out the other day, made the leaves tremble, sending sparks of silver shooting through the night sky. But the beauty of the scene was lost on him. Instead, he thought about soup.

For Marcello there was something pure and magical about soup. No matter how great the chef, soup always remained mysterious and impenetrable. Of all food, soup was the trickiest thing to consistently make well. It was unpredictable. Long ago, he had realized this and stopped trying to control the outcome. Instead, he just let the soup go the way it wanted, trying, like a humble priest, to intuit its desires. All his soups were songs of love dedicated to a single woman: his wife. For she was the only woman who completed him, and made him feel invincible. To make a good soup, one had to know what it was to love and be loved like that. This was the thing he couldn't explain. So he never let anyone else make the soup. And only his wife was allowed to taste it.

But that morning, when his wife had put the first spoonful into her mouth, an alien expression had flashed across her face.

'What's the matter?' he had demanded.

'I don't know. It tastes different today.'

'What do you mean, it tastes different? Every soup tastes different. Every soup *is* different. You should know that by now.'

She had tasted it again, thought a little, then pushed the spoon away and shrugged. 'You're right. It just tastes a little less wonderful than normal, though.' Then she had added, 'But one can't be perfect all the time. Don't worry. The tourists won't be able to tell the difference. Luckily, it's a Saturday today.'

When he had recovered from the insult, he asked her what she meant and she looked away, not meeting his eyes. 'I'm ... not sure, but maybe you should let one of the girls taste it.' She had looked at him then, and he had seen the flash of eagerness there.

That had been too much for him. 'I won't have anyone touching my soup. Do you understand?' he had snapped.

After she had gone, he had tasted the soup himself. But he could taste nothing wrong with it.

By then the first few orders had come in and so he had gone to his workstation. Two appetizers and a main course were waiting to be made. He set to work immediately and was soon absorbed in constructing the morel salad when a nervous voice interrupted him.

'Excuse me.'

He looked up. A red-haired college graduate of a waiter stood before him. Marcello glared at the man.

'What do you want?'

'N-nothing, sir, I was looking for Madame.'

'She's by the soup,' Marcello snapped, not looking up from the salad.

'Yes sir, that is the problem.' The young man put a bowl of soup down on the counter. 'Th-they sent this back,' he stuttered, going red.

'What?' Marcello felt himself grow cold, and then hot. He stared at the soup bowl as if he were looking at a scorpion.

He looked over to where the soup stood. The women were gone. But in his mind's eye he could see them still, whispering over the soup like witches. He grabbed the bowl from the waiter and sniffed it. The soup had grown cold and so its smell had faded. He threw it away and started towards the soup tureen, then, halfway there, changed his mind.

'Give the man a terrine instead. And tell him that soup is for humans, not pigs.'

The waiter's eyes grew round. His jaw fell open.

'Don't stand there looking like a sheep. Get on with it,' Marcello shouted.

The kitchen went quiet. Such a thing had never happened before. The waiter was the first to recover.

'Yes, sir.' He bobbed his head and almost ran to the prep area.

Marcello stalked back to his stoves. His elder child was still missing. He began to prepare the next order, his mind troubled.

When Graciella returned, Marcello was finishing the orange sauce for the duck. He looked up and asked her pointedly if the turnips were ready. She gave him a half-guilty, half-frightened smile and hurriedly set to work. He let her begin, then asked casually, 'What were you doing by the soup?'

Graciella jumped, and a little butter fell out of the pan and sizzled on the flame. 'N-nothing,' she replied. 'Just admiring it.'

Marcello stopped stirring the sauce in irritation. She was lying to him. Even if the waiter hadn't come to him, and if he hadn't seen her by the soup, he would have known she was lying.

'People don't stand around in the middle of a busy luncheon, admiring soup,' he snapped.

Graciella went red. 'Bu-but—'

'Stop stammering and speak properly,' he ordered. 'What about the soup? How is it you don't sniff my soup every day?'

'I wanted them to taste it,' his wife said, appearing suddenly.

He turned around. 'What are you doing here? I wasn't asking you.'

'But it was my decision,' his wife replied. 'It's time the girls learnt how to make your soup. I wanted the girls to taste it so that they can understand and learn.'

That's when the truth had hit Marcello. The secret enemy was none other than his own wife. *And she wanted the girls to learn his secrets so they could take over.*

'Don't be upset, my love, I'm only doing it for the restaurant,' she said, looking anxious.

'I'm not upset. There are three orders on hold. I can't afford to be upset,' he snapped.

She hadn't replied. Instead, she had turned and walked away.

Marcello shifted uncomfortably on his seat. Thinking about it hurt even more. Why the secrecy? If they wanted to take over, all they had to do was ask. He was bored of the routine, the unremitting demands of the kitchen. He would love to give it all up and travel, become a hunter once again, even meet new women. Perhaps he could take his wife on a world tour. They had always wanted to go to Tahiti together.

All of a sudden Marcello went icy cold. He remembered the early days when his father-in-law, the chef, had been the unquestioned ruler of the 'Chauldron a Quatre Pas', as it was then called. Marcello had been a lowly grill boy, the good-for-nothing child of an Italian poacher. But the lowly grill boy married the chef's daughter, and each night, as his father-in-law taught him his secrets, he and his bride had dreamt of the day when it would be their turn to run the restaurant. What wondrous dishes would they not concoct!

A dull singing began in Marcello's brain, spreading through his entire body. He would not give up his restaurant. People came there to eat *his* food, to learn about pleasure, and comfort, and a little sensuality—from *him*. He wouldn't let them down. He stood up. The night was enveloped in stillness. He could hear his heart beating fast and irregular. Suddenly, a cat jumped onto the garbage vat, shattering the silence. It froze there, a black shadow against the sky. He stared at it for a while. The cat looked back, unafraid. It was a new one, jet-black except for the star at its throat. Gently, he put his hand out. He would become a hunter once again, he swore to himself. Then he turned abruptly and stalked into the house, never noticing the worried pair of eyes watching him from the master bedroom.

Marcello's dreams that night were strange and disturbing. Scenes from the past replayed themselves in almost unbearable detail. Twice he woke up in a cold sweat, seeing his father-in-law's accusing face. Then he would remember everything again.

One little detail continued to bother him. He couldn't figure out *who* they were going to replace him with. Amanita was the obvious choice. But he had heard them say that she was not a part of their conspiracy yet. How could they be sure she would go along with it? His wife would never leave such a crucial part of her plan to chance. There had to be someone else. He tossed it around in his mind but couldn't come up with an answer. Eventually he fell asleep. Only to dream again.

The next morning Marcello awoke unrefreshed. He had been dreaming of fennel, its twin cheeks very white, like a woman's bottom. They came together in a sensual curve to form a slim, translucent green waist. He could feel the cool firm vegetable flesh, its sluggish life throbbing under his palm. Then he woke up. Silently, he got out of bed and dressed.

A few minutes later, Graciella was dragged out of an equally troubled and erotic dream.

'Wake up.' She opened her eyes to find her father gently shaking her awake.

'What is it?' she sat up in alarm. 'Is maman all right?'

'Yes, she's fine,' he answered impatiently. 'Get dressed quickly, we're going to the market.'

In the van they were silent. Graciella was still three-quarters asleep, and Marcello, now that he had Graciella with him, didn't know how he should approach her. The market was once again a disappointment. No new scents at all. And even the familiar ones seemed tired and withdrawn. He let her take the lead in the buying, watching her make many of the mistakes of the novice. At last they were finished and he led her to the café at the mouth of the market.

'You have wonderful hands, and a sure eye,' he flattered her. 'Essential ingredients in a chef.'

She looked surprised. 'Thank you, father, but I have a long way to go. And I don't know if I want to be a chef.' Unconsciously she patted her swollen stomach.

'Of course you do,' he agreed. 'There's a lot you still have to learn, but I can teach you everything you need to know.'

She blushed. 'Thank you, but I am quite content doing what I do.'

That was the old Graciella talking. Marcello felt his love for her swamp him. 'Do you love me?' he asked.

She leaned away from him, a worried frown on her face. 'Of course, papa! Why do you ask?'

He was the first to look away, embarrassed. 'Oh. I just wondered.' He began to doubt whether he was being foolish, whether it wasn't just a daylight version of his standard nightmare of a recipe going irretrievably wrong.

But Graciella's next remark put his hopes to flight. 'Papa, you haven't been acting yourself lately,' she said.

'What do you mean?'

'Well,' she licked her lips, 'th-there have been some mistakes.'

'Mistakes? What are you talking about?'

'In the f-food.'

A cold little hand squeezed his heart. He couldn't wait any longer. 'Stop talking nonsense. I never make mistakes.' His eyes narrowed. 'Why is she making you spy on me?' He leaned closer. 'Tell me, what is she planning?'

The effect of his question was spectacular. Graciella,

innocently lifting her coffee to her mouth, spilt it all over herself. She leapt up, muttered something incoherent and rushed away.

Marcello ground his teeth and waited for her to come back. But when she returned she wasn't alone.

'I said we could give him a lift. He has an urgent message for Matthias,' she explained. Matthias was the headwaiter.

'Why can't he just call him later?' Marcello asked suspiciously.

'He says Matthias refuses to speak with him on the telephone.'

Marcello eyed the delicate young man. He hardly seemed the kind of man their muscle-bound headwaiter usually went for.

'You a friend of Matthias?' he asked doubtfully.

'Of course he is,' Graciella replied impatiently, loading their parcels into the boy's arms and pushing him towards the car.

There was nothing for Marcello to do but follow in silence. One thing a hunter could not afford was to be impatient.

Both Amanita and his wife hurried out into the yard to help them unload. His wife looked both worried and furious. Amanita looked serious but serene, like she always did. Marcello wondered if his wife had spoken to Amanita yet. He smiled at his youngest child. She looked surprised, then smiled back shyly. His heart lifted. Not yet. He let them do the unloading and went off to check on his stocks. But halfway down the stairs an idea struck him and he dashed up the stairs into their little sitting room-cum-study. If he knew his wife, as soon as they finished the unloading, she would bring Graciella in there for a little 'talk'.

He entered the room and looked around for a place to hide. At the far end was another door, behind which were the stairs leading up to the bedrooms. He tucked himself into the shallow curve of the stairs, leaving the door slightly ajar. Marcello didn't have to wait for long. He had barely squeezed himself into the alcove when he heard a door opening cautiously.

'What did you tell him?' Madame Tocinelli asked as soon as the door was shut.

'Nothing,' her daughter answered, walking into the centre of the room.

'But you were with him for the better part of two hours. What did you talk of?'

'We didn't talk much. We just shopped. He showed me what to look for in the market and what to avoid.'

'Good. You had better learn that side of the business, too. Marcello always swears all suppliers are cheats. Did you ask him about the orange sauce?'

'No. Because then he asked me if I loved him and … and I spilled the coffee all over myself.'

'What? That's crazy.'

'That's what I thought myself,' Graciella agreed.

'Maybe he's sensed something,' his wife's voice faltered.

'I'm sure he hasn't. He's always been emotional,' Graciella said quickly.

Why is she not telling her mother the rest, Marcello wondered, intrigued. He leaned forward to push open the door a little more so he could get a glimpse of them. Then he remembered that the door creaked and pulled his hand back. But something squeaked anyway. He froze, his hand still extended.

'What was that?' his wife asked sharply.

'What?'

'That sound—like a footstep on the stairs.'

'Oh, don't worry, that's probably a rat, or Amanita moving about upstairs.'

'Amanita hasn't gone upstairs.'

'Then it's a rat. I see them when I come down at night to turn the dough.' Suddenly, Graciella changed the subject. 'What about Amanita? Have you told her?'

There was a pause. 'I forgot,' his wife admitted finally.

Graciella let out an exasperated sigh. 'My god, you had all the time in the world to do it and you forgot? It's your restaurant, too, maman. Do you want to save it or not?'

'I know, but I can't bear to tell her. Guilt is such a heavy burden.'

'But you have to, we don't have a choice. She must be made to keep her mouth shut.'

Marcello felt sick. How had he given birth to such a snake, such an actress?

His wife sighed heavily. 'You're right. I'm sorry. I'll tell her as soon as I can. You're sure he suspects nothing?'

'I'm sure.'

'Thank god, I was so worried when I woke up and found the two of you missing.'

Marcello heard their footsteps move towards the other door. It creaked as one of them pushed it open. He waited for the door to click so he could get out of his hiding place. But the sound never came. He waited, meditating on the perfidy of women. His back began to cramp and he became conscious of his body and the awkward position it was in. He listened to the distant sounds coming down the hallway. Nothing was what it seemed any more. At last the pain outweighed his fear of discovery. He eased himself into the recently vacated room and sat down heavily on one of his wife's flowered sofas. A thoroughly colonized room, he thought disgustedly. His wife had left her mark on everything except the wooden panelling. Things seemed far worse than he had imagined. Clearly Amanita was not the fulcrum of their plan, someone else was. But who? The father of Graciella's child was in Australia. Besides, he was a hopeless cook. The cramp got worse instead of better. Marcello grimaced in pain, wondering how he would cook. Could Jean, his butter-fingered third year from Lausanne, be allowed to take over? Or should he try to train his Turkish grill man? Then he remembered Amanita and brightened.

Suddenly, his wife put her head through the door.

'What is it?' he barked.

'There you are. The butcher was looking for you.'

'Tell him to go to hell.' The pain in his back was excruciating.

She looked at him curiously. 'What are you doing here?'

'I got a cramp coming up the stairs, so I came in here.'

Immediately, she was all concern. 'Where is it? What did you do to it? Shall I call a doctor? Were you trying to carry something too heavy? Here, let me see.'

He flinched at her touch, but she pretended not to notice, her clever fingers finding the twisted muscles at once and kneading them lovingly. The muscles began to respond and with them something else awoke too: an avalanche of memories, long-dormant feelings, and finally desire—sharp and spicy. Her fingers trembled suddenly, then they went on moving as if nothing had changed. Neither of them spoke. Why didn't she say something, Marcello thought unhappily. Didn't she know he would happily step down if she wanted him to?

'There.' She stopped.

When it dawned on his astonished brain that his back no longer hurt, he got up and walked out of the room without a backward glance. How dare his wife try to seduce him even as she cut his throat?

The door banged. Madame Tocinelli hardly moved. She stared at her hands for a long time. Then she got up and left, too.

His mind in a whirl, Marcello went hunting for his daughter. But it was almost eleven before he could get to her. First, the butcher had to be coffee-d and fed while Matthias, his assistant, checked the meats. Then there were other things to be inventoried, orders to be given, stocks prepared, meats to be hung and others marinated. By the time Marcello entered the pantry, it was almost time for the show to begin. Quickly, he called his younger daughter to him. 'I want you to work beside me today. Let's see what your fancy hotel school has taught you,' he told her. She looked surprised but followed him without another word.

Seeing him enter the room, Graciella had stood up. She watched her sister walk away with the chef and sensed what he was going to do. She bit her lip in frustration. Why had she hesitated? She should have spoken to Amanita herself, not left it to her sentimental mother. She resolved to speak to her sister the first chance she got.

Though his wife and daughter hovered over them like anxious bees around the queen, Marcello ignored them. He concentrated on his youngest one, keeping a sharp eye on her as they worked silently, side by side. Twenty minutes into the second service, he realized he was enjoying himself. Having Amanita's dark, intelligent eyes follow his smallest gesture, sparkle with understanding at his clever little short cuts and glow with approval at his inspired and complex moves, brought back a pleasure in cooking that had been missing for some time.

But towards the end of the meal he remembered why he had brought her there in the first place. He looked around. Miraculously, both his wife and eldest daughter were absent. Marcello seized his opportunity.

'Has your mother spoken to you?' he whispered to his youngest daughter.

She looked up in surprise. 'About what?'

'About the *plan*.'

'What plan?'

He smiled, scenting an opening. 'So you really don't know?'

She frowned. 'Know what?'

'What your mother and sister are up to.'

'No. What do you mean?' Amanita bit her lip in confusion.

Just then his wife returned, suspicion written all over her face. 'Everything all right here?' she asked. She turned to her daughter. 'Your father hasn't been drinking too much of the wine, has he?'

She pulled out a near-empty bottle of their best Bordeaux from under the table.

Marcello didn't react. She's trying to discredit me, he thought. Make me seem like an alcoholic. Clever woman.

'I was asking my daughter here if she truly loved me,' he said to his wife. Then he turned to his daughter. 'Do you?'

Amanita looked from one to the other. 'Of course I do,' she said at last, 'but ...'

Marcello interrupted. 'And you'd do anything for me, anything I asked you?'

She looked even more confused, even a little scared. 'I ... uh ... I don't know ... probably. What's going on, why are you asking me these questions?'

Suddenly, his wife lost her temper.

'Stop this,' she snapped, her voice rising. 'Don't drag her into your stupid games. I don't know what you think you're doing, Marcello, but you've got to stop. You are going to ruin the restaurant.'

'I thought that was your idea,' he replied calmly, seething inwardly.

Amanita stared at the two of them. She had never seen them fight in the kitchen.

Madame Tocinelli flushed. 'You're impossible,' she muttered, giving up unexpectedly.

Before Marcello could savour his victory, a rush of new orders swamped them.

Orders came in an unrelenting stream and they all worked solidly till the meal was almost over. Then Graciella wandered off to take care of desserts. Marcello wiped the sweat from his eyes and went in search of some beer. Summer was a nightmare for chefs, the heat outside adding to the torture of the kitchen. Suddenly, he felt ready to give it all up.

When he returned with his beer, he had come to a decision. 'I'm going out,' he told his daughter abruptly.

But she stopped him. 'Papa, what's happening? Are you and maman fighting? Is it important?' Her voice faltered over the last question.

Marcello paused in the process of untying his apron. He looked into her worried eyes and felt a surge of sadness. But also of relief. In a low voice, he told her what he knew. Then he told her the rest, how he had overheard his wife and Graciella plotting, culminating in the incident of the soup.

Amanita was horrified. 'But why? And who would they put in your place? No one can cook like you,' she cried.

'You,' he replied.

'Me? But I'm just—'

'No,' he cut her short, 'you have the nose, you'll be every bit as good as I am—in time.'

'But I'm happy where I am.' She began to look mulish. 'I don't want to come back. Besides, I could never take your place.'

Marcello felt a rush of relief. Suddenly, his wife reappeared.

'We're almost done,' she said unnecessarily.

'Good. Then I'm going for a smoke,' he replied, trying to sound normal. He decided to leave and let his wife hammer the last few nails into her coffin.

'Good,' she said absently, her attention concentrated on their youngest daughter.

Marcello smiled secretly and left.

After he was out of sight, mother and daughter faced each other. 'By now you must have noticed how strangely your father's behaving,' Madame Tocinelli began. She caught sight of the beer. 'Has he been drinking too much? Is that the problem?' Amanita looked at the veal reduction she was making and didn't reply. Her heart felt cold.

'I didn't want to tell you earlier because I didn't want to worry you,' Madame Tocinelli continued. 'But he's been doing strange things. His cooking … there have been mistakes.'

'I know what you're doing,' Amanita cut her off coldly.

'Has Graciella spoken to you already?' she asked eagerly. 'Thank god.'

She looked at Amanita's troubled face and explained, 'I know you don't approve, but we have no choice. It's just till we know what's wrong with him.'

'Maman, I know,' Amanita cut her off. 'I know about the plan,' she added unhappily.

'So Graciella already spoke to you. I am so happy. We need you, my dear. I'm so glad you're back.'

Amanita could bear it no longer. 'I won't do it!' she shouted and rushed out.

Outside, in the sunshine, Marcello hummed a little song as he trimmed his cigar. Things were going well, he reckoned. Cracks were appearing in the ranks of his adversaries. He felt suddenly young again. He was the hunter once more, the one who knew how to be as still as a rock and wait for his prey to come to him. That was the strangest thing about hunting, he thought to himself, the hunted always came to the hunter. He never understood why others hadn't noticed this. Perhaps because it was so inexplicable, so bizarre—the fascination of the living for death. He had never had to chase his prey, ever.

Suddenly, his youngest daughter burst onto the terrace, her face red with unshed tears. She came and sat on the bench beside him. After a minute, Amanita had mastered herself enough to speak. 'You were right, papa,' she said, 'I'm sorry I didn't believe you at first.'

He continued to smoke and waited for her to go on. After a pause, Amanita told him about her conversation with her mother, her words coming out hesitantly.

'But why? Did she tell you that?' Marcello asked when she had finished.

Amanita shook her head.

'Did you ask her?'

She looked down at her hands.

Marcello wanted to shake her, but controlled himself. 'Did you at least find out a little more about the plan?'

She looked bewildered. 'I thought you knew everything already,' she answered.

'I do ... almost,' he said gruffly. 'But I wanted to be sure. I wanted to hear it from her mouth.'

'Ask her then.' His daughter looked beseechingly at him.

Marcello looked away. He didn't want the game to end now, just when he was beginning to enjoy it.

Amanita chewed at her lips and looked frowningly at the lake.

'But you're right. And they're wrong.' She turned to him, her expression bleak. 'I will help you, papa. Tell me what I have to do.'

Suddenly, she no longer looked a child. Remorse twisted his gut. But it wasn't his game. *She* had started it. Marcello pulled Amanita to him and gave her a big hug. 'Don't worry. It'll be easy, you'll see. We're going to win this together. Just stay close to me when I'm cooking, watch my back at all times, and spy on them when they are not looking. That's all.' He said it as matter-of-factly as possible.

She gave a long shudder. He felt the tremors enter his own

body and his anger flared. How could his wife do this to them? Had she fallen for another man? Was that why she had lost her head so completely?

'When they talk to you again, pretend to be convinced. Let them think you're on their side.'

She snuggled closer to him, trying to stop the tremors that ran through her body.

'Good,' he told her briskly, 'now go inside and begin. I'm counting on you.'

He finished his cigar.

It was a hot day and all the French windows leading into the dining room were open. Reluctantly, Amanita entered. She was immediately pounced upon and dragged into the little anteroom. Graciella put a hand over Amanita's mouth to keep her quiet. 'Wait. I must talk to you in private,' she whispered. Then, satisfied that Amanita would not run away, she went over to the windows, shut them and hurriedly drew the curtains.

Marcello watched the curtains being drawn. He sat very still. It had begun. He looked across the terrace to the windows on the other side of the room. The curtains were already drawn on that side, but someone had forgotten to shut one of the windows. He got up, flattened himself against the brick wall, and inched his way along it till he came to the open dining-room windows. Then, lifting his considerable bulk onto his toes, he ran till he reached the safety of the other wall. As he drew nearer, he heard the low murmur of voices. He crept closer until he could almost touch the curtains. But he couldn't make out what the voices were saying. He touched the joint between the curtains and wondered if he dared open it. Too risky, he decided, light pouring into a dark room would immediately attract attention. So, instead, he pressed his ear against the heavy cloth.

Inside the room, Graciella faced her sister.

'By now you've probably got some idea of what's going on here,' she began, 'but I doubt you've any idea of what's really happening.'

Amanita shook her head obediently. She knew she wasn't

expected to reply—she was a nobody, an upstart who had come six years later.

'Good.' Graciella gave her a superior 'just-do-what-I-say-and-things-will-work-out' look. 'The restaurant is in terrible danger. And the danger is our father. Luckily, I've been managing to control the damage so far, so no one knows.'

She began to stride up and down the carpet as she told her story. 'It began with the customers. We noticed funny expressions on some of our regulars' faces as the food was put before them. This turned to confusion after the first few bites and plates were left half-finished. Then there were the strange silences when maman asked them if they'd enjoyed their meal. And then some of our regulars stopped coming altogether. Then M. Fabius told mother that rumours had begun to multiply in Geneva about the food not being what it used to be. When mother told me, I didn't believe her. I told her it had to be a plot. Maybe the trainee sous-chef was trying to give the restaurant a bad name. Then one day I tasted something father had made. You know, a quick finger in the pan when he wasn't looking, like we did so often as children.' She gave a bitter laugh. 'It was off. Something was missing. I couldn't figure it out at first, I don't have your nose. It came to me as I was baking that night. He'd forgotten to put celery in the liqueur for the béchamel sauce. Can you imagine that?'

She told the story well, Amanita thought bitterly. 'How terrible,' she agreed docilely. 'What can I do?'

'You can help us by staying close to him and making sure he makes no more mistakes. Tell us what he's thinking. Find out why he's doing it. I think he suspects maman and me. But you, you are still the apple of his eye.'

Thus, you keep me occupied spying on my father while you and maman do your mischief, Amanita thought silently.

A gust of wind off the lake blew the curtains wide open. Marcello pressed himself back against the stone wall hastily. But he caught Graciella's last words and felt both angry and sad. She was such a convincing liar. He gripped a bit of the curtain so he could hear better, wishing he had heard what had been said before.

But the curtains swallowed half the syllables, turning the words into gibberish.

Suddenly, a hand touched his shoulder. He leapt backwards.

'What are you doing here?' his wife asked.

'What are *you* doing here?' he returned. 'You almost gave me a heart attack, I thought you were inside, too.'

She looked perplexed. 'I was in the corridor when I saw you cross the terrace on your toes. I was about to call out to you, but you suddenly disappeared. I thought something must have happened to you, so I came out,' she explained.

'I was looking for you, that's all,' Marcello said grumpily, 'and I was exercising.'

'Then why are you standing outside if you thought I was inside?'

'I—' Marcello stopped. 'I was thinking of going inside.' He felt his ears burning. But his wife didn't seem to notice. She pushed aside the curtains and walked inside.

'I found him, he was just outside.'

They all stared at him. She's trying to make me look stupid, Marcello thought angrily. He sat down as casually as he could in his favourite armchair. It felt alien and hard. No one spoke, or moved. He shifted uncomfortably and tried to find a neutral space of wall to look at.

'What's the matter?' he growled, giving up and glaring at them. 'What are you staring at?'

They looked away hurriedly.

'Would you like some lunch?' his wife asked after a few minutes.

'I'm not hungry.'

'Are you feeling ill? Maybe you are catching a cold. Would you like to lie down and rest a little?' she suggested.

'I'm fine. I went for a walk, I feel better than ever before, full of energy and good spirits,' he replied impatiently. At least the last bit wasn't a lie, he told himself fiercely. He was enjoying this.

'But you've never gone for a walk at lunch time,' his wife pointed out.

'So what? I am not a farmer … I don't have habits. Habits can get you killed. I will go for a walk whenever I feel like it. The restaurant can manage without me.' He laughed in what he hoped was a masterful manner. 'You'd like that, wouldn't you, to manage without me?'

Silence descended upon the room. Amanita began to knead her hands together nervously.

'Shall we watch some TV?' Marcello asked innocently.

They looked stunned. 'But you … you never watch television!' his wife exclaimed.

'My family does. So now I will, too. I am joining my family at last.'

Amanita looked bewildered and opened her mouth to say something, but her sister nudged her in the ribs. Madame Tocinelli hurriedly switched on the television. On the screen, someone was beating egg yolks in a large stainless steel bowl.

'You mustn't forget to separate the white and the yellow of the eggs,' a creamy voice said.

Marcello stared at the screen in fascination. The yellow liquid looked unbelievably yellow and each little bubble on its surface glistened with a dozen rainbows. It looked like an enormous lake of egg yolk set into a curved silver moonscape.

'How wonderful, a cooking show! You can learn everything on TV these days,' he remarked to the room. None of the family responded. He continued to stare at the screen. Beaten egg whites, forming stiff white peaks, were added to the bowl of egg yolk and allowed to float atop the yellow lake like virgin icebergs.

'I always like my omelettes really fluffy,' the smooth voice said.

Omelettes? Marcello sat up. The man was going to make omelettes like that? Omelettes weren't beaten, they were given a few lazy turns with a pair of forks. Marcello stared at the screen disbelievingly. The bowl with eggs was suddenly replaced by a frying pan containing something minced that had been browned to death, sitting in an orange liquid.

'Now we start stage two,' the voice said authoritatively.

Marcello stared hard. You didn't drown the ingredients of an omelette in a sauce. What was the man doing? His irritation mounted as Chinese mushroom, shrimp, basil, coriander and mint were added to the mixture. Suddenly, he realized what the orange colour of the liquid came from. It was paprika. The man was putting foreign spices into a French omelette!

'What is the man doing?' he burst out, unable to contain himself any more.

'Omelette Indo-Chine,' Graciella replied.

He turned and glared at her. 'Omelette *what*?'

'Indo-Chine. It's very fashionable in Sydney, I believe. They even make it in Paris now,' Graciella said, her eyes intent on the screen.

'That's an abomination.' He watched in horror as mussels were added to the mess in the pan. He tried to shut his eyes. But some terrible force kept them wide open and fixed on the screen.

'Keep stirring so that there is a nice exchange of fluids,' the buttery voice continued. 'There, now! The ingredients are nicely sated, oops, I mean saturated.' He laughed and an invisible audience roared. 'And now we can put it aside and get on with the making of the omelette. Hold on, it's almost ready now. But first we break for a few commercials.'

Marcello began to feel ill and was about to switch off the television when suddenly the screen opened out and the cook came into view. Marcello goggled at the owner of the smooth voice. For it was none other than Hubert, Graciella's fiancé.

'Oh my God, no!' he groaned, closing his eyes at last. The soothing music of a commercial felt like lime being applied on his already lacerated heart. Marcello couldn't bear it any more. He switched off the TV. The others looked at him angrily.

What are you looking at me like that for?' he demanded.

'Why did you do that?' Graciella demanded. 'Just because you're in a bad mood, don't turn it on us.'

'He's a fake! You can't make an omelette like that. Even you should know that.'

'So what? That's Hubert's new programme. He looks great

on TV,' Graciella replied.

'But he can't cook. That's why he left.'

'Of course he can cook, that was just for TV. He had to make it look good. And look how well he did it,' Graciella defended Hubert.

'He's lying about the food. He's not a cook if he can lie about food.'

'So what, it's TV. Everybody knows it's not real,' Graciella snapped.

'All the more reason not to lie! Thousands of people, including children and young women, will try to make an omelette like that and will be heartbroken when it doesn't work.'

'No one will be heartbroken. Don't be so dramatic. No one tries these recipes at home anyway. They're far too complicated and too expensive.'

'They aren't complicated. They don't work.'

'How do you know? You've never made anything except boring French food all your life. You don't even know there's a world outside France and Switzerland, and maybe Italy.'

'And just because he's stolen a few of the slit-eyed people's spices, he thinks he's a genius. That's not how you create a dish. He's just pretending. *Menteur*. Just because he has to show he's original, different,' he spat out the two words, 'he is deliberately destroying our cuisine, mixing Oriental spices into an ordinary seafood omelette and giving it an exotic name, and you think that's okay? That's theft firstly, lying second, and third, it's vandalism. He's destroying history there. Now millions of people will think that the Orientals conquered France sometime in the last four hundred years and that's where we got our food from,' Marcello shot back.

'You exaggerate, Marcello. Hubert is a good man,' Madame Tocinelli defended him. 'He's your daughter's fiancé, remember?'

Marcello couldn't believe his ears—his own wife was defending the impostor, the destroyer of civilizations, against him. He turned on her, ready to fire a blast so strong that it would send her to China. Then it hit him. She had just given herself away. The pattern lay before him in all its diabolical simplicity. Hubert, the baby-faced, butter-mouthed slug, was to be his replacement at the Chauldron d'Or!

'So, it's the money then,' he said bitterly.

His wife looked bewildered. 'What money?'

'I'm not able to bring in the customers the way I used to. So you want to replace me with a TV cook who'll bring in the sheep and the cows to graze on TV food.'

'I didn't want to tell you, but you leave me no choice.' She looked pained. 'There have been complaints, and some of our customers have stopped coming as regularly as they used to.'

Marcello turned away. He began to feel sick. 'So you want me to leave, then?' he asked.

'Leave? What are you talking about? Marcello, are you unwell?'

'There's nothing wrong with me,' he snapped. 'Don't turn your guilt into a disease and inflict it on me.'

'You've been acting strange all week. Maybe you should rest.'

'So that you can do all the cooking,' he sneered. 'Do you think you can really do that?'

She looked at him, perplexed. Then she turned to the girls. 'Go outside for a minute, girls,' she ordered. They got up and left the room through the French windows. Then she turned to him again. 'Marcello, what are you talking about? I can't seem to follow you at all.' She lowered her voice. 'Tell me what the matter is. I'll call a doctor. You've upset the girls enough today, already. Graciella says she's unable to concentrate on what she's doing because you've been behaving so erratically.'

Aha! She's played her trump. The children. Now she knows I'll melt, I'll begin to doubt, and to fear. Then I'll be in her power. Suddenly, he was overwhelmed by sadness at the way she was shamelessly manipulating him, using her knowledge of him, acquired through years of togetherness, to shred his resolve.

'Why are you bringing the children into this?' he asked. 'If you want me to leave so you can take over, just say so. I don't mind. You're my wife.'

'What are you talking about? Have you gone mad, Marcello?' Now she was angry. 'Why on earth would I want you to leave?'

Why was she denying it? Marcello's eyes narrowed. The game was more complex than it seemed. He needed to think. 'Maybe I just need some food,' he muttered and walked towards the kitchen.

Once in the kitchen, he turned around, half expecting her to have followed him. But she hadn't. His shoulders sagged, partly in relief and partly out of disappointment. He wandered aimlessly through the kitchen. His hands touched the cold counters with a new awareness. His eyes lingered on the shining curves of the copper-bottomed pots, the saucepans, the frying pans, and came to rest on the old, blackened cast-iron frying pan, wiped, never washed, sitting proudly on the gas range. His kingdom. Would he ever forget it, once it was no longer his?

He decided on an omelette, so he could wipe out the image of the 'other' one. He broke three eggs into a bowl and beat them lightly with a double fork. He added the seasonings and beat it a few more times. He took fresh goat's cheese, some spring onions, parsley and a little leftover watercress and kept it ready. To it, he added a little ham. He heated the butter and then slid the eggs lovingly into the pan. He tilted the pan and let the liquid coat the surface. He let the flame do its work. When the eggs began to firm, he dropped in a spoonful of crème fraiche, waited till it merged with the liquid at the centre, and then threw in the rest of the ingredients. He watched the omelette thicken and rise. Ah, perfection! He looked up, wishing there was someone to see it. But all he was met with was silence. He slipped the omelette onto a plate and went outside. But the patio felt too exposed, too visible, and so he walked down the garden, through the neighbours' vineyard, to the lake. He sat down on the small wooden jetty and began to eat his omelette. But such was his emotional upheaval that he couldn't taste it. Marcello gave up and threw the remaining bit at a raven sitting on a wooden mooring at the end of the jetty.

The omelette flew past the bird and landed with a soft plop in the water. The bird didn't move. It just looked at Marcello with a steady black stare. Marcello shivered suddenly. He didn't like ravens. The only hunter a raven was intimate with was death. And that was one hunter Marcello was afraid of. He scowled at the bird. Somehow, the way it was staring at him so calmly, so confidently, reminded him of his wife. He winced.

'Papa.'

He gave a start. Amanita appeared at the top of the vineyard, searching for him. For a second he contemplated staying where he was. 'I'm here,' he answered, getting to his feet.

Amanita's face brightened. She ran to him and gave him a hug.

He put his arm around her shoulders and together they walked back to the house.

'So it's Hubert, isn't it?' he asked when they were nearing the top.

'What are you talking about?'

'He's the one who'll replace me, isn't it?'

'I-I ... don't know. They didn't say.'

He dug his fingers into her shoulders. 'You lie. They must have told you.'

With a small cry Amanita tore herself from his grasp and disappeared.

'What were you doing to her?' his wife demanded, suddenly appearing on the terrace.

They stared at each other in silence.

'Don't hurt the children, or I'll put you into the asylum myself.'

Suddenly he smiled. 'I'm changing the menu for the wedding party tonight,' he told her.

Her face froze. 'What do you mean? You can't do that. I already discussed the menu with Madame Martin last night.'

'I don't see why I let you make the menu when you can't cook to save your life.'

'You asked me to make the menu,' she reminded him coldly.

He refused to be distracted. 'Well, I've changed my mind. Menus are too important to be left to an amateur. I'll give the

Martins a menu they won't forget.'

Her face tightened, but she cleverly changed tack. 'But what about the ingredients?'

'Leave it to me,' he said, waving his hand grandly. 'I will contrive.'

He began to walk inside. But she caught his arm, her expression beseeching.

'What do you mean to do?' she asked.

Marcello felt a tremendous sadness well up inside. When had their love died? Why hadn't he seen it?

'Maria...'

'Yes?' she said softly. But her face had changed. A certain calculation had come into it. Marcello pulled back.

'Don't worry,' he said gruffly. 'You'll see, I'm not as dispensable as you think.'

'What do you mean?' She pulled away. 'I never thought you were dispensable. I always—' Spots of colour rode her cheekbones.

He cut her short impatiently. 'I am going to make a meal no one will ever forget.'

'But why? Why now? Do it ... do it some other time, when we can plan things.'

'Plan things!' he spat. 'Farmers plan for cows, sheep, vegetables, wheat. If they could, they'd plan the weather. But a human being is different. He is like wind, fire, and water. A human being doesn't plan things, he changes things.'

His wife backed away from him, looking uncertain. He felt a surge of triumph. 'Now leave me alone. I have to concentrate,' he ordered.

In the silent study, Marcello stared at a sheet of blank paper, pen in hand. Menus were like clothes, he thought disdainfully. They could hide what they were supposed to show, or show what they were supposed to hide. An Omelette Indo-Chine, for example, was a name so enormously rich and seductive in meaning that just the name alone whipped up a gargantuan appetite in the most birdlike of stomachs. You ate a continent. You cannibalized a people, a race, an entire culture. But it was made easy and digestible by the homely egg, barnyard friend and foot soldier, hardened by many a culinary adventure. The brave omelette domesticated the East, wrapped it in clean linen and made it digestible. That was the secret of the 'Omelette Indo-Chine'. He grunted disgustedly. But did anyone stop to think of what that did to the brave Norman farmer's wife?

What it did was to bury her contribution to history in oblivion, he thought grimly. So that now an omelette no longer evoked Mont St. Michel, or huge bowls of apple cider and cream. French cuisine was no longer about the traditions of its people, but about its conquest and absorption of others—like the slit-eyed races, and the Arabs, and the Africans. Hubert! What a disgrace to his country the man was. He spat in disgust.

He looked at his wife's menu sitting on the blotter and sat up straight in anger. It was boring. She was making his restaurant seem boring. It was an invitation to tourist pigs! A discerning palate, one with imagination, would lose its hunger out of sheer boredom.

He stopped reading. He had trusted her, and his trust had blinded him. Never again, he promised himself, never again would he trust anyone. Trust was the trap. That's why his father had lived and died at the edge of the forest, never coming into the village, never tying himself down to people. He looked at the menu, grimacing. They were going to replace him with that baby-faced fluff ball who could not cook but who looked good in front of a television camera! But he could probably write an excellent menu. He had gone to university. Omelette Indo-Chine! He had probably studied literature to be able to invent a name like that. Everything began to make sense.

After a few moments of intense thought, he wrote down carefully in his rather childish handwriting, *Soupe a l'odeur sacree*.

Then he thought for a few minutes more.

Salade de chevre au soupirs innocents. (For the vegetarians.)

He paused. People would want to know what they were eating under the fancy name, all the same. Warm goat cheese salad with pine nut and herb crust, he wrote. He hated having to explain himself, but if fantasy was to take the place of history, explanations, even lies, were necessary.

Salade sphinx.

Cold beef and artichoke salad with a sesame lemon dressing.

Bateau farci a l'orient.

Crepes stuffed with roast duck, served with a ginger-orange sauce. That would show them. Hubert was not the only one who knew about Orientals.

Mousse de canard 'mort subite'.

Duck pate en croute with raspberry hazelnut coulis, served on a bed of fried potato straws.

He drew a line and went on to the main courses.

Medaillons de veau au jus des soldats morts.

Medallions of veal topped with two-coloured sauce. Accompanied by fresh green peas simmered in cream and pommes Maria. He would name the potatoes after his wife, he decided. She would know he was insulting her, letting unknown men consume her, not even as the main course, but as a side dish, used as an adjunct to not one but many different dishes.

Feuilles d'Automne sur tombeau printanier.

Fricassee of prawns on a bed of wild mushroom risotto, accompanied by delicate spears of fresh asparagus.

Cotelets de porc coeurs brises.

Pan-fried pork chops with a herb mustard crust and a creamy cherry-calvados sauce, served on a bed of braised carrots and turnips and accompanied by spring vegetables and pommes Maria.

Poulet a la seductrice.

Chicken breast stuffed with pork, apple, walnut mince, and served on a bed of spinach tagliatelle with a creamy fennel sauce.

The desserts he left untouched. Graciella and his wife could take care of those.

He sat back and stretched luxuriously, well pleased with his efforts. He ran his eye down his new menu and grinned. Perhaps he should have gone to university and studied to be a poet. Taking the sheet of paper with him, he rushed out to find his wife.

He found her preparing the *salade verte*. The girls were there, too, eating leftovers.

There was a sudden silence when he entered. They all looked at him. He noticed their slightly guilty expressions and knew they had been talking about him. Some of his new-found elation left him.

'Here,' he thrust the new menu at his wife, 'print this out on your computer.'

She put down her knife with great calm, took it from him and began reading. He waited, unable to see her face clearly. At last she looked up. Her mouth twitched, but she said nothing.

'So, what do you think?' he demanded. 'You wanted something new, something exotic to bring in the customers, didn't you? This is more original than your Omelette Indo-Chine. Even if it comes from an old man.'

'But this is twice as big as the one we agreed on!'

'They don't have to eat everything, I give them a choice.'

'But you don't believe in choice.'

'Now I do. I even watch television.'

'You'll go mad making all that, no one is going to help.'

For a second Marcello was nonplussed. Then he said, 'Someone is going to help me. Amanita. You remember our daughter, don't you? The others can look after the rest of the restaurant.'

'And what about the ingredients,' she said angrily. 'Where do you think we'll get those from?'

'So cautious! That's all you care about, isn't it? The quantity of things: how much, how many, how big. Of course I have thought of everything.'

'Well, make sure, because there's no one to send out for ingredients in the evening, your highness.'

He stared at her in dislike. Always so practical!

'Plan, plan, plan,' he mocked her. 'It's because of people like you that the shops close so early. On second thoughts, I will close the rest of the restaurant. Then we won't fall short. And you can all watch me so I don't make any mistakes.' He turned and began to walk towards the pantry.

'One last thing,' she called after him, 'what is a *salade sphinx*?'

'I can't tell you. It's the chef's secret,' he replied in what he hoped was a light-hearted manner.

'Is that what you want me to tell Madame Martin also? And what about *feuilles d'Automne sur tombeau printanier*? No one will want to eat something with such an absurd name. As for this *medaillons de veau au jus des soldats morts*, our guests aren't cannibals.'

He turned around slowly and drew himself up to his full height. 'I am still chef here, and you will print that menu,' he ordered. 'As for absurd names, you think any of mine could be more absurd than Omelette Indo-Chine? Yet, you sit like cows before the television and gobble that up.'

Her lips thinned and set in a mask of refusal. He looked anxiously at her, knowing the expression well.

Suddenly, Graciella came and took the menu out of her hands. 'Let's see, maman.' She read through the menu and looked up, her eyes shining with laughter. 'This is really good, papa. I didn't know you had such an imagination. Such menus are all the rage in Sydney, in New York.'

'New York? But this is not New York!' Madame Tocinelli threw up her hands in despair.

Marcello gave her a long look. This is what you wanted, it said. 'An entirely original menu will delight our clients. I am going to make human beings out of the sheep. It is time we changed things from the bottom up, or else our society will be destroyed. And anyway, I am still the chef here.' There was a stunned silence, but no one challenged him. He smiled triumphantly. 'Now listen, here's what you all have to do.'

Like well-trained sheepdogs, they set to work. He had made sure that they were kept occupied in different parts of the kitchen and that the list of tasks for each one was so complicated that they wouldn't have a minute to spare to think. The restaurant was a well-oiled machine, and that placed certain limits upon them. Ultimately, only a man was strong enough to throw off the shackles of habit. Only a man could be a hunter. And only a hunter could be a creator.

Cooking was the mirror image of hunting, he realized suddenly, except that where the hunter sought to drive the last whiff of breath out of his victim's body, the chef hunted the soul of the animal, trying to catch it and impale it in a bed of complementary flavours of equal strength and power to hold it there. Both hunters and chefs relied on the sense of smell. Smell was the silent intimation of a creature's soul, and also the traitor and enemy of its body.

A chef, like a high priest, purified the body and set the soul free. And then he told God to go to hell, and trapped the soul again in a magic potion of his creation. The soup epitomized this. That's why, to be a chef, one had to be the master of the soup. A soup was nothing less than a soul leached out and presented to the palate as a taste, the eternal imprisoned in a fragile, ordinary base. He shook his head, amazed at the sheer brilliance of his insight. Why hadn't he seen it before?

His body began to feel light, and as he wielded the chopper on the meats, his fingers tingled and his head felt as if it would burst. Then, when he was almost done, he felt eyes boring into his back. His hands tightened around the meat cleaver. His wife and Graciella were standing there watching him.

'What is it? Have you finished what you had to do?' he asked edgily.

'What exactly goes into a seductive chicken?' Graciella asked, smiling nervously at him.

'Ah, yes. Of course you will be wanting to write it down, won't you? Have you finished the reduction yet?' He glared at her.

'Though it is boring,' she stared him down, 'it is necessary for the continuing success of the restaurant and must be done.'

He felt deflated by her control. He would have preferred knives thrown at him, meat cleavers wrenched out of his hands, tears, total capitulation, fear, sweat, terror.

'I don't know yet,' he answered honestly, 'but since the art of seduction is based upon deception, the bird will have to be stuffed. And since seduction depends upon passion and jealousy and evil, I will stuff it with green, red and black things, and lay the white breast flesh on the top.' He stopped, and looked at their stupefied faces mockingly. 'But surely, you cannot already have finished everything I asked of you?'

Reluctantly, they moved away.

'Let us know what you stuff the bird with so we can write it down later,' his wife called over her shoulder.

Marcello didn't answer. Write it down, indeed. She wanted to steal his imagination, he thought. But she was a fool. She didn't see that the thinking organ where food was concerned was the nose.

As Marcello was removing the last breastbone, he heard a gentle step behind him. He turned sharply and saw his younger child standing there. She looked as if she were about to ask him a question. Is she really on my side, Marcello wondered. He decided to find out. 'Come, my child, let me show you how I marinade the chicken,' he said, taking her hand and pulling her over to the other side of the room.

The second stage of separating the flavour from the flesh was the marinade. Marcello believed firmly in the importance of the marinade, though some cooks had dispensed with it altogether. Now he finally understood why. The marinade tempted the chicken's own secret juices to come out. Gleefully, he prepared a simple marinade of oil, wine, herbs, garlic and orange peels and placed the chickens inside. The orange and the garlic would bring out the sweetness and the passion of the bird respectively, while the wine would purify the flavours. The oil was the great sympathizer, reconciling the soul of the bird to its new partners. He sighed, longing to share his insights with his wife. They had always been so close, they would have built a great restaurant together. And now, when his genius was in its final flowering, his greatest triumph, that which would surely make him the greatest chef ever, would never be shared.

'Damn her,' he muttered under his breath.

'Yes, papa?' Amanita responded politely.

'What?' He had forgotten about her. She was always so silent. He frowned at her, wishing it was his wife beside him, instead.

'Did you want something?' she asked.

'No.' He frowned.

'Shall I go away?' she asked nervously.

'No.' He looked at her standing poised for flight and was suddenly, forcibly, reminded of a little brown bird. He laughed and grabbed her by the shoulders. 'Oh, you little bird. Can I trust you?'

She looked back out of frightened eyes.

Marcello let go of her abruptly. 'Oh, what the hell, every fox has a friend. Now listen carefully.' He banged his fist on the counter to scare the fear from her eyes.

'The secret of good cooking is to catch that last breath of life and impale it in a complementary bed of flavours so that it lies there inert and helpless as it is consumed,' he told Amanita in a whisper.

'How horrid!' Amanita gasped, wondering if her beloved father had indeed gone mad.

'That's life, it's not horrid,' he explained. 'You mustn't be scared of life, or it will hunt you down and eat you up. Life is a hunter, too.'

She said nothing, so he continued, 'The marinade is the first step in that fixing process. You surround the victim with strong opponents. You intimidate him with their presence, then quietly you pour on the fat. The victim is too busy fighting off the obvious enemies, and fails to see the presence of the traitor until it's too late. The fat opens the gates of the flesh and allows the spices to penetrate. That, my dearest child, is the secret of the marinade.'

Amanita could bear it no more. Mumbling something incoherent, she ran away. Marcello stared after her in frustration. Squeamish child! He decided not to follow her. She would learn the full extent of her loss later.

Next, he turned to the soup. He had decided on a simple consommé of duck. Nothing could be more sacred than a consommé. The consommé's unquestioned authority lay in the fact that it took the essence of a creature, its smell, and fixed it transparently in so humble a foundation as water. One didn't eat or even swallow a consommé—one sniffed it like incense. A consommé was the pure taste of the soul. That's why it was so delicate, so deceptively simple.

He chopped one of the fresh ducks, removed the breasts and the leg meat and, setting aside the fleshy bits, immersed the rest in cold water. Consommés were incredibly difficult to make. The bonds that bound the essence of the creature to the water were fragile—a few vegetables, bouquet garni and a teardrop of garlic and some peppercorns. Which is why restaurant chefs rarely made them. Marcello stared down at the ingredients assembled before him and shivered. Consommés were said to be related to the soul of a cook. If the cook was bad, the consommé would not clarify.

He put the pan on the stove and lit the fire. He hoped the vegetables would be strong enough to trap the soul of the duck. With a sinking heart, he remembered the lacklustre quality of the vegetables he had bought today. He crossed his fingers and prayed that luck would not abandon him.

'Shh, look at him, he's crossed his fingers and is praying. He has to have gone mad—he's never been inside a church in his life,' Graciella whispered to her mother behind the pantry door.

Madame Tocinelli stared through the little window in the pantry door and involuntarily she crossed herself. 'It won't hurt him to pray. He's got a huge job ahead of him this evening.'

'But that's not all. I spoke to Amanita. She's terrified ... poor thing. He keeps on about hunting and killing things and eating their souls. I think he's ... he's become a cannibal.'

'Don't be silly. He's your father,' Madame Tocinelli snapped.

'He doesn't sound like it any more,' Graciella grumbled.

Madame Tocinelli turned back to the little glass window and watched her husband anxiously.

From the soup, Marcello had turned to the prawn fricassee. He set the unpeeled prawns in a basic stock base, added white wine and a bouquet garni and let them simmer gently. For

Marcello, this was the most spiritual stage of all cooking. For here the magic ingredient was wine. Wine became the sacrificial offering that made the rest of the meal a success. On its own, water could not hold the flavours of bone and vegetables which were freed by the boiling. But when wine was added, the wine evaporated and took the place of the taste, and tricked the bones and vegetables into giving up their essences to the water instead of the air. In the process, little of the wine remained, but what one got was a delicious base of taste that could be refined or diluted, and used as holy water to revive the spirits of the dead.

At last Madame Tocinelli turned back to her daughter. 'Look at him, he's fine. Don't be so imaginative. Go and watch him carefully. Learn what he has to teach.'

Reluctantly, Graciella pushed open the pantry door and went into the kitchen.

Marcello had just finished seasoning the veal and the pork. 'Ah, there you are,' he said, much to her surprise. Then he began preparing the stuffing for the chicken. He chopped the braised fennel and green onions. Next, he minced the pork and the apples, while the breadcrumbs and nuts roasted under the grill. Meanwhile, he took the prawns off the heat and let them cool and skimmed the impurities off the top of the consommé. He realized that he was sweating profusely. He wiped his forehead, and cursed under his breath. Graciella handed him a towel and gave him a small smile.

He took it gratefully. 'So you're feeling better then?' he said gruffly.

She nodded, refusing to trust her voice.

'Good.' He heated the butter and threw in the onions. 'Get me the chicken breasts.'

When she returned with them, he quickly cut them into little pieces and tossed them into the pan along with the pork and the other ingredients. He stared at the contents of the pan and smiled. Inside there, elements, opposite and incompatible, were about to engage in a most violent conflict. But even the most violent conflicts, he thought regretfully, ended in the re-establishment of harmony. Even death was a kind of harmony, he reflected.

The contents of the pan sizzled and immediately Marcello's attention fixed upon them. The onions were the first to enter the fray, giving off a haze of green vitriol. The apples and fennel followed suit. Marcello threw in the herbed breadcrumbs, and the three turned upon the newcomers and attacked them jointly. Meanwhile, the pork and the chicken held back. He added a little goose fat to spur them on. The pork was the first to react, drawing the fat into itself, sucking in the false friend. With the fat went the other flavours and before the pork could defend itself, the battle was over. Together they turned on the chicken. But it was no match for the combined strength of the others.

Who was the winner? Marcello laughed. None of them. They had all collapsed into a single mass, still seething and chaotic and unstable inwardly, but outwardly, the battle was over.

He added a few drops of wine to fix the taste and put in some more seasoning. Judging from the smell, it was still a little bland, he guessed.

'From this point on,' he told Graciella, putting the pan back on the fire, 'all cooking is about dissolution and reconstitution. Having tricked the flesh into giving up its essential living flavour, you then dissolve that in butter or wine or cream and then reduce it to reconstitute the flavour—isolated in a new base.'

Graciella shook her head. 'I don't understand,' she whispered miserably, wondering what had happened to her father to make him talk like this.

'Because then, what you have is ten times more powerful than what you had in the beginning ... having lost its essence, lost its body, the flavour is pure. Unalloyed. But in that pure state, it is too much for the human palate to accept, it's like a poison and therefore it has to be diluted again. So we mix it with a complementary ingredient so that the taste remains but it is now palatable, because it has that key element of difference hidden inside, the black spot in the centre of the sun.' He paused and looked at her eagerly, waiting for her to say the words of praise he expected to hear.

Instead, he heard her say, 'Papa, I think it's beginning to burn.'

'Of course it isn't. What you're sensing, you clever girl, is the inner fire that is awakened by the cooking, the black smoking fire of putrefaction that forces the taste out of the body. A good cook knows this and waits for the slight burning to tell him that all is well with his ingredients, and that the fire has done its work. Now we must moisten it, so that the taste gets fixed.' He reached for the stock and looked down, and to his horror, the stuff in the pan was indeed beginning to burn around the edges and underneath. He yanked it off the stove, and saw that he had forgotten to damp the flame down. He cursed softly. Cautiously, he sniffed it and gave a relieved sigh. 'No, not burnt.' He took it off the stove and mixed in the walnuts and fresh herbs. In a little saucepan, he cooked the morels in butter and fennel, and then he cooked the red peppers.

Once the ingredients had cooled sufficiently, he mixed them— green, red and black—and took the stuffing over to where the hollowed-out chickens waited. Graciella followed him unhappily. Marcello then proceeded with the delicate task of stuffing and sewing the birds up. Next, he rubbed the skin thoroughly with goose fat, enjoying the slippery feel of the skinned bird and imagining the taste of the finished product.

'The secret to good cooking,' he told her expansively, 'is fat. Without it, there can be no food. It is the great sympathizer, the spy, the secret weapon of the cook. Just as love is the secret weapon of the hunter.' He watched her closely as he said it, hoping to surprise a hint of guilt.

But it never came. Women, he thought bitterly, they were as slippery as fish. He stopped rubbing the carcass, remembering the prawns. 'Finish these and put them into the casserole with the vegetables, and don't let anyone touch them,' he ordered and dashed off to where the prawns were. But Amanita was already standing there. 'What are you doing here?' he barked.

'Nothing. I just turned off the stove for you,' she answered, wiping her hands nervously on her apron. It had fresh stains on it, he noticed.

'Are you sure that's all you did?' He tried to sound menacing and snatched the pan away, sniffing it suspiciously. Something felt different, but he couldn't tell what exactly had gone wrong. He cursed her under his breath.

Carefully, he peeled the prawns and immersed them in butter to keep them moist. The evening yawned before him, full of treachery and danger.

By quarter to six, the kitchen began to fill up. The waiters came first. Then came the dishwashers, moving more slowly, and talking to each other in a medley of foreign tongues. Marcello removed the vegetables from the pan and put them into a bowl, covering them carefully. One couldn't be too careful with foreigners. Their alien languages, if nothing else, could corrupt his carefully constructed food. He returned to the ovens. The chickens were waiting for him, with the washed chicken giblets and vegetables arranged around them. He added the wine and stock and the herbs, and a little more salt. Then he set the birds carefully in the oven and, satisfied, returned to the soup.

Quickly, he strained the soup and put it back on the burner. The liquid was translucent already. Satisfied, he then prepared the quenelles and the clarification mixture. After cooking the quenelles, he added the clarification mixture to the liquid and let it come slowly to a boil, stirring constantly. When the egg white had formed a soft crust, he stopped and breathed a sigh of relief.

'How is it?' his wife asked, appearing suddenly at his elbow.

'Huh?' His train of thought stopped. He looked into his wife's face and burst into laughter. Suddenly, the humour of the situation struck him.

She began to look uneasy. 'What's so funny?'

'Actually, I was thinking about this,' he said, nodding at the soup. 'The essence of a living creature trapped inside ordinary water. It's a miracle. And I only realized how it works because of you.'

She looked doubtful, then her face cleared. 'C-can I taste it?' she asked eagerly.

'No. It's sacred. I don't want you to taste it.'

'But you always let me taste the soup.'

'Rituals are for the religious. I don't need them.'

For a second, her face crumpled. Then she pulled herself together. 'You enjoyed our little ritual for thirty years. You'll pay for destroying it.' And she stalked off.

Marcello stared after her worriedly. What was she planning? She was certainly his equal in hunting, maybe his superior. By the end of the evening, he would know. Then he remembered Amanita. So innocent and birdlike. So silent. He had nothing to worry about, he decided.

His wife arrived, her eyes bright. 'The Martins have come. I hope you know what you're doing,' she hissed. Before leaving, she bent down and pulled out the bottle of champagne he had been hiding and took it with her.

Good riddance, Marcello told himself. Staying sober would help keep him ahead of them. Quickly, he poured the soup through a sieve and added the Cognac and a drop of thyme oil. The resulting liquid, he thought triumphantly, was more than sacred. It was divine. He replaced the soup in the cauldron and placed the lid on it. 'Watch this. Let no one touch it,' he told his loyal Turkish grill man who had held the sieve for him. The man nodded nervously. Marcello next went to the ovens to check on the roasting birds. He opened the door of the oven and let the scent of the birds come to him. Tonight they seemed to be taking a very long time. He turned up the heat slightly and went over to the stoves. The last stage in the game was about to begin. And so far, he decided, he was winning.

He walked regally to the stoves. Graciella and Amanita were already in their places. The air hummed with suppressed emotion. Both girls looked slightly scared. They wouldn't look at each other. The first course was the consommé. 'You get it ready,' he told his elder daughter. Graciella nodded obediently and disappeared. The two of them were left at the stoves, caught in a tiny pocket of time. Marcello wondered where his second daughter had been for so long. Had they caught her, turned her into a double agent?

'Do you know what your name means?' Marcello asked his younger daughter.

Amanita blinked. 'A kind of mushroom?'

'It's a hunter's favourite mushroom. Do you know why?'

Amanita shook her head.

'Because there are so many kinds of Amanita sisters. Some are deadly poisonous, some are delicious, some, like *Amanita muscaria*, are hallucinogens and were used by the ancients to get directly in touch with God. The *Amanita caesarea*, on the other hand, is a delicious mushroom highly prized on any hunter's table. But hunters who aren't so good often mistake its sibling *Amanita halloides* for the *caesarea* and end up mysteriously dead.'

'My god, but what if—?' Amanita went pale.

'Don't worry. I could never get them confused. But humans are harder to know than mushrooms.' He paused, suddenly nervous. 'Tell me, my wild silent child, what kind are you?'

Amanita jumped back and looked around wildly. There was no one nearby, no one to rescue her.

'What do you mean, papa?' she asked.

'What is there to understand?' Marcello asked, annoyed. 'I've told you my secrets. Things I wouldn't reveal to anyone, not even to your mother or your sister. I want you on my side. And I'm willing to pay for it with my secrets.'

'Of course I am on your side, papa.'

But she didn't look at him as she spoke. Marcello tried again. 'Good girl ... I trust you. By and by I will tell you the secret of my greatness.' He licked his lips. 'Now, tell me, what is it they're planning?'

A look of fear spread across her face.

'Don't worry. Nobody will know except me. To be a great artist one must pay the price. And sometimes that price is betrayal. Often that is the price for the best of us,' he reassured her.

Her mouth opened and shut like a fish.

Marcello turned around. Graciella was right behind him.

'What do you want?' he growled, turning to face her. 'Can't I talk to my own child in private without someone trying to listen?'

I said I would write everything down, didn't I? But I can't do that in the middle of a meal. Not this meal, at any rate.'

Graciella looked hurt. 'You're mad. Absolutely mad,' she burst out and dashed back to the hors d'oeuvre area.

'Of course, that's what you'd like everyone to think, wouldn't you?' he shouted after her, wanting to wring her neck.

But there was no time to be distracted, he told himself firmly. He had hungry people outside waiting for his genius. A wedding feast had to be something to remember. He glanced at the order card before him. Three salad sphinxes, two *soupirs d'innocents*, and the rest duck crepes. To be followed by three veal, three pork and two prawn fricassee and the rest for the *poulet*. That would keep them busy—even Graciella. He whispered loudly to Amanita, 'Come and watch me cook. It's time you learnt all my secrets.'

She nodded reluctantly, not looking up.

When she arrived, he was already sautéing the veal. For a second he wondered what had taken her so long. Then he thrust the thought aside. 'Ah, you've come just in time. I was about to begin the sauce.' He took out the veal and put it onto a separate plate. Then he added shallots to the veal juices and a little walnut butter. 'The key to a good sauce,' he told Amanita, 'is to make sure there is lots of butter to moisten it. That's what captures the flavour and keeps it fresh. It is the same principle as in embalming. The fat preserves whatever is put in it.' He added the vermouth and the brown sauce and boiled them down till there were two cups of it. 'Now watch,' he told her, 'here's where the sauces, like two children of the same parents, become different, change character.' He divided the sauce into two. He added tarragon and fennel to one lot and let it boil down until the liquid was fragrant and steaming, while in the other he put garlic, tomatoes and mustard. Just before he took it off the stove, he added cream. It became a lovely rosy colour. He sighed, unable to contain his admiration.

'Aren't you going to taste it?' Amanita asked him.

'Of course not, my nose would have told me if there was

anything to add. Taste is a creation of the imagination, not the mouth.'

'Can … can I taste it then?' she asked, overcome by curiosity.

Marcello felt irritated and was about to refuse. Then he remembered that he had to keep her on his side. 'All right, just so you know what it should taste like in the future. Once we've got rid of the others, it will be just you and me doing everything.'

Amanita blinked rapidly. 'J-just you and m-me?' she stammered.

'Of course! That's what you want, isn't it?'

Amanita's mind reeled. Her father wasn't mad, he was evil. She decided she would find her mother and tell her everything. Quickly, she tasted the sauces. She realized immediately that there was too much mustard in the second veal sauce. Her heart began to beat wildly. She was saved by Graciella who called Marcello over to the hors d'oeuvres counter to make the sauce for the crepes l'Orient. Amanita's body went limp with relief. She promptly set to work, diluting the sauce with cream and rectifying the mistake.

Meanwhile, Marcello was needling Graciella, enjoying himself.

'What is in this sauce that is so special I can't do it?' she was saying, looking sulky.

'Creating a sauce requires imagination. It requires unpredictability. You are incapable of either,' he replied

She coloured. 'Really? How can you be so sure?'

'I know you. You're like dough, you cling to others of your kind and wait for a man to tear you away and mould you.' He saw Graciella's face darken and quickly changed the subject. 'Is the ginger ready?'

'Yes, here it is.' She proceeded to hand it to him, looking mutinous. Just as he was about to grasp the glass bowl, she let it slip from her fingers.

'Good god! What is wrong with you?' Marcello snapped.

'You wanted unpredictability. I gave it to you,' she replied coolly.

Marcello snapped, 'Now get out of my sight before I get so angry I ruin the sauce.'

She left him, still laughing.

In the pantry, Graciella collided with her sister and mother.

'I tasted the sauce of the veal escalope, it was all wrong. The tarragon had swamped all the other flavours in one and the mustard had done the same in the other,' Amanita was explaining breathlessly.

Madame Tocinelli gasped. 'That's impossible. He'd have to be ill to make such an obvious mistake and if he was sick I'd have known it.'

'Then maybe it's not a mistake,' Graciella said grimly. 'Maybe he's doing it deliberately.'

Both of them looked shocked. She stared back at them fiercely. Then Amanita slowly went beetroot red, biting her lip guiltily.

Graciella turned on her. 'Aha. I knew it. You know something about this, don't you? You know I'm right.'

'What are you talking about?' Madame Tocinelli turned towards her younger daughter.

'Graciella has a point. I ... it's a long story. Too long to tell just now,' Amanita began wearily. 'But I think papa somehow thinks you and Graciella are trying to get rid of him.'

'So that's what it is.' Light dawned on Madame Tocinelli's face. 'Come, we will end this farce now.'

'Oh maman, please, not now,' Amanita begged, 'or he will know I've told you. He ... he will think I have betrayed him.'

'So what?' Madame Tocinelli was impatient.

'We have to get him out of the kitchen before he ruins us, not afterwards,' Graciella added.

Amanita stared at her sister resentfully. 'You can't. Not when there's still half a meal to go and only he knows how to make most of the dishes.'

'It doesn't matter. We can invent the rest. We should be as good if not better cooks than he is, we've been watching him since we were children,' Graciella replied. 'Besides, he's definitely gone senile already. He thinks he's a hunter. He told me only hunters could cook. Can you imagine that? Fat old papa a hunter.'

'He's not senile,' Amanita shot back. 'As for being a hunter, he was an excellent one. He told me so. His father taught him.'

'Oh, really? Have you ever heard of a hunter being a cook?' Graciella turned on her.

'He ... he hunts mushrooms. He got a whole bag of them yesterday—and he was too shy to tell us. You need a good nose for that, just like ... like ... ' Amanita faltered, her face turning fiery red.

'A mushroom hunter,' Graciella laughed scornfully. 'He was a butcher's assistant before he met mum, you little fool. That's all he's ever been.'

Amanita's face became even redder. 'But he's a good cook. I'll watch over him. See he doesn't make any more mistakes.'

'Oh, really? How will you do that? He'll cut off your head if he sees you messing with his sauces.'

'Enough, enough, both of you, let's not be hasty.' Madame Tocinelli tried to make peace. 'Amanita has a point. Let her watch over him.' She paused and smiled at Graciella. 'And tonight we will talk with him—together.'

Meanwhile, afraid of the mischief Graciella could wreak on his food, Marcello rushed through the rest of the preparations for the sauce. He set the ginger and cinnamon and nutmeg and cumin in the pan. Then he poured in the wine and the brown stock, added the orange liqueur and peppercorns and let the mixture bubble. Once the scents had merged into a single entity, he took the sauce off the flame and added the cream and the saffron. He put it back on the burner for a minute and then took it off the flame and beat in some cherry-walnut butter. Yet, he was dissatisfied, it just felt wrong. His sauce *Orientale* was a fake; he could smell it. He wished he could change the name now. But the menus were outside and circulating among the customers, and he was in the midst of a war desperately trying to hold on to what he loved most. He added some more stock and seasoning to the sauce in the hope that it would revive a little and poured it over the pregnant-looking crepe. He arranged two slices of orange and a mint leaf on the side and rang the bell for the waiter to take it away.

But instead of a waiter, his wife appeared and reached for the plate.

'Oh, no, you don't.' Marcello reached over and grabbed her hand. 'Let the waiter take it.'

'Why? I always serve the special customers. Have you forgotten?'

He was about to let her go. Then he changed his mind. Hunters did not follow other people's habits. That was what had changed him, following his wife's habits.

'No. Let a waiter take it in, or I'll do it myself.'

Suddenly, Amanita appeared at his wife's side. 'I'll take it, maman,' she said quietly.

Marcello watched her go through the doors leading to the dining room and his smile grew. Amanita was such a perfect double agent.

In the corridor leading to the dining room, Madame Tocinelli found her younger daughter waiting for her. Her heart sank.

'What is it now?' she asked.

Quickly Amanita told her.

Madame Tocinelli's face went white. 'Oh, no. How can I keep him away for fifteen minutes?'

'Maman, you have to try,' Amanita insisted. She turned away, biting her lip.

Meanwhile, Marcello was happily sautéing the pork chops. For such an ugly, fearsome animal, he was thinking, this wild boar's flesh was surprisingly sweet, its taste delicate and almost feminine. He couldn't wait to attack the juices, to transform them into something flowery and pungent and hedonistic, a delicate salmon-coloured sauce to match the fragile, rather innocent flavour of the pork. He watched the animal's life juices flow slowly out of the pork.

'Marcello, we have to talk.' Suddenly, his wife was before him.

He turned around and glared at her. 'But we're in the middle of dinner.'

'I don't care. I have to speak with you right now,' she insisted, licking her lips nervously.

His eyes narrowed. What could she want to speak with him about? Did she want a truce, or was she going to trap him again? He remembered one of his father's sayings: Once a man worries, he clings to things, and once he clings he is bound to get exhausted. A hunter never worries. He knows he will lure game into his traps again and again. To worry is to become a victim.

He squared his shoulders. 'All right, give me five minutes and I'll be with you,' he muttered ungraciously.

In the pan, the golden juices were slowly swirling around the chops, unsure of where to go. Quickly, Marcello tipped out the chops and returned the pan to the flame. He deglazed the pan with some vermouth. Separated from the heavy flesh that held it together, the juices began to dance around the pan in an agony of desire. Marcello smiled and threw in the braised onions and braised mushrooms. The languorous scent of the pork clashed violently with the perfumes of onions and mushrooms. Steam rose off the top of the pan. Marcello watched the battle and, unwillingly, his eyes strayed to his wife. This was one fight from which there would emerge no victors, he thought grimly. Just as abruptly as it had begun, the scents collapsed on top of each other. He added a little goose fat to reanimate their passion. The flavours still felt a little underdeveloped. He let the liquid simmer. Marcello felt the scent reaching up towards him, full of yearning and the knowledge of loss, of its incompleteness.

'Aha, it's ready,' he muttered triumphantly, reaching for the cream.

'What?' his wife asked.

He looked up, annoyed. 'Nothing. I just said it's ready.'

'Ready for what?'

He frowned. 'For the next stage.' He poured in the cream and seasoned it with a little nutmeg. The cream formed a tranquil white lake in the midst of the seething liquid. He mixed the two, and felt the easing of tension in the pan as the cream was absorbed into the liquid, seduced by the calm joyousness of the cream. At last he added the saffron-and-honey mixture. He watched the glow of love spread across the face of the liquid. He turned up the heat slightly and felt the impatience of the liquid grow. Marcello felt the joy begin to bubble inside him. Unbidden, the tears welled out of his eyes. No matter how many times he did it, this moment, when the sauce was at last ready for its ultimate reunion, always brought answering emotion bubbling to his eyes. Love was love after all, whatever the breast that held it. Those who knew the difference between passion and love were united forever in its memory.

Involuntarily, his eyes went to his wife. His chest tightened. She was looking away, pretending not to have been watching him. He wiped the tears from his eyes, hoping she would think it was just perspiration.

'Here, finish the plate for me,' he ordered Amanita and followed his wife out of the back door into the yard.

Outside, an orange moon was riding across the sky. He looked at it in surprise. It was years, maybe even a decade, since he had seen an orange moon. It reminded him of the lake of cream in the pan before it had melted into the pork juices.

He looked at his wife. In the old days, when his father-in-law had been in charge, they would rush out and make love every moonlit night. He looked at her face. It was no longer the one he remembered so well, the one he saw each night in his dreams.

'Do you remember,' he burst out, feeling all the pain of a love lost.

'Marcello,' she cut him off, 'you have to stop this at once.'

He groaned. He couldn't help it. He was weak, he was a man.

'Marcello? Are you listening to me?'

'Since when have I not listened to you? Were you to pour poison in my ear, I would still offer it to you,' he said bitterly.

'Stop joking, this is not a game. You're ruining your own reputation, forget the restaurant.'

That was too much for him.

'How dare you?' he roared. 'You are the one plotting behind my back. Trying to throw me out of my own restaurant.'

His wife's eyes opened wide.

In Marcello's breast, satisfaction warred with disappointment. Sometimes, knowing things brought no pleasure.

'You think I didn't notice?'

His wife didn't answer.

But her silence only infuriated him further. 'Why did you do it? Was I not good enough?'

'What do you mean?'

'Do you think I can't see what you're doing? Have you forgotten the way you and I waited, and planned, for the day I would take over from your father?'

She looked guilty. He hurried on, 'Why the secrecy? Surely you could have trusted me? They are my children, too. If they had wanted to take over, I could have helped them.'

'So *that* is what you believe.' His wife sounded sad.

'I don't believe. I know.'

'Know? What can you know?' she spat. 'There is nothing to know.'

'Yes, there is. I heard you after lunch the other day, telling those clients how I was getting old, hinting at a change in the chef.'

'What on earth are you talking about?'

He continued, 'For the rest, Amanita told me everything.'

His wife's eyes flashed. 'Amanita?'

'Of course! She is the true child of my spirit. I will teach her everything. I will make her the world's best cook—even if she's a girl.'

She shook her head. 'I don't believe it.'

'Then let's go and ask her,' he challenged.

She nodded grimly. They walked back inside, this time with Marcello in the lead.

Amanita was so busy repairing the damage to the sauce *Orientale*, she didn't notice Marcello's arrival. Only when he let out a roar and grabbed her by the shoulders did she become aware of the disaster that had burst upon her.

'No-o-o,' her father roared like an animal in pain, 'not you too.'

She looked into his wounded eyes and felt the tears forming in her own. 'I'm s-sorry,' she stammered. 'I w-was only trying to help.'

'Help? I don't need your kind of help.' He let go of her abruptly and turned on his wife. 'So she was your secret weapon? You planned this all along, didn't you? To pry the last few secrets out of me before you threw me out? I congratulate you!'

His wife's face went red. 'I've had enough of this absurd theatre, Marcello. Why can't you accept the truth? You've been making mistakes, that's all. I-I don't know why. But you have been making too many of them to ignore. Either you tell us why or we'll have to taste everything you make for ourselves,' she said firmly.

'You want to muzzle me? I'll never let you do it,' he shouted. 'As for you ... you traitor,' he rounded on Amanita, 'I would have given you all my knowledge if only you'd stayed with me. But you were too greedy, just like the rest of them. You wanted it *now*, didn't you?' He grabbed her by the shoulders and began to shake her. 'Didn't you?'

'Leave her alone.' His wife sprang to her defence like a tigress.

Marcello let go. Amanita let out a huge sob and dashed out of the kitchen. Madame Tocinelli started after her, but Marcello grabbed her arm.

'How could you turn them against me like that?' he whispered hoarsely. 'What did I do to make you hate me so? I am not an ogre like your father was. I'd have happily let you take over. If only—'

'You don't understand,' his wife cut in. 'You've got it all wrong! I was trying—'

Just then, a harassed Matthias burst upon them. 'Excuse me, but where is the *poulet*? They have been waiting now for twenty minutes.'

Both husband and wife looked as if they had been turned to stone.

'See, this is all your fault,' Marcello muttered, recovering first.

'No, it isn't. This would never have happened if you hadn't changed the menu in the first place.'

'How much longer will I have to wait?' the waiter asked irritably.

They turned on him simultaneously. 'Let them wait!' they ordered.

The waiter backed away, still grumbling. They watched him disappear and then faced each other.

'Are you going to let me do this?' Marcello said quietly.

She looked away, biting her lips.

'Look, I'll leave after this evening,' he said, trying to sound conciliatory. 'I promise. I don't want the restaurant. You can have it. But just this time, let me make the food my way.'

'But I don't want—' she shut her mouth abruptly.

'You don't want what? What are you scared of now? You've won,' he said angrily.

She looked at him, and there was sadness and distance in her eyes. She walked away.

Marcello's body slumped. All of a sudden, his desire to cook had vanished. He frowned and forced himself to concentrate. The pink order slip glared up at him. *Poulet Seductrice.* Was it the poor groom who had ordered it? Did he know he was the one who had been hunted and now he would lose his freedom permanently? Marcello pondered the question as he walked through the kitchen to the ovens. Around him there fell a pall of silence. Even the foreign staff seemed to have sensed what was going on. He ignored them all. His loyal Turkish grill master was still guarding the doors of the ovens. He moved aside on seeing his employer.

Inside the oven, the chicken glowed golden. Perfect for the carving, Marcello thought gleefully as he pulled it out.

He decanted the juices into a saucepan to thicken on the stove, and began to carve up the chicken. When he had finished, he lovingly placed the slices on beds of freshly blanched spinach and poured the fennel sauce over them. He arranged the potatoes and the beetroot around the chicken. It looked beautiful. He rang the bell for Matthias and finished dressing the remaining plates by the time he arrived. Then he picked up two of the plates himself and carried them into the restaurant.

The wedding dinner was in full swing, everyone more than a little drunk. They smiled and nodded to each other. Someone had just finished an impromptu speech. Their eyes widened when they saw the chef himself there. M. Martin, his white hair a shining halo around his flushed face, rose.

'A toast to the chef,' he shouted, raising his glass.

'A toast to the chef!' they cheered.

Monsieur Martin raised his hand for silence. 'For twenty-three years, now—' he began.

'Twenty-four,' his wife corrected him, 'you told me twenty-four.'

He frowned down at her. 'No! Twenty-three. I should know, I discovered this restaurant right after I moved to Geneva. I remember I would drive for hours on weekends, alone in my car.'

'Enough, you'll make the food cold,' his daughter shouted from the other table. She was one of those who had ordered the veal, Marcello noticed. It was sitting before her, getting cold.

'Ah, yes. Anyway, to make a long story short, in this restaurant, I asked my wife to marry me. Here, I introduced my son to the pleasures of good living. Perhaps that is why he spends his life travelling and writing about food. I am not a very religious man, but I do feel that, after a lifetime's devotion to food, I may call myself a priest of the temple of good food.'

He gestured to Marcello to put the plates before his son and daughter-in-law.

'A marriage,' he continued, 'is the beginning of a long and sometimes tiring journey. Two people aren't naturally meant to stay together. Like two river stones, they must rub against each other to become smooth.' The guests began to clap, impatient to begin. 'Then, something magical happens, a new person, a single entity, is born where once there were two lonely ones.' He paused briefly, to take hold of his wife's thin hand. Then he resumed, 'I'm almost finished with what I have to say.' He turned to Marcello. 'In life I have learnt, there is nothing that cannot be resolved over good food. A toast to the man who creates it!' He raised his glass and drank it down.

'Hear, hear.' The guests stamped their feet in acknowledgement. Matthias finished the service. Marcello bowed, plucked a rose from a nearby vase and gave it to the bride. There were more cheers. Then silence as people turned inwards to their plates.

Marcello watched their faces, in particular the faces of the newly-weds. This is why I cook, he thought to himself. For this moment.

Their faces alight with expectation, the bride and groom smiled into each other's eyes. He was the first to take a bite. His bride followed. His face paled. He reached for the wine and took a gulp. After a few seconds, she stopped chewing, and swallowed her mouthful instead. They stared at each other and then at Marcello. Their faces mirrored the feeling in his blood vessels.

Marcello turned away. He pulled off his hat. As if they had a life of their own, his hands began to untie his apron. In the foyer he took his old wool coat and hat and slipped them on. Then he opened the front door of the Chauldron d'Or and stepped out.

Outside, the moon rode high in a clear black sky. Marcello looked up, but it was not the same moon. It was not, he realized, had never been, a hunter's moon. He could not get the look on the guests' faces out of his mind. What had gone wrong? What had betrayed him? His faltering steps turned towards the road. Behind him he heard light footsteps on the gravel. It was his wife. Without a word, she took his arm and began walking with him. Slowly, his head sank down on her shoulder.